W9-AWT-275

Shades of gray

JACQUELIN
THOMAS

Steeple
Hill®

Published by Steeple Hill Books™

STEEPLE HILL BOOKS

Steeple
Hill®

ISBN 0-373-78553-4

SHADES OF GRAY

Copyright © 2006 by Jacquelin Thomas

www.SteepleHill.com

Printed in U.S.A.

In loving memory of

SHERITA JAMES

It is said that angels come as thoughts, as visions, as dreams, as animals, as the light on the water or in clouds and rainbows, and as people, too. For me, Sherita was not only a dear friend—she was one of God's angels loaned to me for a short time. My dear friend, you will never be forgotten.

This book is also dedicated to Sherita's children,

KIMBRIA, CHALANDRIA, AKEYLA AND DARIAN

Your mother always said that her daughters were her best work. Losing your mother is tragic, but know that not even death can steal your precious memories of the life you shared with her. She will visit you in your dreams and her love will transcend death. You are Sherita's legacy—through you, she will live on.

DISCUSSION QUESTIONS

1. Sela and the children were devastated by the loss of Rodney and handled their grief in different ways. All of us have experienced grief in our lives at one time or another and each of us handles it in our own way. What advice could you offer to someone grieving now?

2. Sela is jealous of Rodney's relationship with the Lord. Why do you think she feels this way? Is there something present in her husband that she finds lacking within herself?

3. Sela had a bad experience in a church she attended when she was younger. She isn't comfortable attending services, even with Rodney. Are her feelings justified? Why or why not?

4. Bitterness makes us hold on to an offense and makes us prisoners of our hurts and hatred. Job 21:23, 25 described it like this: "One dies in his full strength, being wholly at ease and quiet... And another dies in the bitterness of his soul, and never eats in pleasure." Are you holding bitter feelings in your heart against someone? If so, what should you do about it?

5. All Rodney ever wanted was for his family to come together. His children had the same dream. It finally takes the older children to get Sela, Roman and Ethel to see what the tension is doing to their family and to see that you forgive a person by releasing them from any obligation to make things right. What made Junior and Ayanna speak up? Do you think the children had been trying to tell them that all along?

6. Forgiveness is an attitude that honestly acknowledges an offense and then dismisses it on the basis of God's forgiveness of us. Ephesians 4:32 tells us: "Be ye kind one to another, tenderhearted, forgiving one another, even as God for Christ's sake hath forgiven you." Sela and her in-laws had to truly forgive one another before they could move forward in their relationship. What does it mean when someone says forgiveness must come from the mind *and* the mouth?

7. When Roman brings up the fact that Sela and Rodney should have never gotten married in the first place, Sela calls him a racist. Roman recites II Corinthians 6:14, which says: "Be ye not unequally yoked together with unbelievers, for what fellowship hath righteousness with unrighteousness...?" He states that interracial relationships are wrong because they go against the will of God. What is God truly referring to in this scripture?

Chapter One

✧

"I would like to make a toast…." Rodney's eyes traveled the length of the oversized formal dining room, summoning the attention of his guests.

Standing by him, Sela openly admired Rodney. He stood tall and regal, looking very handsome in a black tux that hugged his body as if it had been designed just for him. His deep blue eyes framed a square face, bronzed by the sun, and the set of his chin suggested a stubborn streak. At the age of forty, while some men were going bald, Rodney still had a wealth of ash blond hair.

There was no doubt in Sela's mind that Rodney Barnes was the best-looking man in the room. She wove her fingers through his, their coppery color a warm contrast against the coolness of his tawny skin. Sela loved her husband more than life itself and never tired of looking at him.

Earlier, they had renewed their vows in a formal ceremony to celebrate their twentieth wedding anniversary and afterward had returned to their new home of six months for the reception.

Sela drew her attention back to Rodney, a smile tugging at her lips. He was still trying to get everyone to quiet down.

He's up to something, she suspected. Knowing him as well as she did, Sela had a feeling that Rodney was about to do something terribly romantic.

Rodney cleared his throat and stated in a louder voice this time, "I'm glad y'all are having such a good time, but I'd like to take a few minutes of your time so that I can make a toast to my wife."

This time everyone in the room heard him, their conversations dying down to a hush.

Sela met her mother's gaze and smiled.

It had taken Althea Johnson a while to warm up to Rodney when they had first gotten married, but now she loved him like a son.

Rodney's gaze swept the room again, making sure everyone had a glass of sparkling cider, before he returned to his wife, taking her right hand in his left.

He looked down into her eyes and said, "Sela, we've been through a lot over the years. The better and the worse… I have to admit that not always the better prevailed. We've seen the richer and the poorer."

Rodney's grin grew wider, making Sela's heart skip a beat.

"The sickness sometimes outran the health, but through it all, I can't say I have any regrets. It has been my highest honor to be your husband. Twenty years ago on this very day,

I pledged my heart to you till death do us part. Earlier, we renewed those vows and tonight I only have one wish, and that's for the rest of our dreams to come true."

Holding up his glass, Rodney continued, "Here's to the beautiful woman I married—to the wonderful mother of my children. Thank you for the past twenty years of marriage and I'm looking forward to the next twenty plus. I love you so much, Sela. You are a dream come true for me." His deep baritone voice died off, watered down by emotion as he tapped his flute gently against hers.

Sela was too choked up to respond amidst the clapping and oohs and aahs. Rodney's words had touched her deeply—she knew he'd meant every word spoken. She and Rodney had been through a lot over the years and their marriage had thrived despite the doom and gloom spouted on a regular basis by Rodney's parents. Sela felt like she was the luckiest woman alive, having found such a loving and wonderful man.

Rodney leaned forward to whisper, "I meant every word I said, honey. I love you and I am so blessed to have you in my life."

"I love you, too," Sela whispered back. There was so much she wanted to say to him, but for the moment she was too overwhelmed to find the right words. When they got married March thirteenth all those years ago, it was in front of a Justice of the Peace and their parents. Rodney had always promised to give her the wedding of her dreams.

Tonight he'd kept that promise, Sela whispered in her heart as her eyes traveled the room, noting friends and family gathered throughout.

The only ones present who didn't share in their joy were Roman and Ethel Barnes, her in-laws. They didn't like that Rodney had married an African-American woman. They had accused her of trapping their son into marriage when she had become pregnant at seventeen. They also blamed Sela for Rodney's dropping out of college at the age of twenty. According to them, she'd ruined his life.

Just thinking about her in-laws soured Sela's mood. Their intense dislike of her felt like clothes that were too tight whenever they were around. She removed her hand from his and began pulling at her sleeves.

"What's wrong, honey?"

Rodney's voice cut into her thoughts, effectively pulling her out of the reach of unpleasant memories. Embracing him, Sela responded, "Nothing's wrong. Everything is just fine. Tonight couldn't be more perfect."

Before she could say more, friends wanting to say goodbye interrupted their private conversation.

Out of the corner of her eye, Sela saw her mother-in-law coming her way and dropped her head.

Although she pretended to be interested in the conversation between Rodney and his friends, Sela's body unconsciously tensed for battle and her trembling fingers fluttered over the rhinestones sewn on her ivory-colored lace jacket, covering the satin gown.

She made herself stop fidgeting; take a deep breath and calm down. Sela cast a quick look over at her mother-in-law, who was patiently waiting her turn to speak with them.

Although Sela wouldn't admit it aloud, she felt inadequate around Ethel. The woman carried herself as if she'd been born with a silver spoon in her mouth, despite Rodney's insistence that his mother had grown up poor. Tonight she was garbed in a beautiful dress Sela recognized as an Adrienne Vittadini design, and a good seven or eight inches taller than her, Ethel used her five ten height to her advantage.

Towering over Sela with hands on her hips, Ethel's voice was filled with censure. "Don't you think it's time you put the twins to bed? Children need consistency in their lives."

Can you say that any louder? Sela wanted to ask. *The people next door couldn't hear you.* Speaking as calmly as she could, Sela instead replied, "The only reason they're still up is because this is a special occasion, Mrs. Barnes. You don't have to worry about your grandchildren. I have everything under control." Ethel knew that the five-year-old girls had a rigid bedtime schedule. She just wanted to ruin Sela's evening.

"Well, I *am* worried, Sela."

Ethel gestured dramatically around the room, drawing unnecessary attention to them. Sela believed this was another one of her regular attempts to publicly humiliate her.

"This is an adult party. If you're not going to use good judgment in this situation, then I'll just take them upstairs and see that they get their proper rest," Ethel threatened as she ran her hand over her hair, smoothing back the chignon at her nape.

"I don't need you to take *my* children anywhere." Sela struggled to keep her voice low. "In case you've forgotten, these are my children, Mrs. Barnes. *Not yours.*"

Looking down at Sela's petite frame, she stated, "Don't you dare take that tone with me. I told Rodney—"

"Whoa," Rodney interrupted. "Come on you two," he pleaded in a harsh whisper. "Why don't you and Sela call a truce—just for tonight? Okay?"

"I'm fine," Sela responded tersely. "It's your mother who has the problem."

"Mother. Sela and I agreed the children could stay up a little while longer. We appreciate your concern, but like Sela said...we have it under control."

It annoyed Sela whenever Rodney tried to act the diplomat. After all, it was his racist parents who were constantly giving her grief. Since they hated her so much, she didn't understand why they'd bothered to come to the ceremony at all.

"I was just concerned over the children getting their rest," Ethel uttered after a moment of tense silence.

Without another word, Ethel stalked off to join her husband, Roman, who had been watching them from his position near the door. Roman never said much to Sela and that suited her just fine. She didn't need the two of them on her back—especially tonight.

Sela heard the familiar sound of her own mother's bracelets jingling as she walked toward them. "Sweetie, is everything all right?" Althea asked.

She gave a slight nod. "Yes, Mama. Everything's fine."

Althea glanced over her shoulder to where Ethel and Roman Barnes were standing and asked, "You sure?"

Nodding, Sela pasted a smile on her face. "Now go on and have a good time. You hear me?"

Althea glanced over at Rodney. "I saw Ethel sashaying from over here. I hope your mama is not upsetting my baby. This is *her* day."

He nodded in understanding. "You don't have to worry, Mom. I'm not gonna let her."

Althea patted Sela on the arm. "I'ma go make sure your father stays away from the shrimp. His cholesterol is sky-high and shellfish has a lot of it—you know how much he loves shrimp."

Hugging Sela, she whispered, "You look so beautiful, sugar. Now don't you worry about that Ethel Barnes. If I catch her bothering you again, I'ma have a li'l talk with her."

"Mrs. Barnes isn't gonna bother me," Sela assured her mother. She didn't relish the thought of a verbal confrontation between Althea and Ethel in the middle of her reception.

"I've known that uppity Ethel Barnes a long time, Sela. I'ma keep my eye on her just the same," Althea whispered before disappearing into the crowded room.

"Honey, don't let anything ruin this evening for us—especially my parents," Rodney pleaded in a low voice.

"You should be over there talking to your mama," Sela responded.

Turning away from Rodney, she mumbled, "I'll be right back."

"Where are you going?"

"I'm going to put the twins to bed before your mother has a fit."

Reaching out, Rodney pulled her back into his embrace. "I'm sorry."

"I know. *You always say that.*" Backing out of his arms, Sela stated, "I have to put—"

"Ayanna can take them upstairs," Rodney suggested. "Or your mother."

Although they lived in Raleigh, their oldest daughter, Ayanna, opted to live in an apartment on the campus of North Carolina State University. Sela's eyes searched the dining room for her. She spotted her daughter talking to another relative and waved to get her attention.

Ayanna immediately excused herself and walked over to where her parents were standing. "What's wrong, Mom?"

"Nothing's wrong, sweetie." Sela brushed a stray curl from her daughter's face. "Could you please take the twins upstairs and make sure they go to bed for me?" She couldn't resist adding, "Your grandmother is worried that they won't get their proper rest." Sela could feel Rodney's gaze on her, but didn't care.

"Yes, ma'am. What about Leon and Marcus?" Ayanna asked, referring to her younger brothers, who were nine and eleven. "Do you want them to go upstairs, too?"

Rodney answered before she could utter a response. "Yeah. Just have them all go on to their rooms now." He leaned forward and planted a kiss on Ayanna's forehead. "Thank you, baby."

"Happy anniversary," Ayanna murmured. "After I get the twins to bed, I'm gonna leave. I've got a lot of studying to do."

Sela tried to hide her disappointment. She really missed having their twenty-year old in the house with them. Ayanna used to come home often when she lived in the dorm. But she and her brother, Rodney Jr., who was now a freshman at the same university, moved into their own apartment a couple of months ago. Since then, Sela hadn't seen much of Ayanna. She was growing up into an independent young woman.

"I have to go to the library tomorrow to meet with my study group. Oh, before I forget, I have a friend I'd like to invite for Sunday dinner." Ayanna pushed her soft brown curls away from her face. "Actually I'll be bringing him to church with me. Is that okay?"

A glint of humor crossed Rodney's face. "Is this friend a close male friend or just a good friend?"

Ayanna grinned like a Cheshire cat. "Daddy, what does it matter?"

"I just want to know whether I should wear my 'mean father' look or not."

Sela's heart exploded with pride as she stood listening to the lighthearted banter between Ayanna and her father. They were very close.

The moment was interrupted when she felt the tiny hairs on the back of her neck stand up. Sela stole a peek across her shoulder, her smile disappearing.

From across the room, Ethel watched them. Sela wondered just how much of the conversation she'd overheard.

"Mom, I'll go get the twins and put them to bed. And I'll come say goodbye before I leave." Ayanna glided over to where Rodney's parents were standing and gave each of them a hug before taking off to gather her siblings.

Sela was grateful her in-laws loved their grandchildren despite their creamy, honey skin color—she would never want her children to face the painful rejection she'd had to face from them. And her children loved them back. Even though mean and vindictive, people like Ethel and Roman Barnes didn't deserve to share in their lives, she thought selfishly.

The warmth of Rodney's arms embracing her radiated through Sela. Her full lips turned upward as she leaned back against him. They stood watching Rodney Jr. talking to one of his cousins. At eighteen, he was the spitting image of his father. Unlike Ayanna, he still came home almost every weekend.

"We're so lucky to have such wonderful children," she murmured softly.

"We're blessed," Rodney corrected. "Luck has nothing to do with it. God has blessed us richly."

Sela chewed on her bottom lip. Since giving his life to Christ four years ago, Rodney never failed to give God credit in every aspect of his life. Despite the fact that Sela believed in God, she and Rodney were in different places when it came to their spiritual journey. She vowed, however, that Rodney's newfound faith would not become an issue in their marriage.

Chapter Two

Two hours after everyone left, Rodney took off his jacket and began unbuttoning his shirt, his fingers fumbling in weariness. He glanced over his shoulder to where his wife was sitting on the padded bench at the foot of their four-poster bed.

He loved the way her thick, black spiral curls fell around her neck. Sela's face was a copper tint and delicate; her high forehead, made to be kissed. She looked years younger than her thirty-seven years.

Right now, she sat with her girlish chin stuck out and her lips puckered. Whenever she was like this, she was usually annoyed about something.

"Did your parents get settled in the guest room?" he asked.

"Yeah."

He waited to see if she would say more, but she didn't. Sela just sat there with her lips pursed, looking upset.

Rodney gritted his teeth before asking, "Honey, are you still upset with my mother?" *I know I'm gonna regret asking,* he thought to himself.

Sela looked up at her husband and replied, "I suppose you think I shouldn't be. I'm just supposed to take her insults in stride, right? Just ignore the way your parents treat me in general."

Without waiting for a response, Sela bent forward to remove her heels.

He stood beside her now, knowing he was treading on thin ice.

When Sela looked up, Rodney studied her openly for a moment, noting the signs of tension in her face. "We've been together twenty-two years—married for twenty of them. Why do you still let Mother get under your skin?"

"Because *Mother* pushes all my buttons," Sela stated without blinking an eye. "The woman doesn't know when to keep her mouth shut. She is pushy, snobbish, prejudiced and just downright mean-spirited. I've done everything I could to be nice to your folks. Frankly, I'm really tired of trying."

Rodney sat down on the edge of the bed near her. "I know she can be a little annoying—"

"A little annoying? Rodney, your mother is just plain hateful." Sela saw the flash of pain in his expression and added, "I'm sorry, but your parents don't like me and I'm not crazy about them, either. This is nothing new. I would be perfectly happy if I never had to deal with them again in my life."

Rodney laid a hand on her shoulder. "They are our children's grandparents, Sela. *They're my parents.* We can't just cut them out of our lives like that."

She rose to her feet. "Humph. If given the chance, they'd cut me out in a heartbeat."

Rodney stood up, too. He took a small breath and began, "Honey, they wouldn't ever do that." Wrapping an arm around Sela, he added, "They know how much I love you." But even as he said the words, he knew how false they sounded. And judging from the knowing expression on Sela's face—the same expression she wore every time the touchy topic of his parents came up—she wasn't buying his words, either.

She broke into a bitter laugh. "You think they care about that? You're the main reason why they hate me so much."

Rodney took another breath, longer this time and slower. "Honey, they don't hate you," he insisted.

"Babe, stop lying to yourself. *Yes, they do.* They wanted you to marry some nice white girl from a good family."

"It doesn't matter. I married the woman I wanted to spend the rest of my life with."

"Rodney, I don't want them coming to the house anymore. I will not tolerate them being so disrespectful to me in my own home. They've done it for years, but tonight, after our ceremony, in front of our friends…" Sela stood. "*I mean it.* They are no longer welcome here."

He struggled to hide his frustration. "Sela, don't be this way. It's not going to solve anything. We can't go around doing evil for evil."

"Rodney, I wouldn't feel this way if they were just a little bit nicer to me," Sela stated. "This is my house. *My sanctuary.* I won't have it tarnished."

He sighed in defeat. Rodney really wished Sela and his parents could get along and stop their constant bickering.

Turning her back to him, Sela asked, "Could you unzip me, please?"

He did as he was told.

Sela turned around to face him. "I'm telling you, Rodney—I just can't take it anymore. You're going to have to choose. It's either me or your parents. You can't have both."

He shook his head no. "I won't do that, Sela. I'm not going to pick one or the other."

She pulled away from him and stalked off to the bathroom, slamming the door behind her.

This was not the way Rodney wanted the evening to end—with his wife mad at him and locked up in their bathroom for who knows how long.

His mother was probably ranting and raving over at their house, driving his father nuts. Rodney hated being caught in the middle of this ongoing feud between his wife and his parents.

A tingling in his fingers drew Rodney's attention down to his hands. They were swollen again. Worry creased his forehead as he wondered at the cause.

The more he thought about his health during the past years, the more Rodney could recall experiencing a gradual loss in energy, appetite and thirst, a swelling in his legs and fingers, and shortness of breath. Lately, he was tired all of the time and now had a persistent cough—the result of his recent bout with the flu.

When Rodney began experiencing pain in his chest and abdominal areas a couple of months ago, his primary doctor told him that he was stressed out and prescribed anti-anxiety medication. He had no reason not to believe him—Rodney had been working twelve- to fifteen-hour days for the past three months or so, since losing two employees. Barnes Trucking had picked up three new customers. Until he could hire more drivers, Rodney delivered on some of the roads himself.

Rodney didn't mind being back in the driver's seat of his eighteen-wheeler. He loved driving because it gave him some alone time to reflect on his life, but lately he'd begun to feel more tired than usual.

Sela had cautioned him not to take on more customers than their small company could handle, but with two kids in college, a bigger mortgage…Rodney wanted to make sure he provided well for his family. Besides, he still had hopes of expanding Barnes Trucking.

A smile touched his lips as he thought of his wife. Sela was a wonderful wife and mother. If only his parents would give her a chance. It wasn't just them. Rodney knew Sela didn't care for them either.

He'd tried for years to sit down with all of them to discuss the situation, but nothing ever came out of it except accusations. Rodney was tired of their bickering and snide comments whenever they were together.

He and Sela just celebrated twenty years of marriage and his mother just couldn't leave well enough alone. Now Sela was mad at him.

What was he supposed to do? Should he have tossed his mother out of the house? Cause a scene? Rodney wasn't that kind of person.

He could hear the shower going behind the closed door. His heart heavy, Rodney fell to his knees.

"Heavenly Father," he prayed. "I come before You to say thank You for Your loving grace and Your many blessings. Please give me the right words and take away any wrong motives on my part. I love Sela and I love my parents. It is my deepest desire to have them get along. There's been too much tension in my family. Lord, please bathe my words in love, so that they might hear the truth. Amen."

Chapter Three

In the shower, Sela regretted the things she'd said to Rodney. She had been terribly unfair to him just now.

She had known Ethel and Roman Barnes most of her life. Over the years, her parents had purchased most of their furniture from Ethel and Roman's store. Sela met Rodney at Barnes Furniture when she went in to make a payment for her parents shortly after her fifteenth birthday. He was working in the store during the summer.

A freshman in college, Rodney would be attending NC State in the fall to study accounting. Sela planned to major in accounting when she graduated high school and threw question after question at him about this college, the courses and what classes she should take before graduating.

From that moment on, the two had become fast friends. Three months later, they began dating secretly. Rodney and

Sela had successfully managed to keep their relationship a secret until she became pregnant.

Rodney's parents would never change, but they were a part of her life—there was no other way around it, Sela decided. There was no way she could force him to choose her over his parents—it would not only be unfair, but Rodney might grow to resent her.

Sighing in resignation, Sela got out of the shower and quickly dressed in a nightgown. "If I didn't love you so much, Rodney…"

Sela brushed her teeth and combed her hair, then took a few minutes to gather herself before walking out.

Rodney stood just as Sela came out of the bathroom. He held out his hands to her as she came closer.

"Babe, I don't want to fight anymore," she murmured. Putting her hands in his, she continued, "I'm sorry about what I said. I wasn't being fair to you."

"You are so beautiful, Sela." He pulled her into his arms. "All I've ever wanted is to make you happy."

"You *have,* Rodney. You've made me very happy."

He stepped back to assess her from head to toe. Rodney smiled his approval. "Looking at you, nobody would believe you'd had six children."

She laughed, pressing a hand to her stomach and feeling the slight bulge. "*I can believe it.* I'm still trying to lose the weight." Sela sighed softly before adding, "My babies are growing up so fast. Ayanna and Junior are in college. Leon is eleven now and Marcus is nine. Pretty soon we're going to have this big house all to ourselves."

"The twins are only five though—they're gonna be home

with us for a long time. A long time…" Rodney let out a mock groan causing Sela to burst into more laughter.

"It was your idea to have another baby," she pointed out.

"I didn't tell you to have twins."

Wagging her finger at Rodney, Sela responded, "Leah and Lacey have you wrapped around their little fingers and you know it. Your daughters are all crazy about you."

"Just like the boys adore you. God is so good, honey."

Rodney was very active in church. He not only sang in the choir but also participated in a mentoring program for boys. They hardly seemed to have any time for themselves anymore because Rodney was always going up to the church for something.

Sela attended church with him every now and then. Mostly, she used Sundays as a day to pamper herself by sleeping in or soaking in a hot bubble bath. Afterwards, she would cook a large meal and have it ready by the time everyone arrived home.

"What are you thinking about?"

Rodney's question had the desired effect, bringing Sela out of her daydreaming. She looked up at him. "I don't want this moment to end."

"Our wedding day… I definitely don't regret the first one but I have to admit I like this one much better."

Sela laughed at the memory. "We didn't have two nickels to rub together back then. There we were—I was seventeen and pregnant, and you were twenty. You'd dropped out of college and was looking for a job…"

"We were living with your parents," Rodney added. "I was so afraid of your father—I couldn't even look at him."

"It took a while for Dad to warm up to you," Sela admitted, remembering how her father had worried about Rodney being a good husband. "But he realized you were a good man. That's why he gave you a job driving trucks for him."

"I owe your father a lot. If it weren't for him, Sela—we wouldn't have our trucking business." When her parents had decided to leave Raleigh and move to Jacksonville, Florida, her father told Rodney that it was time for him to buy a truck and go into business for himself. Rodney had been scared, but her father's encouragement had given him the courage to take the chance.

"He believed in you, Rodney. Dad's really a sweetheart underneath that bear of an exterior."

"He was so funny at the wedding earlier. I couldn't believe that he was standing there about to cry."

"Mama, too," Sela commented. "She cried through the entire ceremony. I'm sure she nearly used up an entire box of tissues."

"This has been one of the best days of my life and it's all because of you, Sela."

"I feel the same way."

Sela allowed her husband to lead her to the bed. She slipped off her robe and climbed in. When Rodney got in from the other side, Sela inquired, "Rodney, do you ever try to imagine what your life would be like if you hadn't met me? Or if you'd stayed in college?"

He shook his head. "Sela, the moment I met you, I knew you were the one for me. I didn't set out to fall in love with an African-American woman. Truth is I really didn't notice your skin color. All I saw was this little cute and sassy girl that had stolen my heart."

"When I used to picture myself getting married—it was to a black man," Sela confessed. "Until I met you. You were kind and generous, not to mention very handsome. You became my best friend, so loving you was easy."

"Do you regret our not moving to Jacksonville? I know how bad you wanted to leave Raleigh."

Sela shook her head. "If we'd moved, I wouldn't have this beautiful house." She leaned over and kissed his lips gently. "As long as I have you in my life—I can handle anything, *including your parents.*"

Saturday morning, Sela woke up to the delicious aroma of turkey bacon, a mushroom and cheese omelet, and hot, buttery biscuits. She stretched and yawned as Rodney entered the room carrying a wooden tray.

"Good morning," he murmured.

"Morning to you, too," Sela responded with a big grin. She covered her mouth to stifle the second yawn. "The food smells delicious."

"Your parents took the kids out to eat, so it's just you and me," Rodney announced as he sat the breakfast tray in front of her. He walked around the bed to the other side and climbed in. "We have the house to ourselves for a few hours."

Sela bowed her head and silently gave thanks before slicing into her omelet. "I love spending time with you like this."

Nodding, Rodney bit into a biscuit and chewed. He swallowed, then replied, "I feel the same way." He took another bite.

"So what are we doing today?" Sela reached for her glass of cranberry juice and took a sip.

"What would you like to do?"

Shrugging, Sela answered, "I don't know. My parents are leaving tonight, so I guess we should do something with them before we have to take them to the airport."

"Like what?"

Sela thought it over for a moment. "They love bowling. Why don't we go bowling? We haven't done that in a while."

"You sure that's what you want to do?"

Nodding, she responded, "Yeah. Let's make the most of our anniversary weekend with the family. After bowling, we'll take everyone to dinner before we drop my parents off at the airport."

"How about we take the kids to the movies afterward?" Rodney suggested. "Or we can rent some movies."

"There's a new movie that the twins want to see but I'm not sure Leon and Marcus will want to see it."

Rodney finished off Sela's omelet. "We'll talk to them when they get back. I may have to bribe them."

Sela chuckled. "Well, they do want those new model airplanes…."

She enjoyed her family and relished every moment they spent together. On days like this—things couldn't be any better. As far as Sela was concerned, she and Rodney had gone through the worst of times and survived.

"What are you smiling about?" Rodney inquired. "What's going on in that head of yours?"

"I was just thinking about the future—our future. After all we've been through…the rest of our lives should be a breeze."

Rodney placed his hand to his mouth before coughing.

Sela gave him a concerned look. "Babe, are you feeling okay? You've had that cough for a while now."

"I'm just a little run-down. When I had the flu or what-ever it was—since then my muscles have been real sore. I sometimes feel sick to my stomach, too. Probably from the stress of working all those hours…."

Sela examined her husband closely, noting the shadows under his eyes. "Are you sure you want to go out today? You really look tired, honey."

Rodney shrugged away her concern. "I'll be fine. Don't worry about me."

"How can I not worry about you, Rodney? This is what I've been telling you all along. Babe, you need to slow down. See how it's affecting you. You were sick a couple of weeks ago and you still haven't gotten rid of it. Promise me that you're gonna take better care of yourself. The children and I need you."

Rodney planted a kiss on her forehead. "Honey, I'm not going anywhere. Don't worry."

After taking a sip of his juice, he pointed to the last piece of bacon, asking, "You plan on finishing that?"

Chapter Four

❧

The next morning, Rodney woke up early.

He finished writing his entry, and then placed the leather-bound journal back into the top drawer of the nightstand on his side of the bed. He'd been keeping a journal since he was ten years old.

The adult choir would be singing during the morning service, so Rodney went downstairs to practice his solo in the family room. He went through it twice before he was satisfied.

He stole a peek at the clock, noting that it was time to wake up Sela and the children. Rodney eased up the stairs and crept into the bedroom.

Mesmerized, he stared down at Sela. She was beautiful even when she was asleep with her mouth slightly open.

While untying the belt on his robe, Rodney made his way over to the walk-in closet to select a tie to wear with his suit.

Once he'd made his choice, he headed back to the bathroom, calling Sela's name as he walked.

Sela opened her eyes and sat up, running her fingers through her hair.

Smiling, Rodney greeted, "Good morning, sleepyhead."

"Morning…" Sela stretched but didn't make a move to get out of bed.

"How did you sleep?"

"Great. I didn't realize I was so tired." She glanced over at the clock. "It's eight fifteen. I didn't expect you to be up already. We didn't get to bed until after one in the morning. Aren't you tired?"

"I'm singing this morning so you need to get up. We need to leave by nine."

"Rodney, let's just stay home today," Sela pleaded. "We could have a late breakfast and…"

"I just told you that the choir is singing this morning. Aren't you going to church with us?"

She shook her head. "Ayanna is bringing someone over for dinner later. I need to go to the store and pick up something to cook."

"We can do that after church."

"I want to have everything prepared by the time you guys get back."

Rodney sat down on the side of the bed to put on his shoes and socks. "I'd really like for you to attend church with us, Sela. I'm singing this morning, and it would mean a lot to me if you were there." Glancing at her from over his shoulder, he added, "This is supposed to be our anniversary weekend with our family, remember?"

A flash of irritation crossed Sela's face. "*I'm tired, Rodney.* I just want to spend some time alone. Is that too much to ask?"

He didn't want to fight before heading out to church, so Rodney backed off. "Just forget it then."

He slowly rose to his feet, still feeling the effects of having stayed up so late.

"Honey…"

"I need to make sure the children are ready," Rodney stated as he strode out of their bedroom, pausing briefly in the hallway to catch his breath.

Sela must have jumped out of bed immediately, because she appeared suddenly beside him before he could make it to the door of Leon's room.

"Rodney, I'm sorry. I didn't mean to snap at you like that. I'm just tired."

Hurt, Rodney managed to sound nonchalant. "Don't worry about it."

Sighing in resignation, Sela uttered, "If it means this much to you, then I'll go. Just give me fifteen minutes to get ready."

He stopped her. "Sela, you don't want to go, so don't worry about it. The children and I will go to church alone."

"I'll go with y'all next Sunday. I promise."

He refrained from responding. Rodney knew how Sela felt about attending church. She didn't see it the same way he did. To her, the church wasn't a haven for the hurting or a place that drew you closer to the Lord. To Sela, the church was a place filled with Christians who only remembered they were Christians on Sunday morning. Sunday Christians she'd called them. She'd had her fill of them when she was growing up.

Intruding into his thoughts, Sela demanded, "Rodney, are you listening to me?"

"I heard you. Now I need to get the children ready."

He turned his back to her, calling out, "Okay kids, time to get up. I don't want to be late for church."

"Rodney, we had a great weekend. I don't want it to end this way." Sela played with the belt of her robe. "We can't let anger destroy all that happened."

"I don't want to discuss this right now." He wasn't going to let Sela bait him into a fight. She was right about one thing: they'd had a wonderful weekend, despite their tense conversation about his parents Friday night.

Rodney glanced down at his wife, meeting her gaze. "I'll talk to you when I get home."

"Whatever," Sela muttered. She turned away from him and headed back to their bedroom, leaving Rodney to get their children up and ready for church.

Sela glanced over at the clock. It was eleven. Rita attended eight o'clock services at her church and was probably home by now. She took a chance and called.

She felt guilty for not supporting Rodney and was now trying to bury those feelings by pleading her case to her best friend.

"Rodney's really upset with me, Rita. I don't know why he wants to make such a big deal out of me not going to church with them this morning. I just didn't feel like it." Sela played with the telephone cord.

"Well, he's probably disappointed, Sela. You guys renewed your wedding vows Friday night…maybe Rodney just wanted y'all to attend church as a family this morning."

"Rita, I can remember when Rodney wouldn't set foot inside of a church. Then in the last four years he's suddenly become so religious. Now, every time the church doors swing open he thinks he's supposed to be there."

"He got saved, Sela. You really should be happy for him."

Rita's words put her on the defensive. "Well, of course I'm happy for Rodney. I just wish he wouldn't look down his nose at me because I don't share his feelings. I don't want to be a hypocrite—the church has enough of those already. You'd think he would understand that."

"Sela, Rodney loves you and he just wants you both to have a relationship with the Lord. And not everyone that goes to church is a hypocrite."

"I know that there are sincere people in church, like Rodney, but there are some of those *other* folks, too. You know the ones I'm talking about—holier than thou." Sela paused a moment before continuing.

"Rita, I know how much Rodney wants me to give my life to the Lord, but I have to do this for me—not for him. I'll come to God when I'm good and ready, but not before. It should be on my own terms."

"Well, I'm sure you two will work it out."

"I hope so. I really don't want God to be an issue between us."

"Sela, maybe you could start attending church more," Rita suggested. "Especially when Rodney asks you. Or does he want you going every Sunday?"

"He doesn't ask me to go every week, but even if I went—it won't change anything. I'm gonna still feel the same way."

"Well, do you feel you have to compete with God for Rodney's attention?"

Sela broke into a short laugh. "Don't be absurd, Rita. I don't have to compete with God. *Rodney is my husband.*"

"But he *has* changed since he became saved," Rita reminded her. "You guys don't do the things you used to do and I know it bothers you—you've told me so."

"I worship God in my own way. I'm just not one of those people who believe you have to go to church every time the doors open." Sela felt compelled to add, "Besides, some of the biggest heathens can be found in church on Sunday, but causing trouble the rest of the week."

"I agree with you. Everybody that's out there calling themselves Christian ain't. But Sela, Rodney truly loves God. He's not there pretending, so why punish him?"

"I'm not punishing him. What in the world would make you say something like that?"

"Look, we've been friends a really long time. I know some things about you even your mama doesn't know. Now this is what I think—you can tell me if I'm wrong, but I believe you're still upset over what the people at Mt. Olive did to you?"

Sela didn't hide her bitterness. "Yeah, I'm still mad. They had no right to make me get up in front of the congregation and confess my sin. Like half of them weren't out there doing the same thing. They just didn't get pregnant. What I did was between me and God."

"I agree with you, but Sela, that happened a long time ago."

"I was humiliated, Rita. Mama was appalled, too. We ended up leaving that church. My parents didn't even find another church until after Rodney and I got married."

"That's just how some of the churches were back then."

"I know a couple of other girls in the church who'd had abortions—they didn't confess that they'd been out there having sex. Only the few of us who dared to have our babies."

"I think a lot has changed since then. The church doesn't sit in judgment of you."

"It's not the church itself I'm worried about—it's the people in the church. I don't want to have to deal with people like that. I can stay in my house and worship God, if I choose."

Rita changed their discussion to a more neutral subject. "What are you cooking for dinner?"

"I'm making a nice roast with all the fixings—collard greens, rice and yeast rolls. Ayanna's bringing a friend for dinner."

"Good for her."

"Yanna must really like this guy to invite him to have dinner with us. She usually keeps them far away from us."

Sela continued to chat with Rita for a few minutes more before hanging up. She got up and headed downstairs to the kitchen. Rodney and the kids would be home in about an hour and she wanted to have dinner started.

Two hours later, Sela met her family at the door. She greeted Rodney with a kiss before asking, "How was the service?"

His mouth went grim. "You missed a wonderful sermon."

"Rodney, we really need to talk, but I want to wait until after dinner."

His blue eyes cool and proud, Rodney nodded. "I'm going upstairs to change."

"Where's Ayanna?"

"She went to pick up her friend. They should be here shortly."

"Rodney…"

He paused on the bottom step. "Yeah?"

"Are you still mad at me?" Sela was careful to keep her voice low. She didn't want the children to know she and Rodney were at odds with each other.

"Like you said, we'll talk about it after dinner."

Sela watched her husband climb the stairs with misty eyes. She could tell from his posture that he was upset with her. *Why do you have to be so rigid?* she wanted to ask.

She heard the timer go off in the kitchen and rushed to take her roast out of the oven. Sela wanted everything to be perfect.

Ayanna and her "friend" arrived half an hour later. Sela met then at the door.

"Mom, this is Jason Meadows. He likes to be called Jay."

Sela shook the young man's hand. "It's nice to meet you, Jay."

She eyed the tall, slender boy towering over her. "Let's sit in the family room," she suggested. "My husband will be down in a few minutes."

Ayanna and Jay followed her through the kitchen and into the family room. She sat on the loveseat while her daughter and Jay sat on the leather sofa.

Sela guessed Jay had to be a good six five. His skin was the color of butter toffee and complemented his dark brown eyes. His dark, shoulder-length hair was pulled back into a ponytail with a black band. She didn't care much for dreadlocks, but his were very neat and well-maintained.

Ayanna's long, warm brown hair flowed in deep waves around her heart-shaped face. Her eyes danced in amusement when Sela met her gaze. Her daughter knew she'd been silently assessing Jay, taking in his Burberry jeans, the NC State jersey and his Pirelli sneakers. Sela had been looking at a pair similar to his for Rodney.

"Jay's pre-med and plans on becoming a doctor," Ayanna announced. "Both his parents are doctors. He's on the basketball team and Mom...you should hear him play a piano. He's great."

Sela could tell from the way Ayanna talked, that she really liked Jay. Giving her daughter a conspiratorial wink, she said, "Ayanna studied piano for almost six years. Have you heard her play?"

"No ma'am. She told me she could play a little bit—I can't get her to play for me though."

"You're not laughing at me," Ayanna responded with a chuckle. "I've heard you play. You put me to shame."

Sela continued to observe Jay and Ayanna. Her daughter's last relationship had ended badly. Her high school sweetheart had gotten another girl pregnant while dating Ayanna.

Rodney and Sela worried how that one heartache would affect their daughter, but Ayanna gracefully moved toward her future with hopes of finding someone who would truly love her.

She never really brought anyone home to meet her parents unless she felt the relationship was becoming serious.

Sela liked the fact that Jay was very respectful and that he couldn't seem to keep his eyes off Ayanna. His gaze followed her every move.

"Here comes Daddy now," Ayanna announced. She introduced Jay to her father.

Sela applied the finishing touches to her dinner while Rodney held a conversation with Ayanna and Jay.

She could hear him firing question after question at the young man. Sela gave her daughter a sympathetic smile.

Junior bounded into the kitchen. "When is dinner gonna be ready?" he asked from across the room.

"In a minute," she responded. "Do me a favor and get your brothers down here. Tell them to turn off that PlayStation. They can play after dinner."

Peeking into one of the pots, Junior uttered, "Yes, ma'am."

Sela heard Rodney's voice and smiled. After dinner they would sit down and have a heart-to-heart discussion about attending church. She didn't want to have this situation spring up Sunday after Sunday. Sela wanted to put the matter to bed once and for all.

Chapter Five

❧

"Yanna has a boyfriend…" Leah teased. Her twin, Lacey, decided to chime in. The identical five-year-old girls ran around the breakfast table singing, "Yanna has a boyfriend…"

"Stop saying that…you're embarrassing me."

Sela burst into laughter. She and Ayanna were in the kitchen putting away the leftovers from their big family dinner. Rodney, Junior and Jay were downstairs in the basement watching the Los Angeles Lakers play the Houston Rockets. She guessed that Leon and Marcus were back upstairs playing video games.

"We'll put the dishes into the dishwasher for now. I'll turn it on before I go to bed tonight."

Ayanna's eyes grew large. "Wow, Mom. I can't believe it. You're gonna actually use the dishwasher?"

"I've used it from time to time."

"I wish we'd used it more when I lived at home. I hated doing the dishes."

Sela chuckled before admitting, "I hated doing them, too, when I was younger. Mama talked about me the whole time she was here. She still doesn't use hers."

"Granny's so funny. She said she's gonna tell all her friends about the new house. She thinks this is a mansion. Granny even took pictures. I took her to get them developed yesterday."

"I guess it is a mansion compared to the house I grew up in. It was a nice one—just on the small side. I've always wanted a big house though. And with six children, we need a mansion."

"But Mom, Junior and I don't live here anymore."

"But you're going to come home from time to time. Just wait and see. Most children do."

"Can I have my bedroom suite? You and Dad were talking about replacing it anyway?"

"You want that old bed?"

Ayanna laughed. "I love my bed and I want to keep it."

"Well, okay. You can take it anytime."

Ayanna hugged Sela. "Thanks, Mom."

"Junior can have his as well. I'm thinking about getting some new furniture for the family room, so you two can have those chairs in there."

"Thank you so much. I can't wait to tell Junior."

The twins were still running around the breakfast table, laughing and singing.

"What do you think of Jay?" Ayanna asked almost shyly.

Sela gave her daughter a reassuring smile. "He seems like a nice boy. How long have you known him?"

"We've been going out for about seven months now."

"I can tell you really like him." She continued to wipe down the marble countertops as she talked.

"Mom, I do. I like Jay a lot.

"I didn't want to tell anyone because I didn't want to jinx it. I guess I wanted to make sure this was the real thing before I made any announcements about it."

"I'm happy for you, sweetie." Sela put away the leftovers in the refrigerator.

"I wonder what Grandma and Grandpa will say when they meet him." Ayanna's smile suddenly disappeared. "I'm not sure they're going to like him. He's probably too dark for them."

"It doesn't matter whether they like him or not, Ayanna. As long as Jay is good to you and treats you with respect—it really shouldn't matter what anyone else thinks. And it *definitely* shouldn't matter what color his skin is."

At that moment, Jay rushed into the room, his eyes wide with panic. "Mrs. Barnes, there's something wrong. I think we need to call 911."

Sela dropped the pot she was holding. "Jay, what's wrong?"

"Mr. Barnes is having trouble breathing. He's in pain and he says his left side is numb."

Ayanna reached for the phone. "I'll call," she yelled. "You check on Daddy."

Sela rushed down the basement stairs and found Rodney gasping for breath and Junior trying to keep him calm.

"Honey, I'm here." She stroked his face gently. Perspiration streamed down his face in rivulets as if someone had poured a pitcher of water over his head.

"It's going to be okay. Just lie back and try to relax." Her heart was pounding so fast she could hardly control her own breathing.

Rodney tried to talk. He squeezed her hand with his right hand and took several deep breaths.

"Take it easy, babe. Ayanna's called the paramedics. They should be here soon."

He nodded and lay back on the couch.

"Where are they?" Sela snapped in frustration. She debated whether or not to just drive him to the hospital herself, but she feared he might be having a heart attack. If that was the case, the paramedics would be able to help him more than her. Sela let out a short sigh of relief when she heard the doorbell ring.

Jay and Ayanna gathered the children together while Junior ran to the front door to let the paramedics inside.

Sela tried to stay out of the way as the EMTs worked on Rodney. One man approached her and began inquiring about her husband's health.

"This just came on kind of sudden," Sela stated, fighting down her panic. "He's had anxiety attacks before but not like this. He's having trouble with his leg and arm on the left side. And he had the flu a couple of weeks ago, and since then he gets tired easy. We thought he was just working too hard."

Ayanna came to her side.

Fumbling, Sela took her daughter's hand for support. "Is he having a heart attack, or a stroke?" she whispered.

"I read somewhere that symptoms like this could be stroke-related."

The EMT tried to calm her fears. All Sela could think about was the possibility of losing Rodney. Just two days ago, they'd celebrated their anniversary by renewing their vows in an elaborate wedding—now her husband was having an attack of some kind.

Life certainly didn't seem fair at the moment.

Ayanna released her hand and went to reassure the other children that their father would be fine. Her daughter had always had a calming nature—just like Rodney.

Tears filled her eyes, causing Sela to blink rapidly. She didn't want the children to see her cry. It would only heighten their own fears. She had to be strong for them.

Sela wiped her face with her hands before going into the other room to talk to the children. "I'm going to ride in the ambulance with your father, okay? Ayanna is going to drive you guys over." To Junior, she said, "Drive my car to the hospital. The keys are…" Sela drew a blank. "Oh, I can't remember where my keys are!"

"I know where they are," Junior told her. "I saw them on your dresser earlier."

Ayanna grabbed her purse and car keys and said, "We'll meet you at the hospital." She embraced her mother and whispered, "Daddy's gonna be fine."

Sela nodded. She waited until the EMTs loaded Rodney on a gurney and followed them out.

This can't be happening. She heard the words over and over in her head. Sela shuddered from the chill brought on by a deep sense of foreboding.

Chapter Six

In the ambulance, Sela held onto her husband's hand for dear life. She kept telling herself that it was to keep Rodney from being afraid, but the truth was that she desperately needed to tap into his great reserve of strength.

Seeing Rodney like this nearly broke her heart.

He lay there, his blue eyes never leaving her face. It amazed her that, even now, he seemed more concerned for her than himself. Rodney gave her hand a tight squeeze to let her know that everything would be all right.

It was only after they arrived at the hospital that Sela considered calling her in-laws. But then again, she didn't want to worry them until she had something to tell them. Right now they had no idea what was happening to Rodney.

"Should I call my grandparents?" Ayanna asked as soon as she arrived at the emergency room.

Sela pulled on the sleeve of her shirt with trembling fingers. "I was just thinking about that, but I really think we should wait until we know what's going on with your father before we call them. I don't want to upset them unnecessarily."

Ayanna nodded in agreement. "Yes, ma'am. I'll give them a call as soon as we find out something."

Sela placed a hand to her stomach and leaned against the wall for support.

"Mama, do you think Daddy had a stroke?"

"Honey, I really don't know."

"It's probably gas," Leon stated matter-of-factly.

Sela released a laugh in spite of her growing fear. "I really hope that's all it is." She ran her fingers through her son's curly hair. Deep down she knew it was something more.

"Mommy, where's Daddy?" Lacey asked. "I wanna see him."

"The doctors are taking care of him right now. We'll be able to see him soon."

"Mom, why don't you go over there and sit down? You look as if you're about to faint."

Pushing a curling tendril from Ayanna's face, Sela murmured, "My responsible daughter…you are so good to me." She dropped her hands to her sides. "I'm fine. I just wish someone would come out and let me know when I can see Rodney."

"It shouldn't be much longer," Junior responded.

Junior wanted to be a doctor—it was all he dreamed of as a child. With his grades, she knew he'd have no problem getting into medical school. Unlike her son, Sela couldn't stand being in hospitals. She didn't know the reason why—she just knew she didn't like being there.

A nurse called her name. She followed the woman to the room where Rodney had been placed.

He gave her a tiny smile when she entered the hospital room.

"Hey you…"

She eyed the various monitors Rodney was hooked up to along with several pouches of fluid attached to his IV. When she saw the patches attached to his chest and torso, her stomach knotted. They were monitoring his blood pressure, breathing and heart performance. He'd already had a CT scan, which meant they suspected it might have been a stroke.

Lord, please watch over my husband. Make him well, she prayed silently.

Rodney lay there watching her, looking as if he wanted to calm her fears, but couldn't. Sela had a feeling he was just as scared as she was.

A nurse came into the room. Smiling, she greeted Sela and worked diligently, printing out several readings. Before leaving, she said, "The doctor will be in to speak with you both in a few minutes."

Sela tried to rub some warmth back into her arms as she stood beside the bed, holding her husband's hand. "Have you been feeling sick?"

"Just feeling real tired. For a while now I've been noticing that my hands and legs were swelling up. When I started having shortness of breath, I just thought I was having panic attacks."

"Why didn't you tell me all this was going on?" Sela knew he'd experienced panic attacks and she'd even commented on his legs swelling one day last week, but Rodney had assured her he was feeling fine.

"I didn't want you to worry, sweetheart. We were planning the wedding and the reception—I didn't want to ruin it for you."

The doctor entered the room before Sela could respond.

"Hello, Mr. and Mrs. Barnes. I'm Doctor Reynolds," he announced.

Sela gave Rodney a look that said they would finish their conversation later. She turned her attention back to the doctor with the balding head and round-shaped glasses.

Doctor Reynolds held Rodney's medical history in his hands. "Mr. Barnes, you suffered a right CVA—cerebrovascular aneurysm."

Sela held back her tears. She couldn't fall apart right now. Sela knew she had to find a way to be strong. Her family needed her.

"I've prescribed a medicine called TPA to contain the bleeding in his brain. We discovered some clots."

She gasped.

"One traveled to his brain and that's what caused the stroke," Doctor Reynolds explained. "I've put him on an anticoagulant drug, Heparin—that should keep any more clots from forming. Based on some of the symptoms Mr. Barnes described, I'm going to order some tests to see if we can find out what's going on."

Numb, Sela gave a slight nod. She could feel the heat of Rodney's gaze on her. "What kind of tests?" she managed to ask in a calm voice.

"An electrocardiogram and an echocardiogram. I've got to take care of some things but I'll be back in a bit." He turned and walked out the door.

His heart. Sela's own heart started to race. They thought something was wrong with his heart. She quickly forced her troubled thoughts to the back of her mind, so that she could pay attention to Dr. Reynolds.

An orderly arrived shortly after the doctor left to check on his other patients. Rodney was soon en route to undergo more tests. Sela kissed him before heading out to the waiting room. While he was gone, she went to check on her children.

"How's Daddy?" Leah asked.

"He's had a mild stroke but he still has to have some more tests done. The doctor wants to try and find out what caused the stroke."

"I prayed for Daddy," Lacey announced. "God's gonna take good care of him."

Sela sat down beside Leon. "You're awfully quiet. Are you okay?"

He nodded.

Leon was eleven years old and trying so hard to be brave. Sela wrapped an arm around him. "You're sure? I can understand how you'd be scared. I'm scared."

He looked up at her. "You are?"

She nodded. "Uh-huh. I'm scared because I don't know why this had to happen to Daddy, but we should know something soon."

Sela gave Ayanna money to get drinks for everyone. She sat in a chair by the window staring out but seeing nothing.

A different orderly returned Rodney to his room forty-five minutes later.

"How soon do you think we'll know anything?" Sela asked, although she wasn't really expecting an answer from Rodney.

He gave her a slight shrug.

"He's making the rounds, I suppose," Rodney answered. "He'll be back when he gets the results from the tests."

The room was soon enveloped in a thick cloud of silence.

Sela's eyes kept darting back and forth from Rodney to the wall clock. Her trembling fingers played with the fringe on her sleeves in nervous tension. Her stomach quivered and she could hear her heart thumping loudly.

Almost an hour later, they were still waiting on the results.

Sighing loudly, Sela changed her position in the chair she was sitting in and glanced over at her husband. His eyes were closed; Rodney appeared to be sleeping.

"What is taking so long?" she whispered. Sela rose to her feet and tiptoed to the door.

"Where're you going?" Rodney asked, opening his eyes.

Glancing over her shoulder, Sela answered, "Just to get a drink of water. I'll be right back."

She walked out of the room and made her way to the water fountain, bent over and took several sips, wiped her mouth and then headed back to Rodney's room.

Before she could go back into the hospital room, she realized she needed a few minutes alone to gather herself. She didn't want Rodney to see just how scared she was.

"Dear Lord, help my husband. Please don't let anything happen to him," she whispered. This was the most she'd prayed in a long time.

Sela spotted the doctor coming towards the room and met him halfway. "Do you have Rodney's test results?" When the doctor nodded, she asked, "Well, is my husband going to be okay?"

The look he gave Sela sent a chill down her spine.

Sela had a strong feeling she wasn't going to like whatever Dr. Reynolds was about to tell her. Her unwavering gaze never left the doctor's face.

"There's more, isn't there? You found something else besides the stroke."

"Mrs. Barnes, when we performed the echocardiogram, we discovered that your husband's heart is dilated and the pumping ability is very poor," Dr. Reynolds announced. "Normally, the human heart ejects fifty percent of the blood it receives from the veins and retains the rest for itself, but your husband's heart is only ejecting about fifteen percent and probably has been for some time now. The official diagnosis is congestive cardiomyopathy."

Dr. Reynolds went on to explain, "Cardiomyopathy is an ongoing process that damages the muscle wall of the lower chambers of the heart. Congestive cardiomyopathy is the most common form of cardiomyopathy. It's sometimes called dilated cardiomyopathy because the walls of the heart chambers dilate to hold a greater volume of blood than normal."

"*What...*" Sela paused to catch her breath. Feeling like the world had dropped out from under her, she swallowed hard before asking, "Doctor, how did this happen?"

"A virus usually causes this type of damage but in many cases the cause is unidentified."

Sela took another deep breath, exhaling slowly. She placed a hand over her racing heart. "Okay. Well, what can you do to fix my husband?"

She would not consider the possibility that this disease couldn't be destroyed. If it couldn't—the doctor could still find a way to make Rodney's heart better. Anything less was unacceptable.

Sela swallowed the scream that threatened to spring forth through her lips. This couldn't be happening.

"DCM is not curable, Mrs. Barnes," Dr. Reynolds replied in a low, composed voice. "We only can treat the condition with drugs and diet changes.

"Our goal is to minimize the symptoms and prevent the development of further complications. We would like to try and slow down the progression of the disease."

"Is there a strong chance of doing that?" Sela wanted to hold on to every shred of hope available. "I can't lose my husband, doctor. I don't want to lose him."

She recalled that Rodney's paternal grandfather died from the same condition and informed Dr. Reynolds. "He died almost eight years ago. It happened suddenly. You should ask my husband about it."

"Your husband has some paralysis on his left side."

"Paralysis…" Sela put a hand to her mouth.

"I believe the paralysis is only temporary, Mrs. Barnes," Dr. Reynolds assure her.

"Please, God," Sela whispered quietly when Dr. Reynolds walked away. "Please heal my husband. Make him well."

Chapter Seven

✤

July twenty-fourth delivered dark clouds and heavy rain on the morning of Rodney's funeral. He lived exactly one hundred and twenty-seven days after his initial diagnosis.

One hundred and twenty-seven days of emotional turmoil and heartache.

"See Mommy…God's crying for Daddy, too," Lacey told her while they dressed for the service. "That's why it's raining."

The rain had stopped an hour before they were supposed to leave for the church, but the clouds insisted on hanging around.

Despite the dreary weather, Sela knew the church would be filled to capacity. Her husband had been a well-liked man and had a lot of friends in the church and surrounding community.

Sela had dressed for Rodney's homegoing service with the

same care she'd given on the day they renewed their wedding vows. Sela wanted to look nice for Rodney. She wanted him to be proud of her.

She'd purchased a nice black suit with white trim, a pair of matching shoes and a hat to wear to the funeral. For the twins, Sela selected dainty white dresses, and for Leon and Marcus, she decided on black suits. Ayanna and Junior both wore black as well.

They were ready to pay their final respects to Rodney when the funeral director arrived. A short time later, Sela's face clouded with uneasiness the moment her in-laws appeared on her doorstep. Fortunately, they didn't say much.

Ethel Barnes looked as if she had aged ten years, Sela thought to herself. It was obvious Rodney's death had taken a toll on all of them.

The thought of a mother grieving the loss of her son was painful—as painful as children suffering the loss of a parent. Sela's eyes traveled to where her children stood, her heart breaking all over again. Life was so unfair.

The funeral director approached her when it was time to leave for the church. "You ready, Mrs. Barnes?"

Sela took one step, then faltered.

Junior was instantly by her side, lending her his support. "I'm right here, Mom. We can do this."

She nodded, unable to say anything.

The limo driver transporting her and the children took a slow scenic route to the church. Normally, Sela enjoyed the picturesque view of the upscale neighborhoods and manicured lawns in north Raleigh, but not today. Today she stared out the window but didn't notice anything.

Two more blocks, Sela counted silently. *Past the construction of brand-new houses and we'll be there. Then I have to say goodbye to Rodney....*

The limo rolled to a slow stop in front of the church. Sela felt anxious, her fingers began pulling at the simple pearl necklace around her neck. Her chest constricted, making breathing difficult.

She took slow, deep breaths until her breathing returned to normal.

Sela's eyes traveled to Lacey's face. Her daughter was staring out of the window, crying softly. She leaned forward to wipe away her tears.

No one said a word during the ride to the church. Her children were hurting and Sela, in agony, couldn't do anything about it. Feeling helpless, she reached again for the string of pearls draping her neck. They were a birthday gift from Rodney.

If she had to describe this very moment, her emotions…all Sela could say is that her world had vanished right before her very eyes. All that was left in its place was numbness. Her pain was so deep that it no longer hurt—instead it had become apart of her. Eternal agony.

She knew without looking out the window that they were nearing the church because her heart began to thump loudly and her chest felt tight.

Sela clutched the pearls as if her life depended on them. Breathe, she told herself. Just breathe…

They pulled to a stop in front of the church.

The door opened.

Sela looked over at Junior. She opened her mouth to speak but no words would come.

He reached over and took her by the hand. "C'mon Mom…we need to get out."

Pulling her hand away, Sela shook her head. "I can't."

On the other side of Sela, Ayanna wrapped an arm around her, saying, "Mama, you don't have to do this alone. We're a family and we're gonna do this together…as a family. Okay?"

She took a steadying breath. "I'm ready," Sela lied.

During the service, each of the children spoke about how much Rodney meant to them. When the time came for Sela to speak, she wasn't sure she could do it, but Junior came to her rescue a second time by escorting her to the podium. He kept his arm around her, lending her his strength.

"Rodney was…is the love of my life. He was a good man— a wonderful husband and father." Sela blinked back tears.

Using the tissue Junior handed to her, Sela dabbed at her eyes. "Rodney celebrated every day of his life. He was a man who loved God and he cherished that relationship, even through his illness. I know that a lot of people would've blamed God and turned away from Him, but my husband wasn't that type of person. In fact, I believe while Rodney was sick, he drew closer to the Lord. I am comforted that Jesus was with him when he drew his last breath. I am comforted knowing that Rodney is in Heaven."

Sela focused her gaze on the huge portrait of her husband. "I thank God for every minute I spent with Rodney. This past March, we celebrated twenty years of marriage…" Her tears were becoming more frequent.

"Rodney, I miss you so much, and I will strive to go on. I want you to know that I love you and you will never be forgotten."

After she finished, Ethel and Roman walked up to the podium together and delivered a moving tribute to their son.

When they were all done, the choir sang one of Rodney's favorite songs.

The pastor, a round man of average height with salt and pepper hair cropped close to his scalp, stood up and began singing. His deep baritone voice blended well with those of the choir. He and other members of the church had been a constant support for Sela during Rodney's illness.

She was grateful for all of their prayers and support. Rodney was well-loved and respected by his church family. The church was filled to capacity as she expected. The audience was a cultural mixing pot of races. One of the things Rodney liked most about the church was the multicultural congregation.

Pastor Grant was mostly a quiet man when not in the pulpit. Because he spent so much time with Rodney over the past months, Sela had gotten to know him pretty well. Rodney counted on his pastor to build him up when his spirit was low. Sela wondered if he could help her through the pain of Rodney's death.

Pastor Grant stood up and began the eulogy by reciting the twenty-third Psalm: "The Lord is my shepherd; I shall not want. He makes me to lie down in green pastures; He leads me beside the still waters. He restores my soul; He leads me in the paths of righteousness for His name's sake. Yea, though I walk through the valley of the shadow of death, I will fear no evil; For You are with me; Your rod and Your staff, they comfort me. You prepare a table before me in the presence of my enemies; You anoint my head with oil; My cup runs over. Surely goodness and mercy shall follow me all the days of my life; And I will dwell in the house of the Lord forever…" He paused to let the audience reflect on his words.

"If you know only one Bible passage by heart, it should be the twenty-third Psalm. This Psalm describes the posture of the human soul before God. The Psalm begins with 'The Lord is my Shepherd, I shall not want.' Those are the words of life. But how do you hear those words today…? I believe more than anything, it is an invitation to a relationship. A relationship that recognizes, when the Lord is my Shepherd, I shall not want."

Sela's eyes kept drifting over to the large portrait of Rodney. Her heart broke into a million pieces every time she allowed herself to relive the memory of his death.

"I can't speak for Brother Rodney, but I have a feeling he would have agreed. The Lord is my Shepherd, He's all that I want. I heard a saying a while back, that if a man loves the Lord, even his dog will know it. I have found that to be a true statement, because I have noticed with people who nurture that relationship with God, there is a certain unmistakable quality about their behavior and their character."

Sela stole a peek at her mother-in-law. Ethel dabbed at her eyes with a handkerchief.

She wiped away her own tears.

"When I think of Brother Rodney, I also think of this particular prayer. 'Heavenly Father, make me an instrument of Your peace; where there is hatred, let me sow love; where there is injury, pardon; where there is doubt, faith; where there is despair, hope; where there is darkness, light; where there is sadness, joy. Grant that I may not so much seek to be consoled as to console; to be understood as to understand; to be loved as to love; for it is in giving that we receive, it is in pardoning that we are pardoned, and it is in dying that we are born to eternal life.'

"If there was anything that Brother Rodney was an instrument of—I believe it was, as this prayer speaks of, an instrument of God's peace…"

Pastor Grant removed his glasses. "The thing that seemed to make it stand out, strangely enough, was a few months back—the first time Brother Rodney entered the hospital. Just to see him there, nothing seemed unusual at all—that was why I noticed it. Brother Rodney had the same calm and peaceful expression that he had any other time I saw him, in spite of facing some serious health issues. Now, let me say, I have seen a lot of people who keep their cool under stress, but I am not talking about that kind of calmness. Nearly everyone I've ever seen on hospital visits, some kinds of little small changes will always be evident as they deal with the disruption to their routines. But it seemed to have absolutely no effect on Brother Rodney at all."

More tears fell from Sela's eyes.

"I've seen very few people who have that kind of serenity," Pastor Grant stated. "It's what I've come to call perfect peace. Isaiah spoke of it—'You will keep those in perfect peace whose minds are focused on You…'

"Brother Rodney knew whatever he faced, God would come and be there with him. He knew that everything was all right."

Sela nodded in agreement.

"July twentieth, the everlasting arms of God gently lifted Brother Rodney up and carried him away to a place that will always be safe and secure, where there will be no more suffering, no sorrow, no more tears, no more sickness, no more pain and no more death. Brother Rodney is with Jesus now. He's up there singing in the choir. Singing and praising Jesus."

Pastor Grant cleared his throat and wiped his forehead with a tissue.

He concluded his eulogy by saying, "We may feel sorrow for now, but I don't think a single one of us would ask that Brother Rodney come back. He is in the presence of our Lord."

Tears streaming down her face, Sela disagreed. She wanted Rodney to come back to her—to their children.

The sound of someone sobbing drew Sela's attention. Leah's crying was becoming louder and louder. Junior picked her up and held her in his lap.

Sela's heart broke as she watched him bury his face in Leah's hair. He could no longer hold back his tears. Ayanna had her arms around Marcus while Leon held Lacey. They were all trying to be so brave.

When the service ended, they were ushered back into the limo by the funeral director.

As they were heading for the cemetery, Junior pointed to the window. "Look, Mom...."

Sela glanced out.

Six black-and-silver trucks bearing the name "Barnes Trucking" were lined up, their headlights on. The drivers all stood beside their trucks, hats in hands. As the limo moved past them, they each saluted, honoring Rodney.

Through her tears, Sela smiled, touched by their gesture.

Ethel, on the other hand, fell apart at the cemetery, setting off a chain reaction with the children.

Holding back her own sobs, Sela picked up Leah, who was crying uncontrollably, and carried her from the grave site to the car.

"It's gonna be okay, sweetie," she murmured.

"I hurt…" Leah moaned. "I want Daddy."

"I know, baby. I know. Mommy hurts, too." Sela wiped away her own tears.

"I don't w-want my d-daddy out there in the dirt. He'll be alone." Leah accepted the tissue Sela held out to her and wiped her eyes. "D-Daddy might get ascared or he might f-feel lonely." She sniffed. "I don't want him to be ascared."

Sela combed her fingers through Leah's warm brown curls. "Sweetie, Daddy isn't really out there in the dirt. He's in Heaven with the Lord."

"Then why are we having a funeral and stuff?"

Leah had stopped crying but her eyes were still bright with tears.

"We just wanted to have a service for Daddy so that everyone who loved him has a chance to say goodbye."

"I didn't say goodbye."

"Would you like to go back out there?"

Leah shook her head. "I don't like it over there. It makes me feel ascared."

"Afraid," Sela murmured.

"Can I say goodbye right here in the car?"

"You sure can, sweetie pie."

"Goodbye, Daddy. I love you and I miss you. Don't forget to visit me in my dreams." Leah peered out the window and blew a kiss towards the heavens.

Turning around to face Sela, she asked, "You think Daddy heard me?"

Sela gathered her daughter in her arms. "I believe he did, baby."

Chapter Eight

After Rodney's interment, Sela and the children rode in silence all the way back to the house.

Ethel and Roman came by briefly but didn't stay long. Everyone assumed that it was because they were overwrought with grief, but Sela believed differently. She was sure they were still upset over the fact that Rodney had been cremated despite the fact that it was his wish. She'd compromised by burying his ashes in a grave, but her in-laws were still very unhappy with her.

Her sister brought a plate of food to her.

Pushing it away, she stated, "I'm not hungry, Shelly."

"Where are the twins?" she asked suddenly. Sela's eyes traveled the room, looking for signs of her children.

"They're upstairs with Mama. Sis, don't worry. They're fine. I think Mama was trying to get them to take a nap."

"Do you know where Junior and the boys are? I need to make sure they're okay."

She made a move to stand, but Shelly stopped her, saying, "Don't get up, Sela. I'll check on them. Ayanna's in the kitchen with—" She frowned. "I think his name is Jay."

Nodding, Sela murmured, "That's her boyfriend."

"I thought as much."

Shelly took a seat beside her sister. "I'm very worried about you." She brushed away a stray curl from Sela's tear-streaked face.

"I'm numb," Sela choked out as salty tears tickled the corners of her mouth.

"That's normal, Sela."

Her eyes bouncing around the room, Sela muttered, "I don't want all these people here. I just want to be alone." Her eyes slid to Shelly. "I'm sorry. I don't mean you—I'm glad to see you and Rusty. Y'all need to visit more."

"My husband fell in love with Raleigh when we came back in March for your anniversary. Ever since, Rusty's been trying to talk me into moving back here. His company wants to transfer him to Research Triangle Park."

"I hope you'll think about it."

"I will." Shelly rose to her feet. "This food is getting cold. I'll go put it away for you in the fridge."

"Can you do me a favor and check on the children for me?"

Her sister nodded. "I will," Shelly promised.

A couple of well-wishers approached Sela.

She politely thanked them for their sympathetic words. Words that meant well but did nothing to stop the heartache and grief that ripped through her heart.

Groaning, Sela rested her forehead in her hand. How was she going to make it without Rodney? How were her kids going to make it without their father?

She was getting a headache.

Three hours later, everyone was gone. Sela's children were upstairs in their rooms; only her parents and sister remained downstairs with her.

Sela hadn't moved since coming home from the funeral. She sat in the formal living room, her hands folded in her lap. She didn't believe that Rodney was gone. She glanced around, eyeing the pictures and mementos of her life with him everywhere.

This can't be happening.

But it is.

I don't want this to be true. I don't want to let go of Rodney.

But you have to.

Sela's mother strolled into the room, putting an end to Sela's conversation with her heart.

"Sugar, why don't you go upstairs and lay down for a while?" she suggested.

Sela nodded. "I think I will, Mama. I'm tired."

She got up and navigated her way to the stairs. "I'll see you in a bit," she said before heading up to her bedroom.

Inside the room, Sela sat on the edge of her bed. "God, I don't really understand why You allowed Rodney to die. I feel so betrayed. I asked You to save him." She paused as if waiting for a response. "I feel as if I'm gonna explode—I'm so angry. I want to vent, but I'm just not sure how to express myself without..." She wiped an escaping tear from her eye. "I don't want to hurt my family, but I just want to be left alone. I need to think. They won't let me think...."

More tears followed.

"I want him back. I want to wake up and find out this has all been a terrible dream. Please give him back to me. Just give him back."

Her only answer was silence.

"Shelly told me you haven't eaten," her mother said as she walked into Sela's bedroom without knocking a few minutes later.

"I'm not hungry."

"You should eat something, sugar."

"I said I'm not hungry," Sela snapped, feeling as if her mother were trying to treat her like a child.

"Sela, I'm just trying to be helpful."

"I know." Sela's voice caught as a new wave of emotion threatened to surface. "I'm sorry for snapping at you."

"I'll leave you alone, then. Just call me or Shelly if you need anything. Otherwise, I'll make sure nobody disturbs you."

Sela got up and prepared to shower. Maybe a few minutes under the spray of water would help calm her. She turned on the shower as hot as she could stand it, then got in.

Rodney would never smile, laugh with the children or hold her in his special way again. Their life together was over.

"I—I'm so mad at You, God. And I'm s—so s—scared. I just don't know how to do this.... How do I live without him?"

She hoped the sound of the running water masked her sobs.

After her shower, Sela put on a pair of Rodney's pajamas, not caring that they hung off her petite body. She held up a sleeve to her nose and sniffed, taking in her husband's scent.

Sela walked over to the dresser and picked up a bottle of Rodney's favorite cologne. She sprayed a little on the pajama shirt.

The four-poster bed was spread with a handmade quilt softened by age to a gentle lavender and ivory color. Drapes in a darker hue hung over the two tall, narrow windows that looked over the porch roof and the front yard.

Sela stepped to the window and peered through, staring out at the half moon. She had no idea how long she stood there.

Rubbing her stinging eyes, Sela turned at the sound of someone knocking. "Yes…"

Ayanna stuck her head inside. "Can I come in?"

Sela nodded. "Sure."

Sniffing, Ayanna stated, "It smells like Daddy in here."

"I sprayed some of his favorite cologne on this shirt." Sela gave her daughter a sad smile. "I just wanted it to smell like him one more time. I thought it might help me sleep."

Ayanna nodded as if she understood.

The twins burst into the room. "Mommy, we want to sleep in here with you," they said in unison.

Sela gestured to the king-sized bed. "Climb in," she responded.

"I bet Marcus and Leon are on their way in here, too," Ayanna whispered.

Since Rodney's death, the children had been sleeping in her bedroom. "It's okay," Sela stated. "Right now it's hard for me to sleep in that huge bed by myself."

She walked over to the bed and climbed in. "Ayanna, there's room for you, too."

Ayanna gave her a grateful smile. "I'll get my pillow. Stephanie is a wild sleeper," she whispered, referring to her cousin who had been spending the last few nights with her in her room. "She kicks me."

On her way out, Ayanna passed her little brothers.

"Can we sleep in your room tonight, Mom?" Marcus inquired.

Sela nodded. "C'mon, sweetie."

When Ayanna returned, she brought Junior with her. Together, they carried extra blankets and pillows with them. While the females settled on the bed, Marcus and Leon made themselves comfortable on the floor beside Junior.

One by one, they drifted off to sleep, all except Sela. She lay in bed listening to the soft sighs and moans her children made as they slept.

She fought back the waves of pain and loneliness that overtook her. Sela reached over and gently brushed away an errant curl off of Leah's face. *My sweet babies… It's so unfair that you have to grow up without your father. It just isn't right.*

Shortly after midnight, Junior woke up and stretched. He glanced over in her direction. "You okay, Mom?"

Sela nodded. "Go back to sleep," she whispered.

Deep down, Sela didn't think she would ever really be okay ever again.

Not without Rodney.

Chapter Nine

⚜

The next morning, Sela woke up fully expecting to find Rodney in bed beside her. When she felt Lacey and Leah's small bodies snuggled against hers, sad memories of what had transpired the day before rushed to the forefront.

Sela felt overwhelming sorrow and closed her eyes. Hearing movement, she opened her eyes and greeted Junior. "Morning, son."

"How you holding up, Mom?"

"I'm trying to manage."

Junior nodded in understanding. He reached over and gave his brother a playful jab. "Wake up, Marcus. Leon, get up."

Sela observed her eldest son quietly. Junior had always been a serious child. But now with Rodney gone, there seemed to be an air of authority about him—even in his voice. He was stepping up to fill the void his father's death left in their lives.

"I'm not playing—y'all need to get up," he repeated. "We got a lot to do today."

Ayanna opened her eyes and sat up. "Good morning," she muttered to no one in particular.

Sela greeted her daughter with a warm smile. "Did you sleep well?"

"I kept waking up, but I slept okay when I did sleep." Ayanna pulled herself off the bed and stood up. "I bet Grandma's downstairs cooking breakfast. I'd planned to get up early to help her…."

Sela climbed out of bed behind her. "Your Aunt Shelly is probably down there with her, too. They both love cooking—I definitely didn't inherit that gene. I only do it out of necessity."

Ayanna gave a short laugh. "I take after you for sure."

Sela walked across the room, where she selected a pair of jeans and a T-shirt to wear. "I'm gonna take a quick shower," she announced.

Junior and his brothers picked up their pillows and blankets before heading out of the bedroom.

"You want me to wake up the girls?" Ayanna asked.

Shaking her head, Sela answered, "I'll get them up after I get dressed."

But a few minutes later in the shower, Sela broke down. "I can't do this, Rodney, I can't do this without you!"

She cried until she could cry no more. Then she stepped out of the shower and dried off.

Sela quickly dressed and combed her hair. She considered

putting on makeup, but changed her mind. There was no point as far as she was concerned. Rodney was no longer around to appreciate her efforts.

Sela's eyes looked around her bedroom. Every piece of furniture had been selected lovingly by her and Rodney. He had painted the sand-colored walls with care. She still couldn't fully digest that her husband was gone and would not be coming back.

"Why did you have to leave me, Rodney? Why?"

"Mommy, you say something?"

Sela turned around to find Lacey sitting up in bed rubbing her eyes.

"Morning, baby," she greeted.

"I want Daddy."

"I know," Sela murmured. "I want him, too."

Lacey eased out of bed. "God has lots of people in heaven already. He don't need Daddy, too."

"I feel the same way, but I guess God needed your daddy for some special purpose. We may not understand it, but we have to trust the Lord."

Sela wasn't sure she really believed a word of what she was telling her daughter, but she couldn't think of anything else to say to offer comfort.

"I saw Daddy last night," Leah muttered as she kicked the covers off her small frame and sat up in bed. "He came to see me in my dreams."

Lacey frowned. "Why don't Daddy visit me? I want to see him, too."

Sela held her arms out to Lacey. "Honey, I'm sure Daddy

will visit you, too. I'm sure all of us will see Daddy in our dreams. He was a big part of our lives."

Lacey cuddled up against her mother. "But why did he visit Leah first?" Peering up at Sela, she asked, "Does that mean that Daddy loves her more than me?"

"Honey, that's not it at all." Sela prayed Lacey wouldn't persist with her questions because she truly didn't have any answers.

Leah stood up in the bed and walked over to the edge where her twin and mother were standing. "Daddy loves us both the same. Daddy came to me because I called for him. I prayed for him and I asked God to let Daddy visit me. You only have to pray and God will answer. They tell us that in church, remember?"

Lacey seemed satisfied with her sister's explanation and let the subject drop.

Sela combed her hair and pulled it back into a ponytail. She turned around to face her daughters. "It's time for you two to take a shower and brush your teeth. I bet Grandma's made a delicious breakfast for y'all."

"Mommy, I don't feel like eating. I'm not hungry," Leah announced.

"What's wrong?" Sela inquired. Leah had always been a finicky eater, but she loved breakfast foods. "Does your tummy hurt?"

Leah shook her head. "No. I just don't want to eat right now."

"Well maybe you'll feel like eating something after you get dressed." Sela opened her bedroom door. "C'mon girls. Let's get you showered."

* * *

Sela didn't have much of an appetite, either, but she managed to force down a muffin and a cup of coffee.

After breakfast, she tried to help Shelly clean the kitchen until her mother forced her out.

Desperate for something to occupy her mind, Sela made her way up the stairs to the home office where Rodney ran Barnes Trucking. She noted the stack of invoices on her desk and shook her head. She would tackle them in due time.

Rodney's desk had a stack of papers on it as well. Those she would have to go through sometime this week because payroll was coming up.

"Lord, I just don't know about this. It's too much." Sela played with her ponytail as she stood in the doorway. "I can't run this business alone. What was Rodney thinking?"

Her mother came up behind her. "Sugar, why don't you let your father help you out with the business?"

Sela turned to look at Althea. "I don't know, Mama. I'd really appreciate the help, but I feel so restless. And tired." She paused and took a deep breath. "Payroll is due next week but I just don't have the energy to deal with it."

"Honey, that's what we're here for—to help you with whatever needs to be done." Althea took Sela by the hand and led her back into the hallway. "All your father knows is trucking—let him take care of this and you go lie down. You don't look as if you slept a wink last night."

"I eventually fell asleep. I kept waking up though."

"I noticed you're not eating."

"Mama, I had a muffin. I just wasn't that hungry."

Althea didn't respond.

When Sela reached her bedroom, she turned suddenly and hugged her mother. "I'm so glad you're here, Mama. I don't think I could make it if you weren't. I love you."

"I love you, too."

A few minutes later, Sela was alone in her room and grateful for the solitude. Her mother amazed her. Life simply seemed to go on for her, while her life had come to a crashing halt.

A surge of anger coursed through her body, motivating Sela to throw a vase that contained fresh flowers across the room.

Shaking uncontrollably, she sat down on the bench at the end of her bed with her face in her hands and tried to silence the sobs coming from her soul. Deep in the recesses of her mind, Sela knew she needed to get a grip on her emotions, but she couldn't quite fathom how to accomplish that particular feat.

When Sela couldn't contain them any longer, loud wails erupted from her throat and overflowed.

Shelly and her daughter, Stephanie, rushed into the room with Ayanna on their heels.

Her sister took in the sight before her and instructed the young women to leave them alone. Shelly sank down to the floor beside her and took Sela in her arms.

"Cry as much as you want, Sela. It's okay to grieve."

Shelly held Sela in her arms until she stopped crying.

"I'm so sorry."

"For what? Grieving your husband? You have nothing to be sorry about."

Sela sat up and wiped her face with her hands. "I didn't mean to break down like that."

"Sis, it's fine. You lost your husband and you're entitled to mourn."

Wiping her eyes, Sela uttered, "I don't want to upset the children."

"Ayanna is practically a grown woman—I'm sure she understands your pain."

"I'm supposed to be strong. How can I help them cope with their loss if I'm crying all the time?"

"You'll take it one day at a time, Sela."

"Yeah."

"Right now it sounds difficult, I know, but sis, you can do it. Just take it day by day."

"Shelly, I wasn't prepared for this. Rodney and I always talked about growing old together." They'd talked about doing many things together...

"I know what you mean. It's not something you really think about. Rusty and I certainly haven't given death much thought. Not until Rodney passed."

Sela eyed her sister. "Shelly, cherish the time you have with Rusty. Don't let a day go by without telling him how much he means to you. Make sure you tell your daughter, too. Death steals our loved ones so quickly."

God, how could you take Rodney from us? What good can come out of this? She railed in her mind.

Chapter Ten

 ❧

Rodney's best friend, Derek Fisher stopped by for a visit two days after the funeral.

Before Rodney died, Sela had overhead him ask Derek to look after her and the children if anything happened to him.

The tall, muscular man with the bald head, sienna complexion and dark friendly eyes would keep his word to Rodney because the two men had been as close as brothers.

Derek was dressed in a T-shirt, a pair of sweatpants and sneakers. He was either coming from or going to the gym to work out, Sela assumed. Derek wasn't one to dress so casual. A lawyer by profession, he was always dressed in suits or dress slacks and silk shirts. In all the years she'd known him, Sela had never seen him in a pair of jeans.

They walked arm in arm toward the back of the house. Derek waited until Sela was seated before sitting down beside her in the family room.

Sela put on a brave face. "We're doing as well as can be. It's a big adjustment," she confessed.

He nodded in understanding.

"I'm angry, Derek," she blurted suddenly. "I feel such rage over Rodney's leaving me. I have the children, the business…his parents." Sela's eyes watered over. "I just want to scream—I'm so mad."

He reached over and took her small hand in his. "Just remember that you're not alone. You have me and you have Rita. You have Rodney's parents. We're not going to abandon you."

"Would it be terrible of me to say that I just want Rodney? I know you're busy—Rita has her own life, and I definitely don't want his parents. *I just want my husband.*"

Derek gave her a sympathetic smile. "Not at all. I do understand."

"I'm considering my mom's suggestion to take the children to Jacksonville to stay with my parents for a few days. If I do, we'll probably leave out tomorrow morning with them."

"You're not going to attend Rodney's memorial service?"

Sela frowned in confusion. "What are you talking about, Derek?"

"Rodney's parents are holding a memorial service for him at their home church."

"That's right. I didn't think they were really serious about it. They never said anything else to me about it."

"It's on the thirtieth of this month," Derek announced.

Folding her arms across her chest, Sela stated, "They were furious with me for having Rodney cremated, even though that's what he wanted me to do. That's why they're having this service. The kids can go, but I think I'll sit this one out. Besides I'm sure they don't want me there anyway."

"You're his wife. It's your place to be there, regardless of how they may feel."

"As far as Mr. and Mrs. Barnes are concerned, I *was* Rodney's wife. Now that he's dead, I'm just his widow and no longer a part of their lives."

"If you decide not to attend the service—just make sure it's because you don't want to be there and for no other reason."

"I will," Sela promised.

They heard the twins talking as they descended the stairs.

"How are the girls?" Derek inquired.

Sela glanced over her shoulder before saying, "They are dealing with Rodney's passing. They don't fight me anymore on staying up. They dream about their father."

"Marcus and Leon handling everything okay?"

"Marcus is really quiet. He doesn't talk much about his dad. I think Leon is trying to be like Junior. He seems to take his cues from him. Overall, I'm really proud of my babies. They're all really trying to be strong."

At the moment, Lacey ran into the room and threw her tiny body into Derek's lap. "Uncle Derek! Uncle Derek!"

"Hello, pretty girl. Have you been behaving?"

"Uh-huh," Lacey muttered. "I been good. Right Mommy?"

Nodding, Sela laughed.

Leah strolled into the room carrying her doll. She walked over to her mother and climbed into her lap. "Mommy, I love you."

"I love you, too." Sela planted a kiss on her forehead. "Did you speak to Uncle Derek?"

"Hey, Uncle Derek," Leah greeted.

"Hello, beauty," he responded. "What you know good?"

"Nothing."

Sela and Derek burst into laughter.

Althea entered the room, asking, "Can I get something for y'all?"

"We're fine, Mama. Thank you." After a bit the girls were ready to do something else, so Sela settled them in front of the television. Derek stayed for another hour talking to Sela.

He left right before lunch, leaving Sela alone with her thoughts.

"I thought Uncle Derek was here," Ayanna uttered when she dropped down onto the sofa beside her mother.

"He just left," Sela responded. "He had a meeting and needed to get back to the office."

"I woulda come down before now if I'd known he was leaving so soon. I was on the phone with Jay. He wants to come by this afternoon. Is that okay with you?"

"Of course, sweetie. I don't mind if you have company."

Althea interrupted them. "Lunch is ready. Y'all c'mon to the table so you can eat."

Shaking her head, Sela stated, "I'm not hungry, Mama."

Althea threw up her hands in resignation. "Oka-ay. Well, if you get hungry later, your food will be in the fridge."

"Thanks."

Ayanna stood up. "I'm starving, Grandma. I missed out on breakfast."

"If you'd stay off the phone with that boy, you might make it down in time to eat. Girl, you're gonna lose weight you can't afford to lose if you keep doing that."

Heat rushed to Ayanna's face. "Grandma, I can't believe you said that."

"Yanna," Sela called out. "Honey, do you know anything about a memorial service for your father?"

"Yes, ma'am. Grandmother wanted to have one."

"Why didn't you tell me?"

"Grandmother said you were too distraught to go through another service. She thought it would be best not to put you through this again."

Sela stood up. "You don't really believe that, do you?"

Ayanna glanced over her shoulder to where the other children were sitting. Lowering her voice, she said, "Mom, I don't really think she meant any harm. Grandmother even said that if it was too much for any of us, we didn't have to attend."

Sela didn't believe Ethel had any good intentions where she was concerned, but, too emotionally wrung-out to argue the point, she decided to let the matter drop for now.

Early the next morning, Sela got up and started breakfast. Shelly and her family had left the evening before and her parents were planning to leave in a couple of hours. Everyone was still upstairs, so she sat down on one of the bar stools and had a cup of coffee.

Lately she seemed to just go through the motions of living. Sela got up each morning, watched the children eat breakfast, then settled in the family room for the rest of the day. She tried to stay strong for her kids, but it was a constant struggle.

Every now and then, Sela would jump up to seek out Rodney, temporarily forgetting that he was gone, but mostly, the pain of her grief was her constant companion.

The telephone rang.

Sela peered at the caller ID, and then decided not to answer it.

There were messages on both the personal and business phones, but she didn't care. She still wasn't ready to deal with anything, including Barnes Trucking. Right now, Sela didn't feel capable enough to be a mother. "Help me, Lord," she pleaded as she prepared a turkey, bacon and cheese quiche. "Even though I'm angry with You, I know I can't do this without You."

Sela thought about the upcoming memorial service for Rodney. After giving it further thought, Sela had made a decision. She planned to attend the service with the children.

Sela told her parents about her decision right after breakfast.

"Mama, Dad, I've changed my mind about going to Florida. The children and I are gonna stay here. We're going to the memorial service Rodney's parents are having for him."

"You sure you want to do that?" Althea questioned. "You barely made it through the funeral. I don't know why Roman and Ethel are trying to put y'all through this all over again. One time is enough."

"They need this service, I think."

"What about the children, Sela? You think they need to be put through another service?"

"I don't know," she answered. "I just think we should be there."

Althea shrugged. "Okay. Do what you feel you must. I just know how they treat you. How they've always treated you."

"I'll be fine, Mama. It's just a small service to honor Rodney's life. My in-laws won't lose sight of that."

"Do you want us to stay here and go with you?" Sela's father asked. "We can stay another week."

Sela shook her head. "You don't have to do that. Thanks, Daddy."

Two hours later, she stood in the doorway waving goodbye to her parents. "Drive safe," Sela called out.

"'Bye Nanny. 'Bye Poppy." Leah and Lacey said in unison.

Marcus waved from the door, then turned and walked back inside the house. Leon stood on the lawn just staring after them.

Sela folded her arms across her chest and leaned against the front door. *What am I gonna do now? Everybody's gone.*

And somehow life must go on.

Chapter Eleven

❧

Before Sela's parents left for Florida, they tried to get her to leave the house for a little while, but she staunchly refused.

She wasn't ready and told them so. Instead, Sela chose to spend her day in the family room going through photo album after photo album.

Later that evening, she lay in bed reliving the day that changed her and the children's lives forever.

After Dr. Reynolds gave her Rodney's diagnosis, she immediately went in search of her children.

Sela's eyes watered at the sight of her precious babies huddled together with fearful expressions on their faces.

Ayanna saw her first. "Mama, is Daddy okay? What did the doctor say? Is he gonna recover from the stroke?"

Sela could only nod. She couldn't burden them with something she didn't quite understand herself.

"Can he come home with us?" Lacey asked. "I want Daddy to come home."

"Me, too," Leah contributed. "When can we see Daddy?"

Junior rose to his full height. "Come on y'all. Give Mom a chance to talk." He placed an arm around her. "You okay?"

Sela nodded a second time. "I don't want y'all to worry. Your Daddy is a fighter. He will be fine and home with us real soon. The doctors are gonna give him some more medication and run a couple of more tests. Now I want y'all to go on home. You don't have to worry. He's gonna be fine."

Junior looked down at her. "Mom, you're not trying to spare us—'cause if you are, you don't have to. Dad had a stroke or something, didn't he?"

Sela couldn't lie to her children. She gave a slight nod. "Yes, your daddy had a small stroke, but don't worry. He's gonna be fine," she replied. "He just needs to rest more and eat better." Taking a step backward, she told them, "Y'all go on home. I'm going back to your father's room, but I'll call y'all later." She forced a smile. "I promise."

"What's a stroke?" Marcus asked.

Junior placed a hand on his brother's shoulder. "I'll explain everything when we get home."

"I want to give you a hug and a kiss," Leah uttered. She rushed to her mother, wrapping her arms around her thighs.

Sela picked up her daughter and kissed her. "I love you, baby."

Junior held up Lacey so that Sela could kiss her, too. She embraced each of her children. "I'll give y'all a call in a couple of hours, okay?"

"Mama, I can stay at home tonight if you need me to—" Ayanna pushed a curling tendril away from her face.

"No," Sela interjected quickly. "Honey, you don't have to miss your class."

"It's not like I can really concentrate anyway. With Daddy in the hospital...well..."

"You go back to campus and I'll stay home with the kids," Junior offered. "I have a late class tomorrow."

Ayanna turned back to her mother, her dark, earnest eyes sought Sela's. "You're sure about this?"

"Yes, go on back home, honey. I'll call you if something comes up."

Ayanna nodded. "Give Daddy a hug and a big kiss from all of us."

"I will."

Sela made her way back to her husband's room. She paused just outside the room, long enough to take several deep breaths before walking inside. "Hey, honey."

From the bed, Rodney gave her a weak smile. "You look tired. You should go on home."

She was thankful the stroke had not affected his ability to talk. "I'm not leaving you."

"Sweetheart, I'll be fine. Just take the kids home—"

"I mean it, Rodney. I'm staying here with you. Ayanna and Junior just left with the children." Sela reached for the phone. "I need to call your parents."

Rodney stopped her. "Maybe we should wait until tomorrow morning. It's late."

Before Sela could open her mouth to respond, his parents burst into the room.

Ethel glared at Sela. "At least Ayanna was thoughtful enough to call and tell us our son is in the hospital." Rushing to Rodney's side, she inquired, "Hon, are you okay?"

He nodded.

"Rodney had a stroke," Sela announced.

"Oh, dear Lord," Ethel muttered.

"A stroke?" Roman sputtered. "He's too young to have a stroke."

"I thought the same thing." Sela shook her head. "I guess we're wrong in our assumptions. But that's not—" Sela stopped short when Rodney shook his head at her. She couldn't believe that Rodney wasn't going to tell his parents what was really going on with him. When their eyes met, his gaze pleaded with her to remain silent. She released a soft sigh of resignation.

"What were you going to say?" Roman prompted. "Now what I'd really like to know is why you didn't call us."

Sela saw the frown set into his features. "I was more concerned with my husband's health. I was just about to give y'all a call before you barged in here."

One corner of Roman's mouth twisted upward but he didn't comment. He turned his attention back to Rodney.

"Sela was about to call you." Rodney paused for a moment before continuing. "I didn't see the point in having y'all drive all the way from Chapel Hill tonight. There was nothing y'all could do except sit around here and worry. You can do that from the house."

"Son, you're in the hospital," Roman pointed out. "We don't want to be anywhere else."

Rodney repositioned himself as best he could. "Thanks for coming. I appreciate it."

When Rodney glanced over at Sela, she forced a smile. She didn't want to do anything to upset him.

"Where are the children?" Ethel asked. "I didn't see them in the waiting room."

"I just sent them home."

"Well, we're here with Rodney now," Ethel stated while straightening the covers on the bed. "You can go home to them. I'm sure they're scared out of their wits."

"Junior is there with them," Sela responded. "I promised to give them a call later."

"I think it would be best if you went home to them, Sela. Junior is a child—you can't expect him to take on your responsibility as a parent." Tilting her chin in a haughty manner, Ethel added, "I would think you'd know that."

Sela's strained smile vanished, wiped away by her astonishment.

"Mother, don't start," Rodney warned. "If you're going to harass my wife, then it's best that you be the one to leave."

She gave her son a wounded look. "Excuse me?"

Sela surprised everyone, including herself by coming to Ethel's defense. "Babe, I don't think she was trying to harass me. Your mother is just very worried and concerned. I can understand that."

Rodney began to cough, bringing Sela quickly to his side.

"Is he okay?" Ethel questioned.

"He just needs to rest," Sela stated.

Rodney dropped his head back. "I...I'm okay."

A tense silence surrounded them.

Clearing her throat, Sela uttered, "I'll be right back. I need to get something to drink." She paused long enough to ask, "Can I bring y'all something back?"

"No, thanks," they replied in unison.

She hoped that Ethel and Roman would be gone by the time she returned, but was disappointed. They had set up camp in Rodney's hospital room. Sela knew they were worried about him just as much as she was.

Inside the room, she strolled past her in-laws, moving to reclaim her position by her husband's bedside.

"Did you check on the children?" he asked.

"I did," Sela confirmed. "They're fine. Just very worried about you."

He seemed relieved.

When the nurse entered the room, Sela said, "I really think you and Mrs. Barnes should go home. I promise I'll call you if anything happens with Rodney. The doctor says that he should recover—he even thinks that the paralysis on his left side is gonna go away."

Ethel shook her head. "I don't feel right about leaving my son."

"I do understand," Sela stated. "But you don't have to worry because I'm not going anywhere. I'm staying with Rodney."

Although Ethel looked like she wanted to protest, Roman stopped her by saying, "All right. We'll leave, but we'll be back first thing in the morning."

"I'll call you," Sela promised. "But I don't foresee anything happening. Dr. Reynolds…he seemed optimistic."

At that time, Sela truly believed that Rodney would recover.

How wrong she'd been.

Chapter Twelve

❦

Rodney had only been buried for one week.

Sela stood outside the sanctuary for a moment. She waited a few seconds to catch her breath before entering the church.

She'd rushed ahead of the others because she wanted to catch Roman and Ethel alone inside the sanctuary. Sela knew there was a chance that they would be angry over her coming but she refused to be deterred.

Roman spotted her first and whispered something to Ethel, who confronted her in the foyer.

"Sela, I didn't really expect to see you here."

She lifted her chin, meeting her mother-in-law's icy gaze straight on. "This is Rodney's memorial service and I wouldn't be anywhere else, Mrs. Barnes. I was his wife."

"Where are the children?"

Sela tossed a look over her shoulder. "Junior's bringing the children inside now." Turning back to face Ethel, she stated in a low whisper, "We should probably join everyone in the sanctuary, Mrs. Barnes."

Ethel glared at her with burning, reproachful eyes. "I don't need you to tell me what to do, Sela."

"Mrs. Barnes, I didn't come here to fight with you. This is hard enough as it is. Let's just call a truce for today. Okay?"

"I lost my s-son…and you had the nerve to cremate him, after we begged and pleaded with you not to…."

Sela held up her hand to stop Ethel. "Mrs. Barnes, I understand how you must feel. I didn't want to cremate Rodney's body, but I had to honor his final wishes. I'm sure you would've done the same thing in my position." Sela's eyes raked over Ethel. She wanted to say something—anything to take away some of her mother-in-law's pain.

Ethel glowered at Sela. "It's over and done with now. We can't turn back the clock, can we?"

"I really am sorry, Mrs. Barnes. I just wanted to do what Rodney wanted. That's all."

Ethel responded with, "We're going to be starting in a few minutes."

"Let's find a seat," Sela whispered to Ayanna as the children entered the foyer. "They're getting ready to start the service."

Sela left right after the service while the children went to their grandparents' house for a light repast.

Instead of driving home, Sela went to Rita's house.

"How was the service?" Rita asked when they were settled on the sofa in her family room.

"Mrs. Barnes is really upset over Rodney being cremated. It's not like I really wanted that, but I promised Rodney. It was his request and she just doesn't seem to understand that."

Rita poured two glasses of lemonade for herself and Sela. "I'm sure she'll realize that sooner or later."

"I know they're grieving—so am I. I just don't understand why they don't get it that instead of fighting, we should be comforting each other?"

"I guess you just have to keep communicating with them," Rita suggested before taking a sip of her lemonade. "One day they'll have no choice but to listen."

Sela's lips thinned with anger. "I've tried for twenty years." She played with her glass. "I'm tired, Rita. I've given it my all—now I'm just sick of trying. What do you think is gonna happen with Rodney gone? Things are not gonna get any better—not between us."

Rita shrugged. "You never know. You still have their grandchildren. Ethel and Roman love them to death."

Sela agreed. "Yeah, they do love the kids. It's the only thing I have in common with them—we all love the children like crazy."

"Maybe that'll be the bond to bring you all together."

She looked over at Rita in astonishment. "I know you don't believe that."

Rita broke into a short laugh. "Stranger things have happened."

"It would take a miracle for us to ever bond. Rodney would practically have to come back from the dead."

Chapter Thirteen

$\maltese$

Sela stared down at the black, leather-bound journal in her hands that once belonged to Rodney. It was one of the few things besides his study Bible that he'd asked Sela to bring to the hospital for him. She felt a shred of guilt at the thought of reading his entries.

This is all I have left of him. It won't hurt just to read a little, she decided.

March 27
"This is my first week at rehab. I had a stroke on March 15th. Two days after my twentieth wedding anniversary. I have never been so scared in my life. But I wasn't just scared for myself. I was scared for Sela. The look of fear on her face tore at my heart.

The doctor told me that I have cardiomyopathy. Sela

wanted to tell my parents, but I told her no. It's just too much to handle at once. My grandfather died from this disease. What does it mean for me?

Although I won't admit this to Sela, I am afraid at times. But the truth is that my faith is not in the doctors—only in God."

Sela closed the journal and laid it on the bedside table. She never suspected that Rodney was afraid because he always seemed so calm and...and brave. He had been the one to keep her from panicking.

"Everything is gonna be fine, baby," Rodney always would assure her. "I'm a fighter. Don't you know that about me? I don't intend to just give into this disease. I'm gonna fight it every step of the way."

Sela had swallowed with difficulty before finding her voice. "But how do you know you can beat it? Isn't this the same condition your grandfather had?"

He nodded. "I'm not worried because I believe that God will pull us through."

"God is responsible for this, don't you agree? You're sick because of Him, Rodney?" She clenched her hand until her nails entered her palm.

His expression darkened with an unreadable emotion. "He allowed this for a reason, Sela."

"Then it must be because of me. You're sick because I left the church. This is God's way of punishing me."

Rodney wore a look of confusion. "Why would He be punishing you?"

Shrugging, Sela answered, "Because I stopped going to church, I guess. Because I'm not saved, like you."

"God's not like that, Sela. This condition I have— It's just that—a condition. God isn't dishing out vengeance."

How do you know? she wanted to ask. Instead, she bent down and planted a gentle kiss on his forehead. "Let's not talk about this anymore. There's been way too much excitement in here." Her voice drifted into a hushed whisper. "Close your eyes and get some rest."

"I love you, Sela."

"I love you, too, babe."

As she watched Rodney sleep, all her nervousness and fear slipped back to grip her. *Am I right, God? Is this happening because I left the church? Please don't punish Rodney for my sins. Oh, Father God, I beg You to step in and make my husband well.*

While Rodney was sleeping, Sela stepped outside of the room to stretch her legs.

"Hey…"

Sela turned around to find Rita standing there. She hugged her friend. "What are you doing here?"

"Ayanna called and told me that Rodney was in the hospital and that he'd had a stroke. How is he?"

"Oh, Rita, I'm so glad you're here." She folded her arms across her chest. "I don't know if I can handle this by myself."

"Sweetie, I'm here." Rita led her over to the waiting area. "Sela, you're trembling. Why don't you take a seat and let me get you something to drink?"

The contents of Sela's stomach rose, causing her to break loose and to rush to the nearest bathroom. Bile burned her throat as she emptied everything she'd eaten into the toilet.

Later, a weakened Sela rinsed out her mouth with water from the sink before leaving the bathroom. Rita was instantly by her side.

"You okay, Sela?"

She nodded, breathing in shallow, quick gasps. "Just need to sit down for a minute."

Her eyes traveled to the clock. "I can't believe this is happening. Rodney had a stroke and if that isn't enough, he has a problem with his heart. It's called dilated cardiomyopathy or something like that. His grandfather died of that same disease. He died months after he was diagnosed. That's why it scares me so much."

"What do we know about this disease?"

"Not a whole lot," she admitted. "But I plan to do some research. The only thing I know is that heart disease is the leading cause of death for African-Americans."

"It's the leading cause of death for *all* Americans, Sela," Rita corrected her. "You know it's also the leading cause of death for women, too."

Sela nodded. "You hear these statistics all the time, but you don't really take them in until something like this happens." She shivered slightly. "I can't lose him."

"You won't. We just have to think positive and have faith that the Lord will carry Rodney through. Everything will be all right. Prayer is powerful, you know?"

Sela pressed pale knuckles to her mouth. After a moment, she muttered, "I can't help but feel that all this is my fault."

"How in the world did you come to this conclusion?" Rita questioned. "You talking about your cooking? We know you can't…" her attempt at light humor evaporated at the look on Sela's face.

"I stopped going to church. I think God is punishing me."

Shaking her head, Rita stated, "I don't believe that."

"You sound like Rodney."

"He's right, then. God doesn't punish us with sickness—He's not like that at all."

Sela walked over to a nearby window and stared out, her mind fluttering away in anxiety.

Rita followed her.

They stood there together for what seemed like an eternity to Sela.

"I need to go back and check on Rodney," Sela announced.

"I'll be in the waiting room if you need to talk."

"Rita, you don't have to stay. Go home. I'll call you if I need you."

"You're sure?"

"No," Sela answered. "But it's the fair thing to do. I don't want you sitting out here all night while I'm in there with Rodney." She embraced Rita. "Thanks so much for coming. I really appreciate it."

"Give Rodney my best."

"I will," Sela promised. She waited for her nervous stomach to settle before going back to Rodney's room.

Sela's mind returned to the present. That night while Rodney slept, she had a long talk with God and she made promises, she'd yet kept.

* * *

"Honey, you've got to put some real food in your belly," Sela advised Leah. "Mommy doesn't want you to get sick. Why don't you try some soup for lunch today?"

Shaking her head, Leah stated, "Ice cream is all I want. It makes me feel better."

Sela remained silent. She understood on some level what Leah was going through. She really couldn't eat anything herself. Every time she tried, Sela ended up sick.

Rodney had been gone for twelve days. She'd gone from one hundred thirty pounds down to one fifteen. Rita had prepared a big pot of chicken soup two days ago and brought it over, so Sela nibbled on that to keep food in her stomach.

Even Junior had experienced a loss of appetite, Sela noticed. He normally ate several times a day—now he was eating once or twice.

"Do whatever it takes to make it through one day at a time," her mother had told her when Sela confided Leah's sudden fondness for ice cream. The little girl never cared for it in the past.

"What do you guys feel like doing today?" Sela asked her children. "It's Saturday. We've got the whole day to ourselves."

Lacey raised her hand, prompting giggles and chuckles from her siblings.

"Yes, baby."

"Can we watch some of the family videos? Like the one from when we went to Disney World."

Sela glanced at the other children.

They nodded in agreement.

"Sure."

"I'm up for that," Junior confessed. "We have all those movies here—let's just watch them. We don't even have to get dressed. We can stay in our pajamas."

The telephone rang and Ayanna jumped up to answer it.

"It's Aunt Rita."

Sela made a face before taking the phone. Putting a finger to her mouth, she murmured, "Shh."

"Hey, Rita."

"What are y'all up to?"

"Nothing much. We're going to lie around in our pajamas and watch family videos and some movies. I'm gonna order pizza for dinner. We're doing a lock-in this weekend."

"Sounds like fun. Since I'm practically family—can I join y'all?"

"Aunt Rita wants to join us," Sela announced. "Should we let her?"

"Yeah," they all chorused.

"Just tell her to wear pajamas," Ayanna stated.

"And they have to be appropriate ones," Junior chimed in. "Tell her it's young children over here."

Sela could hear her friend laughing on the other end of the phone line.

"I'll be there shortly. How about I bring some burgers and fries for lunch?"

Sela repeated Rita's offer.

"I just want some ice cream," Leah responded. "I don't want nothing else. I want a chocolate milk shake. That's what I want."

"I heard her," Rita said to Sela's ear. "I'll get the food and I'll see y'all in a few minutes. Don't start nothing until I get there."

Sela was grateful that Rita was coming over. She would need the strength of her best friend to help her make it through this walk of memories.

"This turned out better than I thought it would," Sela confessed when she and Rita were alone in the kitchen. "I thought seeing those old videos would tear the children apart, but now I think they helped them some."

Rita agreed. "I know what you mean. I wanted to come over because I didn't know what would happen."

"It's hard to imagine that we'll never see Rodney again."

"You can see him anytime you want," Rita countered. "Just pull out a video. You guys have millions."

Sela laughed. "He used to get on my nerves with that camcorder."

Rita embraced her. "I'm so proud of you."

"For what?"

"I can see how hard you're working to keep your family together and how you're trying to be so strong for your children."

Sela turned around to face her friend. "Marcus doesn't say much, but I see that he's hurting. When I try to get him to talk to me, he just shrugs everything off. I think he's trying to be so strong, but he's just a little boy. What can I do to help him?"

"Just give him time and be there for him. That's all you can do."

Chapter Fourteen

❧

April 15

"Since I have been here in rehab, I have been meeting with members of a cardiac rehabilitation team who are counseling me on how to manage this condition. Sela sits in on most of the meetings, taking notes on nutrition, weight reduction, stress reduction and physical activity. She's not gonna allow me to cheat.

I am thankful for being able to sit up on my own again. The paralysis disappeared before I left the hospital. Thank You, God. I believe that my healing is on the way. I no longer need to use a cane for walking and the doctors say that I'll be able to go home in a day or so.

This makes me happy because I know Sela is exhausted.

I keep telling her that she doesn't have to come out

here every day, but my wife is stubborn. I've noticed the dark circles under her eyes and I know she's tired, but once she's made up her mind to do something—there's no stopping her.

I am tired of this room and long to sleep in my big, comfortable king-sized bed. Although my family has been here to visit regularly, I prefer being home with them.

I miss my children and spending time with them. Lacey and Leah are growing up and I feel like I'm missing it. I can't even take my sons to a basketball game.

I know they understand that I would be with them if I could. My children are wonderful and they make me so proud. I have been truly blessed with a great family. I couldn't ask for anything more.

If I could go home, maybe Sela could relax some. I worry about her and all she's doing to keep the family together. We have always been a team—I'm not sure she can handle everything by herself.

If only I could count on my parents to help her. I am thankful they are at least being civil towards one another. I guess I can't ask for anything more."

"All I wanted to do was help you, Rodney," Sela murmured after reading his entry in the journal. Back then, they were so full of hope and determination. She wanted to learn everything she could about the condition. "Knowledge is power. At least that's what everybody says."

Her eyes traveled downward. Sela reread Rodney's entry from April fifteenth.

"I was so glad when you told me you were coming home," she said, as if Rodney were there with her. "It was a dream come true for me. It meant that you were getting better. That was the one day your parents and I truly put our differences aside…"

She had called Rodney's parents and told them the good news, that Rodney was coming home. Grinning, she listened as Roman repeated the news to Ethel, who immediately took the phone from her husband.

"Sela, this is wonderful news. Thank you for calling us."

"I'm going to pick Rodney up around ten. I was thinking you and Mr. Barnes should come over tomorrow and even have dinner with us. We'll make it a small celebration."

"Do you need me to bring anything?"

"I have everything. I'm going to make a couple of Rodney's favorites."

"But isn't he on a special diet?"

"Yes. He can have grilled chicken, which he loves, and I'll make some rice and broccoli."

"I'll bring some yeast rolls," Ethel offered. "Rodney loves my yeast rolls. And I can bring him some of my cinnamon raisin muffins. He used to love having them for breakfast."

Sela held her tongue. Deep down, she knew Ethel wasn't trying to be as pushy as she sounded. She simply wanted to do something special for her son. "That's fine, Mrs. Barnes."

Sela hummed softly as she moved about the house, cleaning up. Rodney was coming home…things couldn't be any better.

* * *

April seventeenth, Sela brought Rodney home from the rehabilitation center.

"I want you to go right on upstairs and get in bed," she ordered the moment they set foot in the house. "The doctor said that resting is a large part of your recovery process."

"He didn't say that I had to stay in bed, sweetheart," Rodney argued. "He just wants me to take it easy."

Sela wasn't backing down. "I want you to stay in bed for the rest of today. Tomorrow you can get up, but not today. You just got out of the hospital."

Rodney let out a long sigh. "Whatever you say, *Doctor*."

Leah and Lacey rushed down the stairs screaming, "Daddy!"

He put on a big smile and held open his arms, embracing them both. "My babies," he murmured. "I missed you darlings."

"I missed you so much, Daddy," Leah announced. "I was so scared."

"Me, too," Lacey contributed. "I'm so glad you're home now. I don't want you to be sick anymore."

Sela watched her husband with his daughters. Rodney loved his children more than his own life. He was a good father. Her eyes watered at the thought of losing him. She had believed her family could never survive without him.

The moment Ethel walked through the front door, she tried to take charge.

"Rodney, you go on upstairs and get in bed," she ordered.

"You just got out of the hospital and you need to rest. Remember what the doctor said."

Sela gritted her teeth to keep from losing her temper. Fuming, she stalked off toward the kitchen to check on dinner.

She slowed her steps when she heard Rodney call her name. Turning around, she inquired, "Did you need something, hon?"

"You okay?"

Her eyes traveled to Ethel, who was standing next to him, then back to Rodney. "I just need to check on dinner."

"Sela can take care of herself," Ethel stated. "It's you that we're worried about. Roman, help your son up to his room. He shouldn't have been up this long."

Ayanna followed Sela into the kitchen. "Grandmother's just trying to help."

"I know. That's why I haven't killed her yet," Sela grumbled. "It never fails—she always finds a way to put me down." She released a long sigh. "The woman gets on my last nerve."

Ayanna remained silent.

"Can you check on the chicken for me, sweetie?"

"Yes, ma'am."

Sela opened the plastic container Ethel brought over. "The rolls look delicious," she said. "I've tried to make them from scratch but they never turn out the way your grandmother's do."

"Have you asked her how she does them?"

Sela gave her daughter a sidelong glance. "I'm not crazy. She would never give me her recipe."

"Have you asked Grandmother?" Ayanna asked a second time.

"No, and I'm not gonna give her the satisfaction of asking." Sela released a dry chuckle. "Boy, she'd love that."

"Maybe something like this could build a bond between the two of you," Ayanna suggested. "This thing between you and Grandmother is crazy."

"It's not me."

"Mom, you don't help the situation though."

Folding her arms across her chest, Sela questioned, "Whose side are you on?"

"I'm on the side of right. Mom, I love you. I love my grandparents. It doesn't make me feel comfortable when you guys don't get along. Please try…."

Sela eyed her daughter for a moment.

"I know Grandmother can get on your nerves. But that's just a part of who she is and what she does."

"Do I get on your nerves?"

"Mom…"

Smiling, Sela said, "C'mon. You can be honest."

"A little," Ayanna admitted. "Especially when you and my grandparents are at each other. I want all of us to try to get along. Okay?"

"I'll try." Sela held up her hand. "But if your grandmother starts up…" her words died at the expression on Ayanna's face. "Honey, I'll give it my best shot. I promise."

Sela prayed she could keep her word to both Rodney and Ayanna. For years she'd tried to get along with her in-laws, but Ethel and Roman made it very difficult.

For Rodney, she told herself. She would try one more time. For her children.

Chapter Fifteen

❧

Rodney's first day home was spent with Sela, his parents and the children. After dinner, when Roman and Ethel left, they went upstairs and settled into the master bedroom.

Junior had to leave to work the evening shift at the hospital, but Ayanna and the other children joined Sela and Rodney in their parents' room, watching television and talking.

Leaning back against the headboard, Sela picked up the notebook containing information on cardiac rehabilitation and began to read. She wanted to do whatever it took to aid in Rodney's recovery, especially since learning that twenty-five percent of people who have had a stroke were prone to have another within five years.

After reading several articles on cardiomyopathy, Sela worried that Rodney would never be the same—despite the doctor's positive attitude. There was a chance that he wouldn't survive.

Sela chided herself silently for thinking negatively. She would need stronger faith to get through this.

The next day Roman and Ethel arrived shortly before 9:00 a.m.

"Did you know your parents were coming by?" Sela inquired when Junior announced that they were downstairs.

Sitting on the side of the bed, Rodney shook his head. "They didn't tell me anything."

"I wish they woulda called or something," Sela grunted.

Rodney tied the belt on his robe and headed to the door. "I'll go downstairs and keep them company until you get dressed."

Sela gave him an appreciative smile. "I'll be down shortly. See if they want breakfast."

When she was alone, Sela wondered aloud, "Why do they keep popping over here without calling? This is not their house and they certainly wouldn't appreciate me doing that to them."

For as long as she'd been married to Rodney, his parents had basically done as they pleased. It didn't matter whether she and Rodney wanted to spend time alone or just with the children. Roman and Ethel showed up whenever they felt like it.

Rodney would speak to Ethel and Roman about their actions, but it didn't deter them. A few times, her husband became so furious, he demanded they leave.

Sela pushed her irritation with Ethel and Roman aside because Rodney was ill. They were his parents and therefore, concerned about him. But it was only because of his condition that she would be so charitable.

While she showered and dressed, Sela's memories of her early dealings with her in-laws rushed to the forefront.

"Sela, you shouldn't just sit there and hold the baby all the time," Ethel advised during one of her visits to see her granddaughter. "Every time I come over here—you're holding Ayanna."

"That's because she cries when I lay her down. She'll fall asleep if I rock her."

"You're spoiling that child."

"Mrs. Barnes, I only hold Ayanna when she's fussy," Sela tried to explain.

Ethel didn't want to hear it. "You young folks go around having babies and don't know what to do with them... Humph... I just don't know what to say."

"I don't like to hear her cry."

"Crying won't hurt that child," Ethel uttered.

Sela chewed on her lip to keep from responding.

"Didn't your mother tell you anything about babies? Or buy you books on parenting?"

"My mother said that you learn how to be a parent through trial and error. She says no one can really prepare you on how to be a mother."

"Perhaps it wouldn't be so difficult if you'd waited a little longer."

"Mrs. Barnes, what would my being older have changed? I still wouldn't know what to do or have all the answers."

"But you're now pregnant again. It seems to me that you should get a handle on raising one child before you go out and get another...."

Sela had wanted her in-law's approval so badly. Being a young mother and wife had been a challenge for Sela, and being constantly criticized by Rodney's parent only made things harder. And Rodney... Rodney was caught in the middle.

With her husband trying to recover, she had to be strong for her family's sake. And if that meant keeping the peace with her in-laws, then she'd find a way to do it.

For Rodney.

April 20

"Sela is downstairs with the children and I have to admit I'm grateful for the time alone. I need some time to deal with my own feelings. I'm scared—really scared.

I can't tell Sela this, but I'm scared that the chest pains will come back and that I won't ever be able to work again. I am afraid of dying. Doctor Reynolds has assured me that most people are able to recover and return to work following heart problems, but some of the articles I've read on my condition only serve to depress me. I want that steadfast faith—I thought I had it...until now. When I feel my chest tighten, my body seems to suddenly go on alert. It's still kind of unusual to acknowledge that I have heart problems. I have a heart condition. Me...Rodney Barnes.

This is not how I pictured the rest of my life."

The doorbell rang, drawing Sela's attention from the journal. She laid it on the coffee table before getting up.

Sela was surprised to find Ethel on her doorstep. She hadn't seen her mother-in-law since the memorial service a week ago. "Hello Mrs. Barnes," she said with feigned cheerfulness.

"I was on my way to the furniture store and I thought I'd just stop by," she announced.

"I see…" Sela stepped aside to let her mother-in-law enter the house. She was sick and tired of Ethel just showing up whenever she pleased. Her arms folded across her chest, Sela questioned, "What can I do for you, Mrs. Barnes?"

"I came by to check on the children." Ethel sat down on the sofa in the living room. "I know that they're taking Rodney's death pretty hard." She shook her head sadly. "Haven't we all…." Ethel's voice was thick, as if she were about to cry.

Sela took a seat opposite her. "I'm very proud of them. They are handling this as best and as bravely as they can."

Ethel met her gaze. "How are you?"

Sela was tired of being asked that particular question.

"Sela, did you hear me?"

"I'm sorry. Mrs. Barnes, I'm doing the best I can. Like the children, I'm trying to cope."

"Me, too." Ethel laid her purse down on the coffee table as if she planned to stay awhile. "People tell you that in time, the pain will ease up, but Rodney was my only child. I won't ever stop grieving for him."

"I've never lost anyone really close to me," Sela stated softly. "My grandparents either died before I was born or when I was very young."

"It's never easy. Death is a painful part of our lives. When I lost my father, I thought I would never survive it and even today, I still feel the ache of his death. We were close…."

Sela watched Ethel, who seemed caught up in her memories for the moment.

Ethel ran a hand through her shoulder-length hair. "I miss my father very much, and now with losing Rodney… Life just doesn't seem fair at the moment."

"I know just what you mean," Sela blurted. "I feel the very same way. Right now I'm very angry over losing Rodney. I don't understand why it had to turn out this way. We worked so hard to keep him alive."

"It was never about us—it was all about God," Ethel offered. "He knew long before I had Rodney what would be the outcome."

"I still don't like it, Mrs. Barnes. My children deserve to have their father watch them grow up."

"I agree. It's just out of our hands."

Sela rose to her feet. "I'll go up and wake up the children."

"They're still sleeping? At this hour?"

"It's only nine-thirty in the morning And it's Saturday. Besides, they're still not sleeping very well. The twins sometimes wake up in the middle of the night and the boys, well, they don't go to bed until late."

"Why is that?"

"They say they can't sleep."

"Have you considered taking them to see a therapist?" Ethel asked.

"I have, but I'd rather have Pastor Grant speak to them."

"There's nothing wrong with seeing a therapist or grief counselor. I had to see one right after my father died."

Sela met Ethel's gaze. "I didn't say anything is wrong, Mrs. Barnes. I would just prefer a spiritual counselor instead."

"I didn't think you were that enamored with church."

Bristling, Sela uttered, "I better go up and get the children."

"If you don't mind, I'd like to take them out for a *late* breakfast. I could take them to IHOP or Cracker Barrel."

"I don't mind at all. However, I have to warn you that Leah isn't gonna want anything outside of ice cream."

"She's still not eating?"

Sela shook her head. "You might be able to get her to eat some yogurt." She navigated to the staircase. "They'll be down shortly."

She returned later to find Ethel about to open up Rodney's journal.

"Please leave that alone," Sela blurted. "That's Rodney's journal."

"Excuse me?"

"You can't read Rodney's journal." Sela walked over and took the leather-bound book out of her mother-in-law's hand.

"How dare you…"

"This belongs to me and I don't want you reading it," Sela stated. "Not just yet anyway. Rodney never let me read his journals—he said I would get to read them once he was gone. Right now, I just don't want to share them with anyone else. I hope you can understand my feelings."

Sullen, Ethel nodded. "I guess I'd feel the same way."

Chapter Sixteen

✤

"I need to get started on the paperwork," Sela announced as she headed to her office. "It's not gonna do itself."

Sighing softly, she sat down at the desk staring at the tall pile of paperwork. "This is going to take all week."

Sela eyed the worn devotional Bible on the corner of Rodney's desk and made a mental note to take it with her when she left the office. She didn't really know where to find comfort in the Word but decided to give it a try.

Rodney had read the Bible daily while Sela hardly ever picked it up. It wasn't until he became ill that she sought comfort in the scriptures.

She yearned for that same peace God had given Rodney. Sela wanted God to take away her pain with His word. She wanted to be embraced by the knowledge that God would stand by her side as she struggled to pick up the pieces of her life—pieces shattered by the death of her spouse.

She needed the same God who carried her beloved Rodney away on wings of love to heal her broken heart. Sela wanted God to mend the rip in the fabric of her family.

Didn't He owe her that much?

Sela toyed with the phone's cord before summoning up the strength to turn on her computer monitor. Reluctantly, she began to do the invoicing.

Several checks had come in the mail, so she needed to post those payments before running out to the bank to make the deposit.

She'd reached a stopping point when the doorbell rang. Sela pushed away from the desk and jumped up to answer the door.

Ethel had returned with the children.

Lacey and Leah rushed to her. "Hey, Mommy," they shouted in unison.

"Did you guys have a good breakfast?" Sela ran her fingers across Marcus's freshly cropped hair as he strode past her.

"I see you took the boys for a haircut."

"I felt they needed one badly. Their hair is so unruly when it grows out, don't you agree?"

Sela chose not to respond. She just stared coldly into Ethel's eyes. She was fuming inside. Ethel shouldn't have taken such liberties with the boys. She never would've done this if Rodney were still alive.

"Well, I need to get to the store," Ethel announced. To the children, she said, "Thanks for having breakfast with me."

"Bye, Grandmother," the children called out before heading towards the back of the house.

"Thanks for taking them to breakfast, Mrs. Barnes." Sela uttered the words stiffly.

"I love spending time with them," Ethel stated with a smile. "I hope you'll continue letting us spend time with them."

"Of course," Sela responded. "Why would you think otherwise?"

"I'm just making sure we're on the same page."

"Mrs. Barnes, I would never keep the children away from you. Or Ms. Barnes. They're your grandchildren."

Ethel checked her watch. "I must be on my way. I have a lot of errands to run."

When her mother-in-law left, Sela strode into the family room where the children were seated, watching television.

Marcus glanced at her when she entered the room. "Where's Grandmother?"

"She left," Sela answered. "She had to run some errands."

"Mommy, can we do something special today?" Leah questioned.

Folding her arms across her chest, Sela wanted to know, "What would you like to do?"

"I dunno. Just something special. Maybe we could go to the mall or something."

"Maybe we can go see a movie," Lacey suggested.

"I don't want to go nowhere," Marcus announced. "I just want to stay home."

Sela walked over and took a seat beside him. "Marcus, is something bothering you?"

"No, ma'am."

"Honey, look at me, please."

Marcus turned to look at her. "I'm okay, Mama."

Sela ran a hand through his thick curls. "If something's bothering you, I want you to know that you can come talk to me. You can tell me anything. Okay?"

"Yes, ma'am."

Leon moved to sit beside her. He leaned against her.

Smiling, Sela planted a kiss on his forehead. "I love you, baby."

"I love you, too."

Leah leaned against the door, sighing loudly. "Mom, can we pleeze go somewhere?"

"Leah, your brother wants to stay home. Why don't we pop in a video and watch a movie?"

Shaking her head, she responded. "I don't wanna watch a movie."

"Then let's go outside and sit on the patio. How about that?" Sela suggested.

"Can we plant some flowers?" Lacey suggested.

"You want to plant flowers?"

"Yes, ma'am. Some roses. Daddy liked roses a lot. I want to plant some for him."

Sela grinned. "Well, I have to tell you, sweetie, I don't know much about roses or planting anything. We need to do some research first."

"We can do it on the computer."

"We sure can."

"Can I help y'all plant the flowers?" Leah questioned.

"Me, too?" Leon chimed in.

"Sure. We'll make it a family project." Sela glanced over at Marcus. "You want to help us?"

He shook his head.

Marcus was the shyest of her children and while he was quiet by nature, he had a wonderful sense of humor and was often witty in his responses. He had been very close to Rodney. As long as his father was somewhere nearby, Marcus was happy.

He was the only one of her children who accompanied Rodney from time to time in the truck. Marcus even planned on becoming a truck driver like his father and one day running Barnes Trucking.

Sela noted he seemed more quiet than usual. She was concerned that he was keeping his feelings bottled inside. She made a mental note to call Pastor Grant and set up an appointment for Marcus.

"I can't get Marcus to open up to me," Sela told Junior while sitting in her office. He'd come by to help her with some administrative work. "I was thinking that you could talk to him."

"I'll come by and get him and Leon this weekend. I'm off, so I can do some things with them."

Sela smiled at her oldest son. "Thanks so much, sweetie. I'm so worried about them—all of you, actually."

"Mom, we'll be okay. Dad and I had some long talks about what might happen. He did what he could to prepare all of us. Yeah, it hurts a lot, but we'll get through. We're family and we're gonna stick together. We'll get through this."

"I know we will. It's been my constant prayer."

"I'ma mow the lawn when I come on Friday after work. I'll show the boys how to do it, too."

"Since when do you voluntarily mow lawns? You used to hate doing yard work."

"I still hate it," Junior confessed. "But with Dad gone, somebody has to do it. I'll get Marcus and Leon to help me. I'll even pay them an allowance."

"I'll pay the allowance. You save your money."

"I don't mind paying out of my own money. I can handle it, Mom." Junior broke into a big grin. "Besides, what you give them definitely won't break the bank."

"All right smarty-pants…" Sela reached over and embraced her son. "I love you, son."

"I love you, too." Junior paused a heartbeat before saying, "If you want, we can pack up Dad's stuff when I come this weekend."

"I'll let you know." Sela wasn't really sure she was ready to pack away Rodney's clothes, his shoes—everything that once belonged to him.

"Mom…" Junior prompted.

"Huh?"

"You okay?"

"I am," Sela confirmed. "I was just thinking that no matter how much of your Dad's belongings we pack up, he will always be in our hearts."

Sela sat a moment in her car, summoning up the strength to walk up the hill to the grave where Rodney's ashes were buried.

She inhaled and exhaled slowly. Opening the car, Sela got out.

She hated making this first trip alone, but none of the children were ready to come back to the cemetery.

Sela placed a bouquet of fresh flowers at the head of the grave. Rodney's headstone would be arriving sometime next week.

"Hey, you…" Sela glanced around uneasily. "You know I don't like cemeteries. I know that you're not really here but in a weird way, I feel close to you in this place."

She played with a carnation. "I'm gonna put away your things on Saturday. I'm not gonna wait too long just like I promised."

Sela reached over and pulled out a weed. "Ooh, Rodney, I miss you so much. The kids miss you, too. We're trying to take it one day at a time." She pushed her hair away from her face. "It's not easy, you know. This is not easy at all. Marcus is quieter than usual. Lacey wants to sleep all the time so that you'll visit her, while Leah only wants to eat ice cream or yogurt. Leon seems to be doing okay—on the outside anyway."

Sighing softly, Sela pulled out another weed. "Junior has just stepped into your shoes. He's really trying to fill the void left in our lives by your death. And Ayanna, she's still grieving but she's trying to be strong."

Her eyes watered, causing Sela to blink rapidly. "I've been trying to get along with your parents. They're not exactly making it very easy, but I haven't given up. I know how much you wanted all of us to get along."

Sela stared up toward the heavens. "I haven't been back to church since the memorial service, Rodney. I know I promised to rededicate my life to the Lord before you died, but…" Her voice died to a whisper. "I'm angry that God didn't save you. I hope you can understand how I feel."

She stayed for a few minutes more, arranging the flowers on the grave. "Maybe the children will come with me the next time I visit."

Sela pulled herself up. "I'll be back to make sure your grave looks nice and to…to talk. Even though I know you're not really here anymore, this helps. To come talk to you like this."

"I love you, Rodney." Sela blew a kiss before taking her leave.

Chapter Seventeen

❧

Junior entered the family room where Sela sat folding laundry on Saturday morning. "You ready, Mom?"

"I guess so." Sela rose to her feet. "I don't think any of us will ever be ready to pack up your father's things. It almost feels like I'm trying to erase his memory."

"We don't have to do this right now. We can wait, Mom."

She raised her eyes to study Junior's face. "Would you rather wait for a while?"

He shrugged. "Like you said—it won't ever be easy. Let's just do it now like we planned."

Sela followed her son up the stairs to the second level, and paused. Rodney had been gone now for one month. It was time to put away his things. He wasn't coming home. "Here goes…"

Sela placed her hand on the doorknob and turned slowly.

"Son, you can keep anything you like," she said.

Ayanna strode into the room carrying a couple of cardboard boxes. "I have some more in the car," she announced.

Junior headed to the door. "I'll bring them up."

"I can't believe that we're doing this," Ayanna murmured. "Daddy's not coming back...."

Sela embraced her daughter. "No, he's not coming back, sweetie." Her eyes roamed around the room resting on the forty-two-inch television Rodney had been so excited about; the bedroom furniture she'd talked him into buying because she loved it so much; this room was filled with so many wonderful memories.

Ayanna picked up a bottle of Rodney's cologne. "This smelled so good on Daddy."

Sela agreed.

"You should keep it, Mom."

"One of your brothers might want it."

"Most likely Junior. Leon and Marcus don't want to take baths much less use cologne."

Sela burst into laughter.

Junior returned with two cardboard boxes. He sat them on the floor, then left again.

Sela and Ayanna walked over to the closet.

"You pack up your father's suits and I'll get his other clothes. Junior's more muscular than your father was, so maybe we can donate these to the church. Do they still keep clothing there for people in need?"

"Yes, ma'am," Ayanna responded. "They do." She did as she was told.

Sela neatly folded a sweater and placed it in one of the

boxes. Her eyes traveled to her daughter. Every now and then Ayanna would wipe her eyes.

"Honey, you don't have to do this."

Glancing over her shoulder, Ayanna's gaze met hers. "I can get through it, Mom." She reached for another suit. "I'll be okay."

Junior returned with more boxes. "What do you want me to do?"

"Why don't you start with the dresser?" Sela suggested. "His things are on the left."

When she finished in the closet, Sela walked over to the nightstand where Rodney kept his Bible and some other mementos.

Sela picked up the black, leather-bound book lying on the nightstand beside the bed. She felt closer to Rodney somehow whenever she read the entries, so she decided to hold off on packing the journal.

Two hours later, all Rodney's possessions were packed away except for a few items Junior and his siblings kept; there were also some mementos Sela thought her in-laws would appreciate.

After dinner, Sela sat in bed watching television. During a commercial break, her attention was drawn back to the journal. She picked it up and opening it, began to read.

April 24
"Sela is finally allowing me out of the house. We took a nice walk. I got tired but I enjoyed being outdoors. We are so blessed that we don't have to leave the neigh-

borhood to enjoy tree-lined sidewalks, parks and green-
ways throughout the community.

I've never really appreciated taking walks in the park
like this before. I just took things like this for granted.

My Sela's a wonderful wife, but she's so protective of
me right now. She kept asking me the entire time we
were walking if I felt okay. She acts like I'm a fragile person. Although I know she means well, I'm offended. I'm
a man—not some little weakling.

Sometimes I snap at her, even though I don't mean
to. I just want to feel like me again. I just want to be a
normal man.

Sela's running the business for me. She's doing a
good job. I'm not real sure how I feel about it."

Sela closed the journal. "I was just trying to make sure you
weren't overdoing it." She was a little hurt by what Rodney
had written. He'd never shared those feelings with her.

A soft knock on her door took Sela away from her
thoughts.

"You okay?" Ayanna inquired. "You were kinda quiet during the movie and dinner. I thought maybe I should check
on you."

Sela broke into a smile. "Honey, I'm fine. I was reading
your daddy's journal. It makes me feel close to him."

Ayanna sat down beside her mother. "I'd like to read some
of Daddy's journals one day. Not right now because I don't
think I can handle it, but one day."

"I think you should. All of you should. Your father really
loved us. You can tell that just from his entries."

"Well, I'm gonna be leaving soon. I have a date with Jay."

"You two are really spending a lot of time together."

"We never really had a chance to talk about Jay—what do you think of him?" Ayanna asked.

"I guess he's okay. He's on the quiet side though."

"He was like that when I first met him, too." Ayanna chuckled. "He's a lot more talkative now."

"I can tell you really like him. Your face just lights up whenever he's around." She was still adjusting to seeing her oldest daughter so enamoured with a boy.

"I think I'm falling in love with Jay."

"Honey, I'm so happy for you, but I won't lie. The idea of you being in love and maybe even considering marriage… Ayanna, I can still remember the day you were born. Like it happened yesterday."

"I'm growing up." Ayanna made a face when she added, "I'm getting old."

Sela patted her daughter's hand. "Don't you go there. If you're getting old, I must be ancient."

Mother and daughter cracked up in laughter.

Ayanna stayed in Sela's room talking about relationships. After about twenty minutes, she rose to her feet and announced, "I guess I better go take a shower and get dressed. Jay is gonna meet me here in about an hour."

"I think I'll take a little walk." Sela swung her legs out of bed and stood up. "I think the exercise will do me good."

Ayanna agreed.

Sela found Junior sitting in the living room staring off into space.

"Feel like taking a walk with me?"

Junior smiled and nodded. He stood up and stretched. "I could use some fresh air."

He moved to open the front door for her and stepped aside.

On the front porch, Sela let her gaze drift over the wide expanse of fathomless blue sky dotted with sparkling pockets of sunshine.

One of the reasons she and Rodney chose the Bedford at Falls River community was because of the neighborhood parks sprinkled throughout.

"This is so nice," Sela murmured as they walked side by side. "Being out here like this.

"I almost forgot—remind me to call Bobby," Sela said, referring to one of their drivers. "When we get home. I need him to take a load to Virginia next week."

"I talked to Bobby this morning," Junior announced. "Dudley Paper wants us to make three runs a week instead of one now. Can Bobby do it?"

Shrugging, Sela answered, "His wife is due in a couple of months. Their last two babies both came early, so Bobby wants to stay local until after she gives birth."

"What about Johnny?"

"I'll ask him," Sela responded. Giving her son a sidelong glance, she asked, "Since when did you become so interested in the business?"

"Since Dad died. Barnes Trucking was his company and we're not gonna let him down."

They walked down to the park, then turned around.

"I like it over here. I know Marcus and Leon love having a park right here in the community."

"Do you like it enough to move back home?" Sela inquired.

Junior laughed.

Sela slowed her steps. "I'm serious. I've been thinking that you and Yanna should move home."

"Mom, can I ask you something?"

"Of course. What is it?"

"Why do you want us to move back in? Most parents want their children to move away almost as soon as they graduate."

"I miss y'all so much. I just want all my babies home with me. I don't want to lose you—any of you."

Junior embraced her. "Mom, don't be scared. We're gonna be fine. All of us."

"I pray so," Sela murmured. "It's my prayer."

Losing Rodney had broken her heart. Losing her children might kill her.

Chapter Eighteen

May 22

"If I hadn't gotten sick, we would be leaving today for Memorial Day weekend. Sela had wanted to take the children up to Virginia Beach. We were all looking forward to getting away, but now things have changed. Derek invited us over to his house for the holiday. I'm not sure I'll be feeling up to it, but I'll see on Monday.

Instead of getting stronger, I feel like I'm getting weaker. Just walking down the stairs leaves me out of breath.

Sela is still watching me like a hawk. I know that she senses all is not right with me, but I don't want to scare her. I don't know how long I can keep this up but I have to try. She has too much to worry about already. I don't want to be a burden to her.

My parents and Sela are trying very hard to get along and I appreciate their efforts. It is my wish that we all just love each other and finally be the family that I know we can be. I don't like playing referee."

The telephone rang.

Sela laid down Rodney's journal and picked up on the fourth ring. "Hello."

"Sela, it's Ethel."

"Is there something I can do for you, Mrs. Barnes?"

"Roman and I were talking and we came up with an idea."

"What kind of idea?" Sela had a feeling that she wasn't going to like whatever her mother-in-law had to say.

"Roman can take over the business for you. That way you can focus on the children."

"Please don't take this the wrong way, but Mr. Barnes don't know anything about the trucking business. I grew up around trucks and I worked for my father from the time I was fifteen years old. The business is fine."

"We're not trying to take it away from you, Sela. We simply thought it might be a good idea for Roman to take over for a while. Just to make sure things are running smoothly."

Coming from anyone else, she probably wouldn't have been so annoyed. But coming from her mother-in-law, she couldn't help but be defensive. Still, she tried to remain polite. "The business is fine, Mrs. Barnes. Thanks for the offer but we're okay."

"Sela…" Ethel pushed. "Just let us—"

"No, thank you," Sela interrupted. Her words came out forcefully. "I don't need your help. Rodney and I are the ones who started this company. I know exactly what I'm doing."

"We just—"

Sela cut Ethel off a second time. "Let's just drop it, Mrs. Barnes. I'm not gonna change my mind."

The annoying sound of the dial tone caught her off guard. "She hung up on me," Sela said, dumbfounded, as she hung up the telephone.

"Aunt Rita's here," Leon announced from the living room.

Sela picked up her purse and car keys. "Okay guys— let's go."

She followed the children out of the house. "We're taking my car," Sela announced.

"What's wrong, Sela?" Rita questioned when they were at the local burger joint. "You seem a bit distracted." She picked up a French fry and stuck it in her mouth.

"I'm sorry. I was just thinking about a conversation I had earlier with my mother-in-law."

"Ooh boy…" Rita groaned. "What happened?"

"She and Mr. Barnes want to take over the trucking business."

"*What?*"

"You heard me. My in-laws want my company—the one Rodney and I built."

"You can't be serious. How can they even think of doing this?"

"I don't know, Rita. Your guess is as good as mine."

Sela dusted the shelves on the built-in bookcase. When she came across a photograph of Roman and Ethel, she paused.

Rodney wanted us to get along and I tried. I really did. I've been trying from the day I married your son. But now you want to take Barnes Trucking from me. Well, I'm not gonna let that happen.

Sela's mind wandered, searching for a moment in time when she really felt like she was part of the Barnes family.

Her eyes traveled to Ayanna's cap-and-gown photo from when she graduated high school. Sela smiled. Roman and Ethel had thrown a wonderful graduation party for her. They'd rented a large tent and hired caterers to handle the food.

All of them had had a wonderful time. "I felt like family," she murmured softly. "It was a wonderful day."

The following year, they'd done the same thing for Junior when he graduated. They promised to do the same for each of the children.

"Why can't we be like that all the time? That's what Rodney wanted. It's what I want as well."

"How would you guys like to invite your grandparents over for a visit?" Sela hoped she could sit down with Roman and Ethel after dinner to discuss the company. She would make it clear that she was more than capable of running Barnes Trucking. More importantly, it was her company.

"Can we, Mommy?" Lacey asked. "Can we?"

Sela broke into a big smile. "Sure. We just have to call them. They may already have plans."

Marcus and Lacey jumped up and raced to the telephone.

Lacey looked disappointed when she walked into the kitchen a few minutes later. "Grandmother said they already got something to do tonight. She said she'll come get us to-morrow though. Her and Grandfather are gonna take us out to dinner."

Sela didn't believe it. *They just don't want to eat here. They would prefer to take the children out to dinner than sit and have a civil conversation with me,* she decided.

"We can have dinner with them tomorrow, right?"

Marcus's words cut into her thoughts.

"Honey, what did you say?"

"Can we have dinner with Grandpa tomorrow? Please?"

Folding her arms across her chest, Sela leaned against the kitchen counter. "So my cooking is not good enough. You guys want to eat out."

"Mommy, I love your cooking," Leah contributed.

"Baby girl, all you seem to want lately is ice cream."

"I eat yogurt sometimes, too."

"Yes, you do. But I need you to understand that you can't eat ice cream every day."

"It makes me feel good, Mommy."

"Ice cream is good sometimes, but not all the time."

"I eat other food, too. Why can't I have ice cream if I eat my dinner?"

Leah was tearing up.

"Honey, you can have ice cream some time—just not all of the time. Okay?"

"Yes ma'am." Leah sniffed.

"I guess I'll just make some hot dogs tonight. I was gonna do a nice homemade Hawaiian pizza with lots of pepperoni and pineapple."

"Oooh, I want that, Mommy," Lacey stated. She rushed

over to where Sela was standing and wrapped both arms around her. "Pleeze!"

"Oh, I don't know… Y'all don't seem to like homemade meals. You want to go out to restaurants and stuff like that."

Lacey squealed with laughter. "We just want to see Grandmother."

"And Grandfather," Marcus added. "We love your cooking. We promise."

"I don't know. You sure you want a homemade pizza? Maybe we should just order one."

"Nooo!" they yelled in unison.

Sela burst into laughter. "Okay. Okay. I'll make one. You guys just go on in the family room," she instructed. "And watch TV or do some reading while I cook."

When the pizzas were ready, Sela called everyone into the dining room to eat.

After a quick prayer of thanksgiving, she prepared plates for the twins. Sela placed a plate in front of Leah, who ate her pizza quickly.

"More please?"

Sela gave her another slice.

"Dad loved your homemade pizzas," Leon stated. "He used to say it was his favorite foods."

Smiling, Sela nodded. She wiped her mouth with the edge of her napkin and said, "This is what we survived on when we first got married. After we moved out of my parents' house, it was all I really knew how to cook."

"Daddy always tried to get the biggest slice," Lacey interjected with a giggle. "I couldn't never beat him to it."

Sela's gaze met Marcus's. "You okay, sweetie?" she inquired.

"Yes ma'am," he mumbled, dropping his gaze back to his plate.

My babies… No ache compared to the pain a mother felt when she was powerless to help her child.

The next day, Sela washed the twins' hair, then fixed it into two adorable ponytails adorned with ribbons on each little girl.

"Your grandmother's gonna love all over you girls—you look so pretty. Like baby dolls."

Lacey preened in the mirror. "I look so-oo cute…."

Sela burst into laughter. "What about your sister?"

"She's not as cute as me."

"We look just alike, Lacey. Only I got a mole on my top lip."

With her arms folded across her chest, Lacey eyed her twin. "Okay, we're both cute."

"I'm gonna check on your brothers. You two go on downstairs and wait for your grandmother."

She heard the doorbell as the sound reverberated throughout the house. "I'll get the door," she shouted. Sela ran down the stairs.

"The children are dressed and ready," Sela announced when she opened the front door. "They're really looking forward to having dinner with y'all tonight."

"We're looking forward to spending some time with them," Roman responded. "We love our grandchildren."

Sela pulled at her sleeve. "I know you do." She almost sighed out loud when Marcus joined her at the front door. "Where are your sisters and brother?"

"They're coming," he responded. Marcus embraced both his grandparents.

"It's time for another haircut," Ethel noted aloud.

"I'm taking the boys next weekend," Sela interjected. She didn't want her in-laws taking liberties again. She was their mother and she alone would decide when her sons needed a haircut.

Ethel gave her a tight smile. "We won't keep them out too late."

Sela nodded. "Thanks." Her eyes traveled to Roman, who was glancing around the living room, as if trying to detect if something was out of place. "Is something wrong, Mr. Barnes?"

"Huh?"

Her question caught him by surprise. She repeated it.

"No. Nothing's wrong." He tapped Ethel on the arm. "I'm going out to the car."

"What's wrong with him?"

Ethel pressed a hand to her chest. "I think being here without Rodney just...he just couldn't be in here."

Sela glanced over her shoulder into the living room—a room filled with photos of her life with Rodney. Maybe it had been too much for Roman.

She stood by silently while Ethel queried Marcus on school. They were waiting for the rest of the kids to come downstairs. Sela couldn't wait for Ethel to leave. The woman just made her feel uncomfortable.

A few minutes later, the other children joined them. After a round of hugs and kisses, Sela was alone.

Alone with her memories of a happier time.

Chapter Nineteen

✧

"Good morning," Ethel sang into the phone.

Sela struggled to sound cheerful. She'd put this off for two weeks, but she wouldn't chicken out today. "Morning, Mrs. Barnes."

Ethel's tone changed upon hearing Sela's voice. "Sela…"

She ignored her mother-in-law's frosty tone. "Um…I was calling to see if I could bring some of Rodney's stuff over. I thought you and Mr. Barnes might want to keep some things for yourselves."

"When exactly did you have in mind?"

Sela hesitated a moment before answering. *The nerve of Ethel…the woman never thinks twice about coming over to my house.* She took a deep breath and exhaled slowly. "I don't have to come by today. You can just give me a call—"

Ethel cut her off. "Of course we want some of Rodney's

things. We're planning to be home most of the day, but later this evening we have plans to go out."

Sela eyed her watch. "I can be there in about an hour—if that works for you."

"We'll see you then, Sela."

She hung up, wishing she didn't have to do this. She didn't feel like dealing with them.

Sela regretted not taking Junior up on his offer to take the boxes over for her. She just knew Ethel would find a way to undermine her generosity. It wasn't like she really, truly wanted to part with any item that belonged to Rodney—she was simply trying not to be selfish.

Sela wrongly had assumed they would be touched by her kindness, but as always, there was no pleasing Roman and Ethel.

Ethel peeked around Sela when she opened the front door. "Where are the children?"

"They're with Ayanna."

"I thought you'd bring them by for a visit, especially since you were coming here."

"They wanted to spend time with their sister. She's taking them to the movies."

"Humph," Ethel grunted.

Sela folded her arms across her chest. "What's wrong with them spending time with Ayanna?"

Ethel met her gaze with a hostile stare. "There's nothing wrong with them spending time with their sister, but you couldn't bring them here for a few minutes? It's not like you're spending the entire day with us."

"I didn't think about it," Sela confessed. "Besides, you just saw them last weekend. Y'all took them to dinner and to the movies, remember?"

"So we can only see them once a week?" Roman asked. "Is that what you're telling us?"

Sela couldn't understand why the air had suddenly turned antagonistic. "No, that's not what I'm saying at all."

"You know, Sela," Roman began, "we intend on spending as much time with our grandchildren as possible."

"I don't have a problem with that at all. I'm sorry, but I just didn't think about bringing them with me. It wasn't meant to be a slight, so please don't take it that way."

Ethel waved her hand in dismissal. "Well what's done is done. It can't be changed at this point."

"Look, I'm trying to apologize. We are a family and it was your son's dying wish that we get along. I don't want you thinking that I'm trying to keep the children away from you. I'm not like that."

"You and I are not family, Sela," Roman said. "Let's get this clear. Your children—my son's children—are family. Rodney's gone and when he died, so did your ties to this family. We don't need a truce."

Her eyes watered, but Sela was not about to let her in-laws see her cry. Roman's words cut her deep but she refused to show just how much he'd wounded her. "My ch-children…"

"We love our grandchildren. Make no mistake, Sela."

"You have to deal with me when it comes to the children."

"Don't try to threaten us. We *will* see our grandchildren."

"Why are you twisting my words around?" Sela demanded. "Why can't you both see that we're on the same side? We all loved Rodney. Just admit it—Rodney loved me and I loved him. We were good together."

"My son could have done some wonderful things with his life," Roman pointed out. "He could have been an accountant like he wanted, a lawyer—anything that he wanted."

"Rodney was happy with his life, Mr. Barnes. Don't you understand that? Tell me something—do you regret having your grandchildren? Would you rather not have them in your life?"

"I never said no such thing. You're the one who's twisting words around. Ethel and I love our grandchildren. You know that."

"I'm not doing anything like that. I'm just saying that we should make a better effort to get along. For Rodney and for the children. They shouldn't have to deal with the unnecessary tension between us."

"I agree the children shouldn't be involved with this—" Roman stopped short.

"What were you gonna say?" Sela questioned.

"Nothing," he uttered. "It's not important."

"The other reason I came is because I have some of Rodney's things in the car. I knew he would want you to have them."

"My son is barely dead and you've already cleaned out his stuff?" Ethel fumed.

"Rodney didn't want me to prolong it. He asked me and the children to do it as soon as he was gone." Sela turned and headed toward the front door, but her mother-in-law's words stopped her in her tracks.

"We didn't hear him say it," Ethel shot back. "For all we know, you could be lying."

Sela's eyes flashed in her anger. "Do you want this stuff or not?"

"Why couldn't we pick out the stuff we wanted to have? Roman gave him a beautiful watch—I'm sure my husband would like to have it back."

Arms folded across her chest, Sela blurted, "That's too bad because Rodney gave that watch to Junior. He wanted his son to have it. My son plans on passing it to his own son one day."

Roman nodded in approval. "I can live with that."

Ethel picked up the box Sela had sat down on the coffee table. She opened it and went through it as if searching for something.

"What are you looking for?"

"My mother gave Rodney a pendant," she muttered. "I want it back. It belongs in my family." Raising her eyes, she gave Sela a hard look. "I know he gave it to you, but it really belongs in my family. Maybe one day I'll pass it on to Ayanna, but I want it back—it's all I have of my mother."

"You don't have to worry. It's in there, Mrs. Barnes. I'm not much of a necklace person anyway. Rodney tried to give it to me, but I never wanted it."

Ethel found the tiny jewelry box and opened it. She broke into a rare smile and pressed it to her chest.

Sela could tell the necklace really meant something to her.

"We still expect to see the children on a regular basis," Roman announced.

"Of course," Sela agreed. "Just call me and let me know—"

Cutting her off, Roman stated, "We'd like every other weekend and holidays."

"Every other weekend is fine, but I don't know about every single holiday. Some of those will have to be spent with me—maybe we can do half days or something."

"We want them one month out of the summer as well," Ethel interjected. "They can vacation with us."

"That will depend on our summer plans and their other recreational activities."

"Don't try to make this difficult, Sela. We intend to spend a lot of time with our grandchildren. They are all we have left in this world."

"You can't make them a substitute for Rodney. I hope you know that. I'm only telling you this because I'm gonna have to keep that in mind, too." Sela strode over to the front door. "Enjoy your weekend."

By the time she made it to her car, Sela felt the tightness in her chest dissipate. Her anxiety level always went up whenever she was forced to deal with Ethel and Roman.

Sela sat in the car until she felt calm enough to drive. She took slow, deep breaths, then started the engine. Her in-laws would not get the best of her.

Chapter Twenty

After making dinner, Sela sat down and called her mother. "Hey, Mama," she greeted when Althea answered the phone.

"Hey, sugar. How're you doing?"

"Some days are better than others," Sela admitted. "Today wasn't a good day."

"What happened?"

"I tried to do what Rodney would've wanted—I went to see his parents. I wanted to call a truce."

"So, how did things go with them?" Althea inquired.

"I'm not really sure. I guess the same as always." Sela changed her position on the sofa to one she found more comfortable. "His mother wanted the necklace back. You know the one her mother gave Rodney."

"You didn't give it back to her, did you?"

"I didn't want it. Mama, the thing is ugly. I don't like cameo necklaces."

"Humph. I still wouldn't have given it to her. That woman is so mean."

"Mama, that's not very nice."

"Sela, sugar, I just said what you were thinking. Ethel Barnes is a mean uppity woman. Just look at how she's treated you over the years. She practically tried to bar you from the memorial service."

"I know all that, Mama. But I…I made Rodney a promise that I'd give her a chance. I'm going to do my best to get along with his parents. I told Rodney I would and I'm gonna do it."

"They've got to do their part, too. Roman and Ethel have to want to get along with you, Sela."

"I know."

"Sugar, I wouldn't waste none of my time with them. Just take care of your children—leave Ethel and Roman Barnes to their own mess. They never liked you and never will. You don't need them."

"We're still a family—even if they refuse to admit it."

"Why are you trying so hard to be a part of that family, Sela?"

"That's not what I'm doing, Mama."

"What do you call it?"

"I call it trying to be civil. Trying to piece together what family my children have left. Roman and Ethel Barnes are the only remnants left of their father." Sela ran a hand through her curls. "Mama, I can't let them lose their grand-parents, too."

"I don't like the way they treat you. You don't think your children see it, too?"

Sela's head was beginning to throb. She couldn't believe she was actually defending her in-laws. "Let's change the subject. I'm getting a headache." She paused a moment before adding, "I don't care how Ethel and Roman Barnes treat me, I still owe it to Rodney and my children to try and keep the peace."

"Mom, you want to go to church with us?"

Sela shook her head. "I didn't sleep well last night."

Ayanna sat down on the edge of the bed. "I'm not sleeping all that well, either. I keep thinking about Daddy."

"Me, too. I miss him so much." Her eyes traveled the length of the bedroom. "He loved this house—this master suite. This is what sold him on the house. Now he's not here to enjoy it." Sela's eyes grew wet. "It isn't fair. Rodney should be here. We should be growing old together."

Ayanna wrapped her arms around her mother. "I don't understand why he had to leave us. I don't get it."

"I'm so angry. I just want to scream. I want to throw the biggest tantrum I can."

"I do, too," Ayanna confessed. "I've tried to stay strong for everyone else, but it's hard, Mama. I can't do it."

"Baby, we can take one day at a time. Some mornings I wake up and I'm not sure I can make it through the rest of the day. But I do—sometimes it seems as if night is never going to come. It does. On days like today, I feel l-like my h-heart is never gonna stop hurting…." Sela put her hands to her face, wiping away tears. "I hurt so badly."

Ayanna began to cry softly. "There's so much I wanted to say to Daddy, but I didn't get a chance. He won't be the one to walk me down the aisle when I get m-married."

"Ooh, sweetie…" Sela's heart was breaking. "I'm so sorry."

"It's not your fault—it's nobody's fault, I guess. It was Daddy's time to go…." Ayanna paused before adding, "I really hate when people say that."

"I do, too. It doesn't make me feel any better."

"I don't want to lose you, Mom. I'd never really given death much thought until Daddy. Now it's all I seem to think about."

Sela embraced her daughter. "I'm not going anywhere anytime soon. I don't want you or your brothers and sisters worrying about death. As much as it hurts us, it is a natural progression."

"I really miss Daddy."

"I do, too."

"But how do you get through, Mom? Y'all were so close."

"Some days are better than others." Sela pushed away a stray curl from Ayanna's face. "Like today. This isn't a good day for me. Days like this, I don't want to get out of bed. But as for when you get married, Junior and I will give you away when that day comes."

"For now, we just take it one day at a time, I guess."

Sela agreed. "Yeah. We keep Daddy in our hearts and we try to move on. That's the way he would've wanted it. Your father didn't want us to be sad all the time." She broke into a short laugh. "I really need to take my own advice."

Ayanna stole a peek at the clock on the nightstand. "Well, I guess I better get everybody up. We don't want to be late for church."

"I'm gonna rest for a little while. If I feel better, I'll be there after Sunday school."

"Okay, Mom."

"Thanks for staying here last night with us," Sela stated. "I enjoyed having you home."

"Me, too."

Ayanna stood up and walked out of the room.

Groaning, Sela fell back against her pillows. She closed her eyes to block the pain throbbing in her head. She felt dizzy for a moment.

Minutes later, her vision cleared. Sela climbed out of bed and padded barefoot to the bathroom. She hoped to feel better after her shower.

In the end, Sela just couldn't bring herself to go to church. She just wasn't ready.

She'd gone with Rodney during the times he felt strong enough to attend services. But now with him gone...Sela didn't think she could set foot back in church. In the past, she'd gone mostly for Rodney's sake. She still had issues stemming from her youth.

She was disappointing her children, Sela realized. "I'll explain everything to them when they come home," she whispered. "They'll understand."

When the children arrived home around twelve-thirty, Sela was sitting in the family room watching television. She threw up her hand in greeting.

"I thought you were coming to church," Leah fussed. "I kept looking for you and when you didn't show up—I got ascared. I thought something happened to you, Mommy."

Sela picked up her daughter. "Sweetie pie, I'm so sorry. I didn't mean to scare you."

"Leah thought you might be dead," Lacey announced. "She was really ascared for you."

Sela glanced up at Ayanna. "You told them I was coming to church."

"I thought you were."

"I had a bad headache this morning so I wasn't sure."

"I'm sorry," Ayanna stated. "I thought you were coming to church."

Sela eyed her for a moment, trying to decipher her mood. Ayanna sounded irritated. "You okay, Yanna?"

"Yes, ma'am. I just didn't mean to upset Leah."

"I'm okay now, Yanna," Leah interjected. "I'm not ascared anymore."

"Mommy, I think you need to say you're sorry. You have to 'pologize to Leah for scaring her like that."

Ayanna thumped Lacey on the top of her head. "You need to mind your own business. You always trying to tell somebody what to do."

"Leave me alone, Yanna."

"Who are you talking to like that?"

Lacey ran over to where Sela sat holding Leah. "Mommy, tell Yanna to stop bothering me. She needs to 'pologize to me."

"Why don't you two go on upstairs and change clothes? I've laid out some things on your bed for you to put on."

Sela turned her attention to Marcus, who was sitting in the wing chair watching television. "Hey, you can't speak to your mother?"

He gave her a slight smile, then got up and walked over to her. "Hey, Mom," he greeted.

"Did you speak with Pastor Grant?"

"He talked to me some after church. He wants me to come in and talk to him sometime."

"How do you feel about it?"

Marcus shrugged. "I don't know."

"Would you like to go talk to Pastor Grant? Maybe when you really feel like you can't talk to me or Yanna— even Junior?"

"I guess," Marcus responded after a moment.

"Just think about it, sweetie. You don't have to make a decision right now."

Sela glanced around and over her shoulder. "Where's your brother?"

"Leon went straight upstairs."

"You go on and change your clothes, baby."

Ayanna and Sela were suddenly alone in the room.

"Mom, I need to ask you something."

"What is it?"

"Why don't you like going to church? Did something happen?"

"Actually, it did." Sela told her daughter what happened all those years ago. "There I was. Young, scared and pregnant with you, and they just made me feel so badly."

"I guess I'd feel the same way. Mom, I'm so sorry that happened to you. But Pastor Grant—he's nothing like that. He's really nice and a very understanding person. He's not judgmental at all."

"I know he's not. Just give me some time, sweetie. This really affected me."

"I think you should talk to Pastor Grant about what happened, Mom. Maybe he can help you deal with your feelings."

Sela considered her daughter's words. She had gotten to know Pastor Grant pretty well during the months of Rodney's illness.

"I need to leave because I have a date with Jay," Ayanna announced. "His parents are in town and we're supposed to have lunch with them."

"Is this your first time meeting them?"

Ayanna nodded. "I'm so nervous. I really want them to like me."

Sela agreed. "It definitely makes things easier if they do. But why wouldn't they like you? You're a very beautiful and intelligent woman."

Ayanna smiled. "You're supposed to say that because you're my mom. Thanks though—I really needed to hear it."

"Don't worry, Yanna. It's gonna be fine. You'll see."

Chapter Twenty-One

❧

June 1
"I haven't been sleeping well. Been having some pain. Tonight seems worse than the other times. Sela has been asleep for about an hour now. I don't want to wake her, but I might have to if this pain doesn't stop."

Sela remembered that day well. It was when things changed for the worse as far as Rodney's health was concerned.

Around two in the morning Rodney had sat up in bed gasping for air and complaining that his chest felt tight.

He was panting and managed to get out, "C-Can't... b-breathe..."

She'd shot up, saying, "Take it slow, babe." Sela had rubbed his back, trying to calm him. "It's okay."

Rodney took short breaths, his body slowly relaxing.

"Do you want to go to the emergency room?"

"I think I should."

Nodding, Sela climbed out of bed. "I'm gonna call Rita and see if she'll stay with the kids."

She picked up the phone and dialed.

While she was on the phone with Rita, Rodney managed to get up and slip on a pair of jeans and T-shirt.

Feeling breathless, he eased down on the bench in front of their bed to rest for a moment.

Hanging up, Sela announced, "She's on her way over. She should be here in about ten minutes." Walking barefoot, she opened her closet door. "I need to get ready."

When he felt stronger, Rodney rose to his feet, stuck his feet into a pair of slippers and made his way to the bathroom where he washed his face and brushed his teeth.

Sela joined him there a few minutes later after throwing on a pair of jeans and a denim shirt. On her feet, she slipped on a pair of sandals. After brushing her teeth, Sela combed her hair.

When Rita arrived, she took Rodney by the hand. "Let's go." In her heart, she kept praying that nothing was wrong.

They returned home four hours later. Rodney had to return in a couple of days to see Dr. Reynolds and have more tests run.

Sela couldn't help but wonder if things would ever get better for him. Rodney's health was spiraling downward.

June 4

"Today Dr. Reynolds ordered more tests. Sela and I are both a little scared over this recent episode. We have done our best to keep the children out of it. Sela is still after me to tell my parents all that is going on. I will probably tell them after I get the results from these new tests.

The doctor told me that my heart is ejecting at fifteen percent and has grown larger and I'm retaining fluid. Breathing now takes a lot of work and concentration and my chest hurts so bad. We take so much for granted in our lives—what I wouldn't give just to be able to breathe normally again.

I would love to just have a day that I truly could say I felt good, for that matter.

But it is the toll that this is taking on Sela that really bothers me. She is trying so hard to be brave, but I can see the constant fear in her eyes. She isn't really sleeping well, frequently waking up to check on me. I know that she just wants our lives to go back to normal.

I'd promised her that there was a chance, but now—now I just don't know. I guess we'll know more once we meet with this colleague of Doctor Reynolds. He'd mentioned transplantation as an option but suggested that I consult another cardiologist.

I ask my Heavenly Father for strength that I will be able to handle whatever is to come. I ask for courage. Heavenly Father, I do not want to have to go under the knife. I haven't heard a whole lot of good about heart transplants but I trust You, Lord and I want Your will for my life. Amen."

This was the first time Sela had actually seen an entry where Rodney had written out his prayer. He must have been really scared.

Sela put away the journal. "Rodney, babe, why didn't you just talk to me? You didn't have to deal with all this alone."

She felt a little hurt over the fact that Rodney seemed more comfortable writing about his feelings over his condition in this journal than talking to her.

It was because Rodney didn't think she was strong enough to handle everything he was going through emotionally. He probably felt she had enough dealing with his condition.

Rodney knew her well, Sela acknowledged. *I would've tried. I would have given being stronger my best efforts. I wanted to be there for you, Rodney.*

June 5

"Sela found some articles on the Internet. There are several options available for people with heart failure. She and I were thrilled to find out that transplantation isn't the only result.

She found something on left ventricular assist devices. LVAD for short. Sela also found something else on cardiomyoplasty. The procedure is still experimental but is supposed to help shrink the size of the heart. We are going to speak to Dr. Reynolds about these other options.

I am so thankful that we are seeing Dr. Winston next week. He's supposed to be one of the best cardiologists in the country. It's a blessing we were able to get the ap-

pointment so soon. We'll ask him about these other options, too. I would like to avoid transplantation if at all
possible."

The telephone rang.

Sela answered it. "Hello?"

"What are you doing?"

She grinned. "Hey, Rita. I was just reading some of Rodney's journal. At least, the entries after he had the stroke. I
wanted to know what he was thinking during that time since
he really didn't share much with me."

"He was still keeping a journal?"

"He did up until the first transplant," Sela stated. "Nothing after that."

"You okay? You sound kind of funny."

"I...Rita, my feelings are a little hurt. Rodney wrote all
this stuff in this book, but didn't share half of it with me.
I used to ask him all the time if he was scared or worried—he constantly assured me that he had nothing to
fear. He didn't really open up to me like my husband
should have."

"Honey, I think Rodney just didn't want to scare you
more than you already were. He was trying to be strong.
That's all."

"You really think so?"

"Sela, Rodney didn't want you falling to pieces. He
knows you."

"He *knew* me," Sela corrected. "Rodney's gone now. I make
that mistake all the time. Sometimes I still walk into the bed-

room expecting to see him…then I feel this deep emptiness inside."

"It's still too soon, Sela. It's gonna take some time, you know."

"Yeah. I know."

They talked for a few minutes more, then Sela hung up. She got up and went to check on the children. They were downstairs watching television.

"Girls, it's time for you to take your baths and get ready for bed," Sela announced.

Leah frowned. "Mommy, I wanna stay up for a little while with Marcus and Leon. Why can't we stay up until nine?"

"Because little five-year-olds need a lot more sleep."

"Mommy…" Leah pleaded. "Pleeze…"

She laughed. "Not tonight, sweetie."

Sela tapped Lacey on the shoulder. "C'mon. Time to go upstairs."

Ahead of her, Leah stomped, arms folded across her chest and her lips drawn into a pout.

Lacey followed behind Sela, silent.

"If you girls hurry up and get settled, I'll come in and read you a story."

"Yay," Lacey screamed. "I know what I want you to read."

"I don't wanna story. I wanna finish the movie," Leah insisted.

"Leah, baby you've seen that same movie many times. Nothing has changed since you saw it the last time. We have the video."

"But it's on tonight." A tear slipped from Leah's eye. She wiped it away with the back of her hand. "Daddy and I used to watch it together all the time."

At the top of the stairs, Sela reached down and picked up Leah. "Why don't we do this? You take your bath and when you're done, you can watch the movie in your room. I'll read to Lacey, then we can all enjoy the rest of the movie together."

Leah wrapped her tiny arms around Sela's neck. She nodded.

"Lacey, how does that sound to you?" Sela asked.

"I like it," she responded. "Sounds like fun."

Sela carried Leah to her room and put her down. "Get your pajamas," she instructed. "I'll start the bath water."

Ten minutes later, she had Leah and Lacey both in the bathtub splashing away. At their age, they still enjoyed playing in the water and making bubbles.

She stayed with the twins until they fell asleep. Leah missed the last twenty minutes of the movie she wanted so desperately to see.

When Sela left their room, she found Leon wandering in the hall. "What are you up to?" she inquired.

"I'm going to take my bath."

She awarded him a smile. "Thanks for being such a sweetheart," Sela murmured. She was grateful not to have to coax him into getting ready for bed. "Where is your brother?"

"Marcus wanted to get some water before coming up. He should be up here soon."

After Sela made sure all the kids were in their rooms, she took a trip downstairs and double-checked the locks.

She made her way back to her bedroom.

Arms folded across her chest, Sela stood in the middle of the floor staring at the empty bed.

"I miss you so much, Rodney."

She quickly changed into a pair of pajamas and climbed into bed. Sela decided to watch some television until she could fall asleep.

When that didn't work, she reached for Rodney's Bible. Sela closed her eyes and prayed. *Heavenly Father, I know it's been a while and I'm sorry but I was too angry to come to You before. I thank You in advance for Your peace and assurance. I'm asking that You please show me how to allow Your love and grace to fill my heart during this time. Cover me with Your peace and comfort through this time of grief. I'm also coming to You to help me overcome my feelings of bitterness over the way my church treated me. Help me understand why it happened and help me to move past it so that I can attend church with my children. In Jesus's name I pray. Amen.*

Chapter Twenty-Two
❧

God answered her prayer.

Pastor Grant and his wife came by to check on Sela and the children the following Saturday.

"It's good to see you both," Sela stated as she led them to the family room.

When they were seated, she inquired, "Can I get y'all something to drink?"

"No, thank you. We're fine," Mrs. Grant responded with a friendly smile.

Sela took a seat in the overstuffed chair that Rodney loved so much. She settled back against the cushions, trying to recapture the memory of the last time her husband had sat there.

"You have been on my mind," Mrs. Grant stated. "We've seen the children at church…."

"I know. Since Rodney's death…" Sela raised her eyes to

meet Mrs. Grant's gaze. "To tell you the truth, it's not because of my husband dying. I haven't been much of a fan of church because of something that happened a long time ago." She gave them a brief synopsis of what happened when she was seventeen.

Mrs. Grant nodded in understanding. "I'm so sorry about what happened at that other church."

"I just can't understand why churches teach believers that we are accountable to spiritual leadership."

"I can answer that for you. It's because the Bible requires it." Pastor Grant added, "The scripture says, 'Obey those who rule over you, and be submissive, for they watch out for your souls, as those who must give account. Let them do so with joy and not with grief, for that would be unprofitable for you.'"

"Where is that scripture found?" Sela asked.

"The thirteenth chapter of Hebrews. Verse seventeen."

Pastor Grant went on to explain, "Not only are Christians to be accountable to the authority of a spiritual leader, but this passage also shows that believers should be a part of a local church—where such pastors and elders can be found. One cannot really be accountable to spiritual supervision without a commitment to a church."

"I guess that makes sense." Sela ran her fingers through her hair. "Anyway, I'm over it now. I do intend to come to church with the children tomorrow. I've already promised them that I would."

"We look forward to having you worship with us," Pastor Grant stated.

"I appreciate your not making me feel bad about the way I've handled all this."

"So often, the people in the church want their pastor to know all about them—but I believe that it's important to get to know their leaders. That is, know their lifestyle, their sincerity, their integrity. Knowing your pastors and leaders provides a tangible example to follow, and also enables you to have trust and respect in their ministry."

"I agree with that," Sela uttered. "I didn't feel that way about my former pastor. He preached one thing and lived something else."

"Sister Barnes, come worship with us and if you find that our church is not spiritually sound or my teaching is not scripture-based, I charge you to hold me accountable."

Sela's eyes widen in her surprise. "Me?"

Pastor Grant nodded. "Certainly, leaders and pastors must be held accountable for their behavior. I will have to give an account to God."

"Tell me something, Pastor. Why is it so important to attend church services? I mean, I believe in God and I was taught that we have the Holy Spirit in us to guide us. Why isn't that enough?"

"Well, it's true that we have guidance of the Holy Spirit within, but this does not mean we should dismiss the ministry of the church. The church is Christ's plan for His followers. He is the head and has commissioned His church to represent Him and His authority in the world. He has ordained elders, deacons and pastors to supervise and manage His flock. When you get a moment, read the fourteen chapter of Acts. You should also read First Timothy, the third chapter, verses ten to thirteen."

Sela smiled. "It's been really nice talking to you and Mrs.

Grant about this. You've eased my mind some. A lot actually. I'll read those scriptures tonight. Thank you."

"Anytime you have questions about anything, Sister Barnes—just ask."

"Thank you, Pastor."

Feeling more at ease, Sela enjoyed the rest of their visit.

"I had a great conversation earlier with Pastor Grant and his wife. They are really nice people," she told Rita later on that afternoon.

"I told you all church people aren't like the ones at that church you grew up in," Rita responded. "There are still some good people out there."

"I know that, Rita. It's just that what I experienced back then just really hurt me. They made me feel terrible. Like I'd committed some unforgivable sin."

"Did you share that with Pastor Grant?"

"Yeah, I did," Sela answered. "He actually explained that the Bible required us to be accountable to spiritual leadership. He also said that we can't really be accountable without a commitment to church. He said that he and other spiritual leaders are also to be held accountable for their actions as well."

"I didn't know that."

"Pastor Grant gave me some scriptures to read on the subject. I'm gonna study them tonight."

"I'd like to read them myself. I'm glad you talked to the pastor and his wife. I've met them once and they really seemed sincere and on fire for the Lord."

"I think so, too. I have to admit, I really like them and I'm so touched how Pastor Grant never abandoned Rodney. He was right there for him until the end."

Sela and Rita changed the subject.

"I'm going to the Heart Foundation Gala next Friday. Are you up to coming with me?"

"No, not really," Sela answered with a slight shake of her head. "I'm not ready for that. I would like to make a donation, however."

"Sela, you can't stay locked up in your house forever, honey."

"I'm not trying to stay *locked up,* as you put it. I'm just not ready for social events. It's just too soon, Rita."

"Okay. You don't have to bite my head off. Sorry I mentioned it."

"Rita, I didn't mean to snap at you. I apologize."

"Honey, I understand."

"No, you don't, Rita. You didn't lose your husband. You don't know how this feels. I hope you won't ever have to, either."

"I guess you forgot that I lost Chuck back in college? He may not have been my husband, but he was my boyfriend and I loved him just the same. His death nearly killed me."

Sela put a hand to her mouth. "Rita, that's right.... I'm so sorry for being insensitive."

"It's hard for us to imagine someone truly understanding the depths of our pain. Because it's our pain—we think no one has hurt as deeply as us or we feel our heartache is so much more than someone else's."

"You're right," Sela confessed. "It's hard for me to grasp that someone out there is hurting as badly as I am and yet—

going on with their lives and I feel like I'm just going through the motions of living."

"And then you have people like me telling you that it's time to move on with your life. That you can't stop living…"

"It seems so easy for everyone else. I just can't lose my husband and then say—oh well, time to move on." Sela shook her head. "I can't do it, Rita."

"It takes time. Look, do me a favor. If I push you too hard, just tell me. Okay? I don't want to do anything to hurt or upset you, but I can't help wanting to help you through this. We're friends. Please don't take this the wrong way, but some people just give up on living when they lose the love of their life or they wallow in self-pity. I'm sorry but I just refuse to let that happen to you. You have six beautiful children and I won't let them lose you, too."

A lone tear rolled down Sela's face.

"Sela," Rita prompted. "You okay?"

"Y-Yes. I'm just glad to have you for a friend. Thanks for looking out for me."

Chapter Twenty-Three

❧

On Sunday, Sela got up early.

"Mommy, you're coming to church with us?" Leah inquired. "Why?"

"You don't want me to come?"

"I want you to go to church with me," Lacey interjected. "If you don't go to church, we won't see you in heaven."

She smiled. "I'm not gonna miss out on heaven."

Leah hugged her. "I'm glad you're coming to church with me. You can meet my friend, Sarah. She's nice."

"After church, can we go out and water the flowers?" Lacey inquired.

"We watered them yesterday, sweetie. We don't want to drown them."

Sela was dressed and ready for church by the time the children came downstairs.

Ten minutes later, they were in the car and on their way.

The choir was just getting ready to march in when they arrived. Murmuring apologies, Sela and the children made their way into the sanctuary, finding a seat midway the center.

When it was time for the sermon, Pastor Grant stood up, adjusted his glasses and made his way to the podium.

Ayanna pulled out a notebook from her purse. She offered Sela a piece of paper.

Sela took it and smiled her appreciation. She never considered bringing paper to take notes. She recalled how Rodney used to take notes as well. Sela always figured since they were married—they only needed one set.

"This morning, we are going to talk about worship and what it means," Pastor Grant announced. "Worship is not a human invention rather it is divine offering. Worship is as natural for man as it is for him to breathe. Church, when we worship we declare God's worth."

Sela wrote quickly, not wanting to miss anything.

"Worship is an indispensable part of Christian life. It is an act of honoring God because of his great worthiness to be honored," Pastor Grant continued. "I've had people ask me before. 'Pastor, why do we worship?'"

Sela knew he was talking to her, but she didn't shrink in her seat—she sat proudly, her back straight, wanting to hear what Pastor Grant had to say.

"The first reason why we worship is because God commanded it and we want to be obedient to God. The second reason is because God is worthy of it. He is our creator and our Lord. Worship brings us into His presence." He paused, letting the congregation absorb his words.

"Worship forces us to turn our attention from lesser things and focus on that which is ultimate. It gives us His perspective on our situation. When we worship, we begin to understand His power and ability."

When Pastor Grant ended his sermon, Sela had four pages of notes including scriptures. She stole a peek at Leah.

Her heart flooded with love when the little girl blew her a kiss. It would've been a mistake to miss out on church services today, Sela decided.

Not only was the sermon interesting, but just being here with her family—it made her feel whole. Something she hadn't felt in a long time.

After church, Sela came home and prepared dinner. She heard footsteps and spotted Leah coming into the kitchen. She stood at the edge of the counter and peered over it, bringing a distant memory to the forefront—the day the children really realized that something was wrong with their father.

"Is Daddy really okay?" Leah asked as she stood on tiptoe at the end of the kitchen counter.

Sela stuck a large slotted spoon into the pot containing spaghetti. "He's getting stronger every day."

"He sleeps a lot."

"Honey bear, your father is really overworked and he just needs to get some rest."

Rodney eased up behind his daughter and began tickling her neck.

Leah burst into giggles while wiggling to escape his fingers.

Laughing, Sela removed the sauce from the stove and sat it on a trivet. She then drained the spaghetti.

"Daddy, it's your turn…."

Turning, Sela opened her mouth to issue a warning, but Junior had already come out of nowhere and had Leah dangling in the air.

"No, it's my turn. If you tickle anybody, it better be me. I'm the one who had to sleep in your room with you last night because you had a bad dream." Junior gently dropped her down on the sofa.

Leah giggled harder between gasping for air. "I…I was ascared."

"Then you wanted to talk all night long." Junior tickled her.

Rodney sat down gingerly, his hand pressed to his chest. His eyes traveled to where Sela stood.

"I love you," she mouthed. Her heart was breaking because of what Rodney was going through. He couldn't even play with his daughter like he used to do and it was tearing him apart. Bouts of depression were now a constant battle for him.

Sela prepared a bowl of chicken soup for Rodney. It was all he seemed to be able to keep down these days.

When they were all seated around the table fifteen minutes later, Sela announced, "I've made doctor's appointments for all of you. It's that time again."

Making a face, Marcus groaned, "Awww, Mom…"

Her gaze met Rodney's. "I want to make sure my babies are all healthy, that's all. You know we do this every year."

Junior sat at the other end of the table watching her silently. He and Ayanna had moved into their apartment the first weekend in August, but he spent a lot of time at home with them.

Sela could tell by his expression that he wasn't buying her reasoning.

Later he approached her while she was cleaning the kitchen. "What's going on, Mom?"

She put away the last of the plates before replying, "After this recent scare with your father, I just want to make sure my family is healthy. None of you really eat right."

Junior's eyes never left her face. "Mom, I know you better than that. You and Dad are hiding something and I want to know what it is. I've seen the way…" He paused and began again. "I know Dad is sick. You don't have to worry about me telling the others."

Sela reached up to touch her son's cheek. "Why don't you go up and talk to your father?" she suggested. "I think he should be the one you have this discussion with."

Junior nodded and gave her a much-needed hug. "It's gonna be all right, Mom. I've been reading up on cardiomyopathy and there are a lot of drug therapies available. We just have to find the right one for Dad."

"We never did," she murmured softly.

"Mommy, you say something?" Leah asked, bringing Sela back into the present.

"I was just thinking out loud, sweetie. Mommy was thinking about something your brother said to me a while ago."

Leah stood on tiptoe. "Can I help you cook? I can make the rolls."

Sela gave her daughter a sidelong glance. "What do you know about making yeast rolls?"

"I know you put butter on 'em, then put 'em in the oven and then you turn it on. That's what Yanna does when she makes 'em."

Laughing, Sela picked up the dish towel and wiped off a pot. "You can help me with the rolls, sweetie."

"Can I put the butter on them, please?"

"Only if you promise to eat a little dinner. Just a little bit."

Leah walked away from her position at the end of the counter and stood beside Sela. "Mommy, I don't think I can eat all that food."

"I'll give you just a spoonful of barbecue chicken, greens, macaroni and cheese. Okay?"

Leah appeared to be thinking it over. After a moment, she uttered, "Okay…I'll try, Mommy."

Sela bent down and hugged her daughter. "You're such a sweet girl. I just love you to pieces."

Giggling, Leah wrapped her arms around her mother. "I love you, Mommy. To pieces…like you said."

Lacey burst into the kitchen. "Hey…I wanna hug, too. Where's my hug?"

Sela tossed back her head laughing as her twins embraced her around the waist and hips. She reveled in their affection for her.

Twenty minutes later, dinner was ready and they were seated around the table. Ayanna and Jay had arrived ten minutes earlier to have dinner with them.

"Is Junior working?" Sela inquired.

Ayanna nodded. "He went in around eleven this morning. I think he'll be off at seven." She reached for the yeast rolls, and took two for herself.

Jay took the rolls from Ayanna.

"Oh, don't let me forget…." she stated. "I need to take a plate home for Junior."

Sela nodded. "Make sure you take him some of the carrot cake. He loves Rita's carrot cake."

"Aunt Rita made the cake?" Leon asked. "I didn't know that. I love her cakes."

Sela settled in her chair to enjoy her dinner. She loved having her children around her like this. It didn't put an end to her heartache completely—just numbed it a little.

June 10

"I did some thinking last night and I made a decision. I'm going to tell my parents today. Maybe Sela was right. I probably should have done this sooner, but there really isn't a good time to tell someone what I have to say. Lord, I ask for Your strength—not for myself but for my family.

I thought I could beat this condition but now I'm afraid it's beating me. I am not going to give up—I'm just facing the sad reality that I might not live much longer. I am at peace knowing that my soul will rest in Heaven, but I can't deny the feeling of woe that comes with the idea of not seeing my children grow up or being able to see Sela's beautiful smile as we grow old together.

She is my heart and I love her dearly."

Sela believed deep down that Roman and Ethel blamed her in some way for Rodney's decision to keep them in the dark about his condition.

"Just one more thing in a long list of accusations."

Chapter Twenty-Four

❧

June 11

"My appearance speaks for itself.

I have never been so pale or swollen in my face, legs, feet and midsection. When I talk, my words come out in a hoarse whisper and I have to catch my breath every other sentence, it seems.

Earlier today Sela and I went to see Dr. Winston and I had to go through yet another round of X rays and blood work.

Sela was a ball of nerves even though she's trying to act as if everything is okay. She is forever trying to show me how brave she is—she insists on being by my side. It's one of the reasons I love her so much.

I was completely at a loss for words when Dr. Winston told me that I was in no condition to go home. I told him that I didn't want to go back to the hospital.

Dr. Winston was very frank with me. He said that if I want to live to see another sunrise—I will need to be admitted into the hospital immediately.

I had no choice if I wanted to live.

I was taken over from Dr. Winston's office by ambulance. I guess he didn't trust I would actually go.

So now I'm back in the hospital.

The test results came in and they're not good. The echocardiogram showed a decrease in my EF from fifteen percent to ten percent.

According to the doctor, it's a miracle that my heart has lasted as long as it has. The doctor says that my heart would've lasted for maybe another four or five days. He explained that there are four classes based on physical functioning and four stages based on the progression of the disease.

My case is a Class Four, End Stage. I'm dying.

I guess I'm still numb from the news because I feel like this is happening to someone else and not me.

I feel like I've failed my family most of all.

I need comfort so I'll close now and study the Bible. I've asked Sela to bring mine from home but for now I'll read the one here in this room. John 6:33 just came into my mind and so did Romans 8:28. I guess I'll start there."

Sela recalled the way Rodney looked over at her with tears in his eyes, and said, "I'm so sorry, sweetheart. I know you didn't sign on for all this."

"Rodney, I wouldn't be anywhere else," Sela assured him. "You're my husband. *In sickness and in health.* I don't want to ever hear you say something like this again. We are a team—no matter what."

Sela ran her fingers through her hair. That day, the hardest call she had to make was to his parents. The pain she'd heard in Ethel's voice broke her already fragile heart.

"Mrs. Barnes, this is Sela. I'm calling because Rodney has to go back into the hospital."

"Is it...h-his h-heart?" Ethel cried.

"Yes."

Sela could tell Ethel was crying on the other end. "I'm sorry to have to call you with news like this. I know how upsetting this is."

"I'm sure you do," Ethel replied. "You and the children must be scared out of your wits."

"We are," she confessed. "I called Ayanna and Junior. They should be on their way already. I'm almost near the hospital. I'll call you when we find out more."

Sela couldn't forget the overwhelming need to scream, she was so angry. This doctor hadn't offered them hope—instead he'd informed them that Rodney was dying.

Sela picked up Rodney's Bible. It took her a few minutes but she found John 6:33. "I have said these things to you that by means of me you may have peace. In the world you are having tribulation, but take courage. I have conquered the world."

Next she turned to Romans 8:28. "And we know that all things work together for good to them that love God, to them who are called according to his purpose."

Sela once asked Rodney why he thought God had allowed him to get sick.

He had taken her hand in his and answered, "Sela, we experience sickness to remind us that we're not going to live forever. Every illness is a reminder from God of our frail humanity—of the temporary nature of life. God also allows sickness to test us, Sela. To see if our sickness will drive us closer to Him or farther from Him."

"It still doesn't seem fair," she'd responded.

"Sela, I want you to do something for me."

"What is it, babe? I'll do whatever you want."

"There are two prayers I want you to remember. One is this—Heavenly Father, there's still more that my husband can do for the kingdom. Please give him a few more years. In Jesus's name, I pray. Amen."

"What's the other one?"

"Dear Lord, it's been long enough. I don't want to see my husband suffer anymore. Take him home to be with you. In Jesus's name I pray. Amen."

Although Sela had given Rodney her word, she knew she would never pray that second prayer. Rodney knew it, too.

It still amazed her that no matter what, Rodney kept turning to God. He insisted sickness was just a tangible reminder of just how weak God's people were without Him.

"Rita was right, Lord. I was mad at you for taking Rodney's attention from me. I guess you might call it jealousy. I was used to being his world, but then that changed— You became my husband's world, and I didn't like it."

Her eyes filled with tears. "I'm a-ashamed…" Sobs welled up from deep down. "I-I'm…oh, Lord…I'm s-sor…ry."

Sela reached for a tissue and blew her nose. She made an attempt to compose herself. "Father God, please forgive me for my sins. My heart is open…please come back into my life. P-Please…"

Chapter Twenty-Five

❧

The children returned to school after Labor Day.

After seeing them off, Sela returned to her empty house.

She worked in her office most of the day returning phone calls and posting payments and writing up the deposit. Junior would do the invoicing when he came by later.

Sela called it a day around three o'clock and went downstairs, carrying Rodney's journal with her.

June 12
"This is my third day in the hospital and I'm finally able to eat without feeling nauseated. Praise the Lord! Thank God my breathing is coming much easier. The doctor has placed me on a low salt diet like before and has restricted me to drinking one and a half liters of water to prevent further fluid retention.

Sela is such a devoted wife to me. She comes every single day after the kids leave for summer camp. Today is Saturday, so they are probably with Rita or with Ayanna. Sela called earlier to tell me that she was on her way to see me.

She never fails to bring me books and fresh flowers. Sela says the flowers are to remind me of the beautiful and vivid hues of beauty in a world surrounded by shades of gray.

I miss the children so much and I appreciate Sela's efforts to bring them to the hospital to visit me almost every evening. Even though Junior and Ayanna both work full-time jobs, they visit me as much as they can.

I'm so proud of Sela and the children. They are really holding it together—much more than I originally gave them credit for. It's my parents who have me worried.

I'm not sure how they are handling all this. My mother hasn't been looking well. I can tell she's been doing a lot of crying.

Sela has been really reaching out to them since my illness. Something good is coming out of all of my suffering after all."

"Mom, you busy?"

Sela glanced up from Rodney's journal. "No sweetie, what's up?" She patted the empty space beside her. "How was the first day of school, Leon?"

"Okay."

She scanned her son's face. "What's wrong?"

"Mr. Bremen stopped me in the hall today and wanted to

know if Dad would oversee the carnival again this year. I had to tell him that he...that he's gone."

She wrapped an arm around him. "I'm sure that was pretty hard for you."

"Kinda," Leon acknowledged. "I didn't wanna talk about it, but Mr. Bremen—he kept asking me what happened and all."

"He didn't know about your father. I guess he was just curious. Mr. Bremen didn't mean any harm, I'm sure."

"I didn't wanna talk though. I don't like talking about it."

"I'll send Mr. Bremen a note. How about that?"

Leon gave a slight shrug. "I need to get started on my homework."

"You have homework on the first day of school?"

"Yes, ma'am."

"Wow."

Sela heard the front door open and close, followed by laughter.

Marcus blew into the family room with Lacey and Leah on his heels.

"Hey, Mama," he greeted.

Lacey ran over to where Sela sat, her arms outstretched. "Mommy, today was so much fun. I like kindergarten."

"Me, too," Leah contributed.

Hugging Lacey, Sela planted a kiss on her forehead.

"I'm so glad to hear you had a good day." She reached for Leah and kissed her on the cheek.

"Mom, can I make a sandwich?" Leon asked from the arched doorway leading to the kitchen.

"Sure, baby. Go right ahead." Sela stood up. "Marcus, you want one, too?"

"Yes, ma'am."

"Mommy, can I have some ice cream, pleeze?" Leah pleaded. "I don't want no sandwich."

"I don't want a sandwich, either. I just want some potato chips," Lacey interjected.

Sela directed Lacey to the pantry to retrieve a pair of Lay's barbecue chip bags. To Leah, she said, "Why don't you eat some fruit instead, sweetie? After dinner you can have some ice cream."

"Mommy...I don't want dinner. It makes my stomach hurt. I just want some ice cream. Strawberry ice cream."

"Did you eat your lunch today at school?"

Before Leah could respond, her twin answered for her. "No, ma'am. She didn't eat it. She went to the snack line and got ice cream."

Leah suddenly pushed Lacey. "She didn't ask you nothing. Mommy was talking to me."

Sela rushed over to where the girls were standing.

"Hold it right there, Leah Michele Barnes. You apologize to your sister right now. And you can forget about that ice cream now."

Leah burst into tears. "I hate you, Lacey! You made me in trouble."

Just as Sela was about to get on Leah once more, Junior strode into the kitchen. "What's all that crying for?"

"Leah said I made her in trouble." Lacey's voice broke. "I didn't mean to!"

He picked up Leah. "C'mon now... You know your sister loves you and she wouldn't try to get you in trouble on purpose. Right?"

Wiping her eyes, Leah nodded.

"I know I didn't hear you say you hated her when I came into the house. My ears were playing tricks on me—had to be, because my brothers and sisters all love one another. We don't say mean and hurtful things like that. Do we?"

Lacey opened her mouth to speak. "She *did* say she hated me."

"You know Leah didn't mean it," Sela interjected. "Your sister loves you."

"She didn't 'pologize."

Junior glanced over at his mother than back at Leah. "What? You didn't say you were sorry?"

Leah laid her head on his wide shoulders and mumbled, "Sorry."

"I want a hug and a kiss," Lacey demanded with both hands on her hips.

When Junior put Leah down, she ran over and hugged her sister. "I'm sorry, Lacey. I love you forever. Just don't tell on me no more."

"I won't. I promise. I don't want you to stop loving me."

Leon shook his head in disgust. "They so silly."

"I think it's sweet," Sela murmured. She held open her arms. "Come give your mother a hug, young man."

Junior embraced her next. "Hey Mom, I'll work on the invoicing."

Junior was truly stepping into his father's shoes.

"While y'all do some reading, I'll get dinner started." She made her way to the pantry and looked inside, trying to summon an idea of what to cook.

Sela decided on spaghetti.

Marcus and Leon finished their sandwiches and went upstairs with Junior, while the twins settled in the family room.

She turned to find Leah sitting at the breakfast bar watching her.

"I thought you were watching cartoons."

"Mommy, are you still mad with me?"

"I wasn't mad. I just didn't like the way you treated your sister. Family shouldn't act that way."

"You and Grandmother are family, but y'all get mad at each other all the time."

Sela couldn't deny it. Leah had a point.

"Honey, it's not that we're mad with each other. We just don't agree on a lot of things."

"I heard you tell Daddy one time that you didn't like Grandmother."

Sela was speechless for a moment. "I was upset with her, Leah. I didn't mean it."

"Did you 'pologize?"

"I didn't tell her that—I only said it to Daddy. I shouldn't have said that and I did apologize to your father."

"Mommy, I didn't like the way the food at school looked." She frowned. "It didn't look good."

"Would you like for me to make you a lunch?"

"Can I take pudding?"

Sela poured a can of stewed tomatoes into a large pot and stirred. "That's fine. But you have to eat regular food, too."

"I don't want no peanut butter though. I want ham and cheese. And pudding. Chocolate pudding."

Sela awarded her daughter a smile. "Okay. I'll pack a ham and cheese sandwich and chocolate pudding. I'll put an apple in there, too."

"May I pleeze have ice cream after dinner?"

"Are you going to try to eat some spaghetti? I'm making some meatballs to go in it—just the way you like it."

"Mommy, I'll try a little. Just a little tiny bit. Okay?"

"Okay, baby."

Leah held up her thumb and forefinger. "Just this much, Mommy."

Sela bit back her smile and nodded. She worried about Leah and her eating habits, but maybe with just a little more patience and understanding, the little girl would soon regain her appetite.

Sela stopped by Barnes Furniture two days later.

"Shopping for more furniture?" Ethel inquired.

"No, Mrs. Barnes. I was in the store next door and just thought I'd stop in to say hello."

"I was thinking about something," Ethel began. "Did you ever have the children tested for cardiomyopathy?"

"I did," Sela confirmed. "They're fine—all of them."

"That's wonderful news. I was so worried."

"What about Mr. Barnes? Has he spoken with his doctor yet?"

Ethel shook her head. "He is the world's worst patient. He refuses to go to the doctor and he's scared to death of hospitals."

Sela glimpsed Roman coming out of his office and threw up her hand, waving. Lowering her voice, she responded,

"He really needs to get checked out. Rodney's heart was so damaged—there was nothing that could be done."

"I was against Rodney having that heart transplant in the first place," Ethel declared. "Maybe he would still be here if—"

"But the transplant was the only chance Rodney had, Mrs. Barnes," Sela interjected. "He wouldn't have lived as long as he did."

She gave Sela a hard stare. "We'll never know that now."

"Losing Rodney is hard on all of us."

Ethel nodded. "I know."

"I'm very angry, too," Sela confessed. "Like you, I want to blame the transplant or someone—anyone for his death, but it doesn't change anything. Rodney is still gone. He won't ever come back."

Tears rolled down Ethel's cheeks.

Sela wanted to reach out to her, but didn't. She wasn't sure how Ethel would respond. "I'm so sorry for your pain, Mrs. Barnes."

Wiping her face, Ethel responded, "I'll be okay."

Glancing down at her watch, Sela said, "I'd better get going. The kids will be out of school soon. I want to be home before they get there."

"Kiss my darlings for me."

"I will."

"Thank you for stopping in." Ethel gestured to her left. "We just got in a new chair that would go perfectly with your sofa in the living room. You really need to put something in that corner near the window."

Sela released a soft sigh. The woman was always trying

to take over. From the moment she and Rodney rented their first apartment, Ethel appointed herself as interior decorator.

She and Rodney had a big fight when she came home from the hospital with Junior to find that Ethel had totally redecorated the tiny three-bedroom apartment. She'd made Rodney get rid of the furniture given to them by Sela's parents and replaced it all with new items from Barnes Furniture store.

Despite the fact that the apartment was beautifully decorated, Sela didn't like the fact that she hadn't been consulted. To her, this was another slap in the face doled out by her in-laws.

Another one in a long line of many.

Chapter Twenty-Six

❧

"Why remember the times when doubt and depression came up against us like a flood and were ready to drown our souls?" Pastor Grant questioned.

"Why should we remember when we were ostracized and criticized and chastised for no good reason? Why would you want to sing about the times when the bills were too high and the money was so low? Why remember those times when we felt hopeless, helpless and couldn't care less? Why think about the times when we were used, abused and confused?"

Sela glanced up from reading the church bulletin. Pastor Grant had gotten her attention with his words.

"If you only remember the times when you had peace in the home and peace on the job and peace at school, then, church, you are missing something. If you only remember when money was good and the bills were paid on time and you lived in a nice house, you don't have the full story. If all you remember are the times when you felt happy and healthy and holy then you don't have it all. You see, this text lets us know today, that everyone of us in here, everyone of us in here will go through some trouble sometime. It's a guarantee. If yours hasn't come yet—I invite you to keep on living."

I've sure had my share, Sela thought silently.

"But most of us if not all of us can testify that even though there were some good times this past year, we have had some rough times also…"

"Amen," she whispered.

"Some of us know how it feels when the enemies of loneliness and depression arise against us. There were times when no one understands what we are going through. Only God and the pillow that we cry on each night know what we're holding on to so deep inside…. For someone, the death or serious illness of a loved one may be your rushing water. You don't know how to make it. Who to turn to? Where to go?"

Sela felt the beginnings of tears. She blinked rapidly to keep them from falling.

Pastor Grant's eyes traveled all over the sanctuary. His eyes landed on her briefly, moved on, but then returned. She thought she detected just a hint of sympathy in his gaze.

"I must confess today, church, I don't know what trouble you may have seen this year. I don't know what burden you had to bear. I don't know what sorrow might have been yours or pain you had to endure. I don't know how many nights you stayed up counting sheep to fall asleep. I don't know how many times you had to borrow from one credit card to pay another."

He paused a moment before continuing. "But I do know this—after all the trouble in our world, in our country, in our neighborhood this year. After all that has gone on in our church, in our homes, in our lives, the reason we are still here today is because the Lord has been on our side."

Sela wondered where Pastor Grant was going with his sermon.

As if he'd heard her thoughts, the minister said, "My first point today, church, as we look back is that when things are at their worst, God is at His best. When we come to our Red Sea, we find out He can make a highway through the waters. When we get tossed into the fiery furnaces, we realize that He will take the heat for us. When we lose our jobs, we recognize that He can stretch our food and our money."

Sela continued to listen.

"God shows up and shows off in our trouble. You know over this last year that the times when we see God most, are those times when we were down and out and He lifted us up. Those times when we were friendless and He stuck closer than a brother. Those times when our heart was broken and He put it back together again. When our joy was gone and He gave us a song in the night. When we didn't know where to turn and He led the way.

"My second point is when we look back over this year we realize that we have not been perfect, but we have a God who never did leave us nor forsake us. He didn't give up on us. He didn't throw in the towel on our lives. He is slow to anger somebody and plenteous in mercy." Raising his hands towards the heavens, Pastor Grant shouted, "I'm so glad that He lifted me out of the miry clay of my mistakes. He set me free. He set me free."

"He set me free," Sela whispered. A lone tear rolled down her cheek.

"Our help is in the name of the Lord, Who made heaven and earth. Our help doesn't come from where we live or what we drive. Our help doesn't come from the schools we went to. Our help doesn't come from the bottle or some pills…no, our help comes from the Lord."

At the end of the sermon, Sela was weeping openly. Junior reached over and hugged her. One of the ushers came over and began fanning her.

When Pastor Grant called for people to come up for prayer, Ayanna and Junior led Sela to the front of the church.

Surrounded by family and church members, Sela prayed in earnest.

"Lord Jesus, I confess that I have held ill feelings and resentments against You. I'm asking You to help me to forgive the people in my old church and myself. I ask You, Father, to drop in my mind and bring to my remembrance the name of anyone whose actions or words have hurt me, or another person for which I hold or have held ill feelings and resentments, or grudges against. Father, as You forgave me when I did not deserve to be forgiven, so likewise, I forgive, whether they deserve it or not—in Jesus's name, Amen."

Images of Roman and Ethel Barnes floated in her mind when Sela finished her prayer. She accepted the tissue Ayanna held out to her and wiped her face before returning to her seat.

The next day, Sela spent most of the morning making plans for Marcus's upcoming birthday. He would turn ten on Thursday.

She picked up the phone and dialed.

"Mrs. Barnes, this is Sela," she announced when Ethel answered the telephone. "The reason I'm calling is to invite you and Mr. Barnes over for dinner. We're celebrating Marcus's birthday."

"When did you have in mind?"

"Next Sunday around four."

"I'm sorry we won't be able to make it on Sunday, but we would like to take the children out on Saturday, if that's all right with you."

"Sure. That's fine." Secretly, Sela was relieved that her in-laws couldn't make the birthday dinner. Their presence would put a damper on what should be a festive occasion. It was going to be hard enough to celebrate without Rodney.

"Tell them we'll be by to pick them up around noon."

"I will."

"Well, I have to go. Thank you for calling."

Before Sela could respond, the line went dead.

Shaking her head, she hung up the phone. "Rodney, I'm trying, babe. I'm really trying." Sela had extended an olive branch to her in-laws. Since the day she stopped by the furniture store to talk to them, there had been no word from Ethel and Roman. The children had called their house a couple of times and spoke to them, but other than that, no word.

She knew how much they loved their grandparents, so Sela wanted to keep the peace. *This is for my children and Rodney. If it wasn't for them, I wouldn't have anything to do with Roman and Ethel. They have been nothing but mean and just rude to me.*

Sela made a promise to Rodney that she would bridge the gap between herself and his parents. She was determined to do everything she could to make that happen.

Roman and Ethel arrived promptly at noon on Saturday to pick up the children.

"They should be down shortly. Why don't y'all have a seat," Sela suggested.

"We won't be here that long," Ethel uttered tersely.

Sela opened her mouth to respond but when she spied Leah coming down the stairs, she changed her mind.

The other children soon followed.

Sela was grateful when Ethel and Roman left.

When the telephone rang a few minutes later, she had an idea of who the caller was. Sela saw Rita's name on the caller ID and smiled.

"Hey, Rita," she greeted.

"How did it go?"

"They were cold to me as usual. Nothing's changed." Sela chewed on her bottom lip. "I don't care though. I don't need them."

"Maybe you should try talking to them again. This has got to stop."

"I've tried, Rita. I invited them to Marcus's birthday celebration tomorrow and they turned me down. They wanted to take the children today. I'm sure they are gonna take them shopping or something."

"Shopping is a good thing."

Sela laughed. "Yeah, it is."

"They're gonna be fine. You know how much they love those kids. They won't do anything to them."

"Oh, I know that. I just don't want them spoiling my children and trying to turn them against me."

"Sela, that won't ever happen."

"I wouldn't put anything past Roman and Ethel Barnes."

"Your children love you."

"You're right." Sela laughed. "I don't know what I was thinking about."

"Mommy! Mommy! You missed it," Lacey screamed as she ran into the house. "You missed Marcus's birthday party. We had so much fun!"

Confused, Sela asked, "What party?"

"Marcus had a birthday party at Grandma's house. They had balloons and everything."

Leah rushed into the house. "Mommy, why didn't you come to the party? I ate ice cream and a little cake."

Sela was furious. She clenched and unclenched her fists. "Where are your grandparents?"

"They just left," Marcus announced when he walked into the house laden down with presents. "Mom, why didn't you come to my party?"

She swallowed hard. "Sweetie, I would've been there if I'd known about it."

"Grandma didn't tell you?" Leon asked.

"No, she didn't," Sela responded. "Maybe it was because she knew I was planning a special dinner for Marcus on tomorrow."

"Are you mad?" Marcus questioned.

"No, sweetie," she fibbed. Sela didn't want to tell her son that she was furious with his grandparents. She couldn't tell him that they'd deliberately shut her out of his birthday party.

Later that evening, she called Rita and told her what happened. "I'm so angry I could scream."

"Just let it go, Sela. That's what they want you to do. Don't sink to their level—just let it go."

When Sela got off the phone, she wasn't so sure she could just let this slide. If she didn't say something to Ethel and Roman, she might burst.

June 13

"Tomorrow is Father's Day and I will be spending it in the hospital. The children called and asked me what I wanted. I couldn't tell them what I really wanted and that is for my wife and my parents to find a way to peacefully co-exist. It is my deepest desire to bridge this gap between my family. I'm tired of the fighting that has gone on far too long.

I have to admit that since my illness, they have tried on both sides to be cordial, but it is not enough—I want there to be love between the members of my family. If I am to die, I want my parents and Sela to work together to raise my children.

But in order to accomplish this there has to be for-giveness on both sides.

Sela resents the way my parents have always treated her. I can't say I blame her, but it has put me in an im-possible situation. I am tired of feeling like I have to split myself in two just to please my wife and my parents.

Lately it has been on my heart to speak to Sela about building a relationship with my parents. But whenever I even mention their name, I can see the change in her mood. It's the same with my parents. Sela only has to walk into the room and the very air is charged with ac-cusations and bitterness.

They talk at each other and not to each other. Why can't my parents understand that I love my wife above all else. But then, Sela needs to understand that I love my parents despite their faults as well.

I love my family—all of them. I don't want to split myself anymore. I don't have energy to keep doing it. I just can't do it anymore."

Sela decided to hold her tongue after reading Rodney's June thirteenth entry in his journal. Before he died, she'd made a promise to try and build a better relationship with his parents.

"I have to do this for Rodney."

Sela closed the journal and laid it on the nightstand. She got up and walked over to the door, peeking out.

Leon was coming up the stairs.

"Sweetie, where is Marcus?"

"He's playing football on PlayStation."

Sela walked out of her room and followed Leon into the bedroom he shared with Marcus.

"Marcus, can you pause your game, sweetie. I need to talk to you."

He grunted, then stopped his game. Marcus got up and stared at her expectedly.

"Why don't we go to my room," she suggested.

"Am I in trouble?" he wanted to know.

"No, sweetheart. I just want to talk to you."

In her room, Sela had Marcus take a seat on the edge of her bed.

"You didn't tell me much about your party?"

Marcus stared down at the carpet. "I didn't think you'd want to hear about it. Besides, Grandma said that you had something else you wanted to do."

"What?"

"It's okay, Mom. I don't mind."

"Marcus, sweetie, if I'd known about your party, I would've dropped whatever I had to do to be there. I hope you know that."

He looked up at her then. "Mom, I know that you love me. I know that you and Grandma and Grandpa don't like to be around each other. It's okay. I like having two parties...." Marcus broke into a grin. "Twice the presents."

Laughing, Sela ran her fingers through his sandy brown curls. "You're something else."

"I love you, Mom."

She embraced him. "I love you, too."

"Mom."

"Huh?"

"Why don't Grandmother like you?"

"Sweetie, I really don't know. I've done everything I could to make them like me—but you know what? It really doesn't matter. All you need to know is that we all love you and your brothers and sisters. Never forget that. Okay?"

Marcus nodded. "Can I go back and play my game now?"

"You sure can. Make sure you let Leon have his turn. I know how you are…."

He gave her a look of pure innocence. "Who, me?"

Sela burst into laughter. "Go on…get out of here."

Chapter Twenty-Seven
✥

June 14

"I don't care about anything but being able to breathe and drink a nice tall glass of ice water. I'm thirsty all the time because of the Lasix I have to take. My lips are constantly cracked and my tongue feels so raw.

On days like this I wonder if maybe death is better than being alive and suffering like this. My children want to play games when they come to see me at the hospital and I am too tired to even do that. They are young and do not fully understand what's going on with me. We have told them some of what's happening to me, but I don't want to scare them.

Junior and Ayanna are spending more and more time at home these days—I guess they worry that I might die. Sela still hovers over me, and it still irritates me to no end, but I don't say anything. It wouldn't do any good—she's stubborn."

The last sentence in this entry bought a smile to Sela's lips. Rodney used to always say this about her and she never thought she'd come to miss it.

She started when Junior walked into the kitchen. "I didn't know you were here," Sela muttered as she placed a hand over her rapidly beating heart. "You scared me."

"Sorry, Mom. I came over to see if you needed any help with the invoicing or whatever. I'm off today. I'll mow the lawn later on."

"Honey, you don't have to worry about that. I've hired a gardener—he'll be here tomorrow. But yeah, I could use some help with invoicing. Business has picked up so much that I'm gonna have to hire at least two more drivers. Your Grandpa's coming up next week from Florida to conduct some interviews for me." Sela had another thought. "Why don't you look at your schedule and see if you can sit in on some of them?"

"I work three days next week. I've got a paper to write so I took some time off. I'd planned to be here anyway because my computer's acting up."

"What's wrong with it?"

"I think I need a new hard drive."

"Put it in the shop and I'll pay for it."

Junior sat down beside her. "Mom, I can pay for my hard drive. I've got some money saved. I'm fine."

"Okay. Okay. I'm just trying to help."

He laughed. "I know and I love you for it, Mom. I just don't want you worrying about me. You have enough on your plate. Just take care of the twins, Marcus and Leon. I'll let you know if I need help with anything. Okay?"

Sela nodded. "You've grown up so fast. You and Yanna both."

"You raised us well, Mom. You and Dad were great parents. We've heard horror stories, so we know how lucky we are. Yanna and I talk about it all the time."

"I'm the lucky one. I've had the world's greatest husband and six loving children. I can't ask for anything more." Sela broke into a short laugh. "Enough of the mushy stuff. Let's get to work."

The invoicing done, Sela made a couple of calls while Junior took the deposit to the bank.

She glanced up at the clock, noting that the children would be coming home from school soon. Sela leaned back in her chair stretching and yawning.

As usual, she hadn't slept well at all. She had gotten up at the crack of dawn and tried to read a couple of passages from the Bible before waking up the children and preparing breakfast.

Sela had taken a light nap around ten but Rita called twenty minutes later, waking her up. Then Ayanna had called to let her know she would be coming by when she left work.

She heard the front door open and knew Junior had returned. Sela pushed away from the desk and stood up. She stifled her yawn before heading to her bedroom.

Sela met up with Junior outside the office.

"I'm gonna try and take a nap before the children come home. I'm exhausted."

"I'll be here."

"Thanks for helping me out, sweetie. I really appreciate it."

"I told you I'd be here for you, Mom. I made a promise to Dad."

"If I'm not up in an hour, please wake me."

"Okay." Junior walked into the office and placed the plastic pouch on the desk. "The receipts are in this bag," he announced. "I'll leave it right here."

"Thanks," Sela murmured sleepily.

A few minutes later, in her bedroom, Sela climbed into the king-sized bed. Within minutes, she was asleep.

Chapter Twenty-Eight

✧

June 14

"Well, I'm leaving tomorrow morning for Duke University Hospital. I will undergo tests to see if I'm a candidate for a heart transplant. I pray that I am. 'Cause if I'm not—I won't be on this earth much longer. I guess I can confess that I'm scared—more than I've ever been in life.

Sela became very upset with me this evening because I wanted to talk about my death. She felt we were being morbid. She thought I was giving up, but that's not at all what I had in mind.

I want to live.

I just feel we need to discuss the important stuff—insurance policies and other important papers. Sela needs to know what to do if something happens. I've told her that I want to be cremated. I don't want her going to all that expense of an elaborate funeral. There isn't any point to it since I will be in Heaven with the Lord. What's left is nothing but a shell."

Sela had hated having that conversation. Although she felt differently now—back then she believed that Rodney was giving up in some way.

"I was afraid to say it back then, Rodney, but I felt it. I felt like I was gonna lose you when you went to Duke."

Her trembling fingers lightly brushed across the leather-bound journal. "I was right…."

The transplant cardiologist who identified himself as Dr. Avery came by the next morning with a team of first-, second- and third-year students, in addition to a fourth-year intern. All of them took turns listening to his heart and lungs.

After the team of doctors moved on, Sela gave Rodney's room a final survey. "I think this looks pretty good. It's not home—"

"Exactly," Rodney snapped in frustration. "This is not my home."

Concerned, Sela walked over to the bed and sat down on the edge. "Babe, what's wrong? Why are you acting like this?"

"This… This is all…w-wrong…" Rodney's voice broke, and tears rolled down his cheek.

Sela knew he was angry, disappointed and probably scared—all rolled into one. She moved closer to him, so that she could wrap her arms around him. In all the years they'd been together, he'd only cried in front of her on a couple of occasions.

Sela's own eyes filled with water. "You're not alone, babe. Just remember that. We are in this together. We're a team—you and me."

She held onto him until Rodney pulled away.

Handing him a tissue, she whispered, "It's gonna be okay, babe. You'll see."

"I'm not in a real good mood right now. Why don't you go home, Sela? Spend some time with the children."

"I don't want to leave you alone. Especially when you're like this."

Sudden anger flashed in Rodney's eyes. Sela could tell he was irritated.

"I want to be alone," Rodney insisted suddenly. "Please…just do as I ask."

Hurt, Sela shot back, "You don't have to be so nasty, Rodney."

Snatching up her purse, she headed to the door. Pausing, she stood there watching him for a moment.

"I'm sorry," Rodney responded.

She tried, but she wasn't moved by his simple apology.

He went on to explain, "Sela, I just need some time alone. This isn't a good day for me. I was fine in the ambulance, but when I got here…" Shrugging, Rodney said, "I don't know what happened."

Without looking back at him, she threw up a hand to wave and walked out of the room, leaving him in his misery.

June 15

"I met one of the other patients today. His name is Leland Walsh. He came in after Sela left.

I feel bad for hurting her feelings but out of the blue—I just felt this burst of anger. I shouldn't have taken it out on her.

I was feeling real depressed with Sela gone and then this man just walked into my room and introduced himself. He told me that he'd been here for a little over a month now. He told me about some of the other patients here waiting for a transplant. Like Peggy Moore—she's right next door to me and she's been here at Duke for two months. The poor woman thought she had a new heart last week but it was a false alarm.

I can only imagine her disappointment.

I also met the psychologist assigned to my case. Her name is Jessie Daniels and she seemed overly preoccupied with my past—how my parents raised me; how much they cared about me. She asked how well Sela and I get along. I don't want her probing into my thoughts, making me feel vulnerable and sensitive. I don't feel comfortable opening up to a complete stranger."

Sela closed the journal and laid it on the nightstand. It had been quite a challenge to get Rodney to agree to see the psychologist.

She eventually had to convince him that the transplant team was worried about his anxiety level.

"Everyone is worried about you, Rodney. They're not sure

if you're mentally prepared for the surgery. Babe, they want you to agree to therapy twice a week for your mental health. They want to be sure that you—"

"What?" he interrupted. "The team wants to know if I'm on the verge of a nervous breakdown. Well look at me—my heart is broken. Isn't that to be expected?"

"You're hurting, Rodney, I know that. Believe me, everyone knows. There is no way we can truly understand the depth of what you're experiencing." Sela moved closer. "The range of your emotions runs from one extreme to the other—you're allowed, babe. But I need you to understand that you're going to have to find a way to cope with this depression unless you're choosing to die."

Rodney sent Sela a sharp look. "What do you mean by that?"

"Jessie said that transplant centers can legally refuse to list patients if they do not find them suitable for a donated organ."

Rodney gave her a look of disbelief.

"She says it's because they can give the organ—which is hard to come by—to another patient who is ready both mentally and physically and will not put it to waste."

"I'm angry," he confessed. "Why can't people understand this? I'm going through a lot."

"It's understandable, honey. You're tired of being poked on and sleeping in a hospital bed. All the pain and needles—that would spoil anyone's mood. I understand all that. But that's why you have to speak to someone. A therapist can help you sort it all out."

"I've been terrible," Rodney stated after a moment. "I guess I owe everybody here an apology."

Back then, Sela was really worried about Rodney. He was so angry and gave the staff a lot of attitude when they were only trying to help him. She'd never seen him like that until he was admitted into Duke Hospital.

But now... Sela eyed the photo of her in-laws. Standing up, she walked across the room and took it off the fireplace mantel.

Chapter Twenty-Nine

❧

June 29

"I've been here at Duke University Hospital for two weeks now. So far all I've done was take tests and give blood. They told me that these first couple of weeks would consist of my workup and evaluation.

Dr. Avery and his team ran about a dozen different tests on my heart and other major organs to determine if my body is physically a candidate for a donated heart.

I am trying to take everything in stride—that is until the IV in my right inner arm became infected with a clot.

Dr. Avery had tried unsuccessfully to stick a tiny catheter down my right neck vein to conduct a left heart catheterization and read the pressures in my heart, but the tube never made it. Pain unlike any I've ever known shot down my neck like a knife.

I'm about ready to say some very unkind things, but am trying to keep my temper in check. This has become more challenging than I ever expected it to be.

Leland never fails to come by my room offering words of support. We are becoming great friends. One of the ladies here died earlier today. I guess she couldn't wait any longer."

One week passed and Sela was still upset with her in-laws for giving Marcus a party without telling her. When Ethel called to say she was coming by to pick up the children, she didn't bother telling her mother-in-law that they were visiting with some friends from the church.

Ethel arrived promptly at two as promised.

Sela met her at the door.

"Are they ready?" Ethel inquired.

Folding her arms across her chest and wearing a smug expression, Sela stated, "Sorry, they're not here."

"Where are they?"

"Out with friends."

Ethel bristled. "Why didn't you tell me this on the phone when I called?"

"Because I wanted to talk to you. I heard about the party you and Mr. Barnes gave Marcus."

"Well, it wasn't a secret."

"Oh, really? Then why didn't you tell me about it? Why did I have to hear about it after the fact?"

"Roman and I knew you'd planned a celebration of your own, so we just decided to do the same."

"I invited y'all over here. You and your husband weren't excluded."

Ethel waved her hand in dismissal. "Sela, this is pointless."

"I don't agree. I really don't appreciate you and your husband pulling this on me. I have the right to know everything you plan to do with or for *my* children. Actually, I insist on knowing."

"Why must you be so confrontational, Sela?"

"Why do you insist on shutting me out of this family? I was Rodney's wife—I am his widow. I *am* the mother of his children."

"Oh, believe me, Sela. We are well aware that you are the mother of my grandchildren. After all, it was your life's ambition."

Sela struggled within to keep from slapping Ethel. "How dare you!"

"I shouldn't have said that. I'm sorry." Ethel played with her necklace. "Look, Sela, we just wanted to do something special to acknowledge Marcus's birthday. Perhaps we were a bit selfish."

"Mrs. Barnes, I wouldn't have minded so much if you'd just told me about it."

Ethel glanced over at the clock on the wall. "Well, I have to be going. Please tell the children I came by. I'd planned to take them to the movies."

When Ethel turned to leave, Sela stopped her.

"Look, I'm sorry I let you make this trip for nothing. If

you'd like, I can go pick them up, get them dressed and bring them out to your house."

Ethel smiled. "We can have dinner and then catch a later showing. Would you mind if they spent the night?"

Sela shook her head. "No, I don't mind. I'll pack a bag for them."

After making arrangements to pick them up on Sunday evening from her in-laws' house, Sela bid Ethel farewell.

"If we can just keep talking like this," she murmured on her way upstairs. "Maybe we'll be able to get along. Rodney would like that."

Sela stared at the television. She wasn't interested in anything on it.

His eyes traveled to the photograph of Rodney on the mantel of the fireplace. "I miss you so much," she murmured softly.

Her eyes watered and overflowed, tears running down her cheeks. Sela wiped them away with the back of her hand.

The house felt so empty and lonely without the children and Rodney. But at least the children would be home later. She'd made plans to pick them up around seven, but Sela now wished she'd arranged an earlier time.

She'd woken up early to attend church. Sela had thoroughly enjoyed the sermon and believed Pastor Grant had delivered it especially for her. She could still hear his words even now.

"Today's topic is 'What God wants me to be.' Our objective in life should be the same as presented in the Scriptures. Matthew 6:33 says, 'But seek ye first the kingdom of God and

His righteousness; and all these things shall be added unto you." It isn't often that the Lord Jesus told us to seek after something, but here He gives us what is to be our objective in life...."

Sela took careful notes as she listened.

"Seek His kingdom, and His righteousness. If we will do that first, then He will assume the responsibility for the rest of the things we need in life."

She was like a sponge, trying to soak up every word spoken from Pastor Grant's mouth.

"We must have a love for the Word of God. In the life of any servant of God, the Word of God deserves the highest priority. It should truly be our daily bread. We should never grow weary of its study." Pastor Grant paused a moment before continuing. "We then have to ask ourselves, does the Word of God have an active place in our life? The Bible is our instruction manual for life and must be studied thoroughly. The kind of person that God wants us to be not only loves the Word—they also live the Word."

The part of Pastor Grant's sermon that stayed with Sela was toward the end when he said, "We need to have a love for people. To be godly is to be Godlike. And to be like God is to love people. You know a lot of times we are defiled by bitterness springing up. Bitterness comes as a result of real or supposed ill-treatment—it really doesn't matter which. Whether or not we have been wronged is immaterial, we must guard against bitterness in our lives. Jesus said they shall know ye are my disciples if ye have love one to another. Are we the kind of person that God wants us to be today? No more excuses! Let's get honest before God and with ourselves this morning."

He closed his sermon by asking, "Have we made our life objectives those that are represented in the Scripture? Are we willing to pay the price to fulfill the will of God for our lives? Do we have a genuine love for the Word of God? Do we have a servant's heart? Do we really have a love for people?"

Sela pondered those questions even now. She couldn't deny that her heart had been filled with bitterness stemming from the past. Some of it, she'd been able to let go of—but some, she still held on to, even now. Especially when it came to Roman and Ethel Barnes.

All she'd ever wanted from them was acceptance. Instead, they held on to the belief that for various reasons Sela had ruined Rodney's life.

Why couldn't they see that she loved their son with her entire being? She had been a loving and devoted wife to Rodney.

"I've got to let it go," she whispered.

Chapter Thirty

❧

July 4

"Today is Independence Day, but it doesn't really mean anything to me because I'm stuck in this hospital. Sela and the children came by earlier but I sent them out to enjoy the holiday. There is no reason for them to sit around here with me.

Tomorrow is my son's birthday. He is going to be twelve years old. We are having a celebration for him here at the hospital. I am going to bed early tonight so that I will be rested and feeling good. I want to enjoy my son's birthday—it may be the last time I get this chance.

Sela worries that I am feeling like giving up and I have to confess that there are times I do. I have made peace with this illness. My trust is in the Lord and I know that even if I die—it will be for the greater good of His glory."

The day after July fourth, they celebrated Leon's birthday.

Sela decided they would have a picnic in Rodney's room so that he could participate in the celebration. She brought in hot dogs, hamburgers, chips and soda. One of the nurses had even baked a birthday cake for Leon.

On that day, Dr. Waters graciously signed an order allowing Rodney to leave the unit for a short time to walk the hospital grounds with his family.

Sela could tell Rodney was delighted to be able to walk around and just get some fresh air. They walked slowly since there were two big IV dosage bags attached to his IV pole.

"I don't understand why I need someone to push the pole for me. I can do it."

"Dad, it's because they don't want you exerting your upper body," Junior explained. "It makes your heart work harder."

After their walk, everyone returned to the hospital room and sat down to have lunch. Sela invited Leland and some of the other patients to join them.

When Ayanna offered her father a plate, Rodney refused the food. "Thanks, sweetheart, but I'm not very hungry."

"Babe, don't you think you should eat something?" Sela asked before biting into her hot dog.

"I'm okay. I'll eat later."

Sela didn't push Rodney. It wouldn't do any good. He would eat whenever he was ready.

Around four o'clock, Dr. Winston entered the room.

"Hey, Doc," Leland greeted. "Come to join the party?"

"I wish I could," Dr. Winston replied. "Happy birthday, Leon."

"Thank you, Doctor," Leon mumbled.

"I have a very special gift for you today. Something I think you'll really enjoy. In fact I'm sure your whole family will be delighted."

This got Leon's attention. "Wow, what is it?"

"We've found a match for your father. He's getting a new heart."

Leon's face lit up like a candle. "My wish came true." He began to dance around the room. "Yeah! My wish actually came true."

"Doc, are you for real?" Rodney asked.

He nodded. "It's on its way as we speak." Gesturing around the room, he added, "I hate to break this picnic up, but we've got to get you ready for surgery."

Sela's own heart skipped a beat. "Thank You, Jesus," she shouted. "Oh, thank You so much."

While Sela called Ethel and Roman from the telephone in Rodney's room, the children kept running to the windows looking for the incoming helicopter to bring their father's new heart.

At approximately 4:30 p.m., a transplant surgeon came into Rodney's room.

His parents arrived shortly after that. Rodney had enough time to say hello when a stern nurse walked in and ordered, "Strip off those pajamas. We are going to have to wash you."

His bed was changed and cleaned of anything that might be considered contamination. Rodney whispered a silent prayer while he waited for the surgeon to call back from wherever he was inspecting his new heart. Sela murmured a prayer of her own and tried to calm her frazzled nerves by focusing on her children.

"I called Pastor Grant. He's coming over right now."

"This is such a blessing," Ethel uttered. "You've been here for two and a half weeks and now you're getting a heart."

"At the expense of someone dying," Rodney said in a low voice. He peered down at his chest. "Whoever you are—I thank you."

Leah blew him a kiss, bringing a smile to his lips.

Rodney held his hand out to Sela. "Remember what we talked about. Don't forget."

Sela didn't want to hear those words. She never enjoyed discussing his final wishes. Especially now, when he was on his way to have surgery. She wished to remain positive.

Dr. Chin, the anesthesiologist, came in and introduced himself, sparing Sela from having to respond.

Chapter Thirty-One

❧

Sela would never forget the day Rodney died.

It soon became evident that Rodney's new heart was not working properly. Exactly fifteen days after the first one, Rodney was wheeled down for a second transplant.

Sela was a ball of nerves. She couldn't seem to shake the dark sense of foreboding that held her in its viselike grip. Her body trembled and she couldn't keep any food on her stomach.

She heard the sound of someone shuffling down the corridor and looked up. It was Leland.

"God will take care of Rodney," he uttered as he neared her. Sela helped him with his IV pole.

"I know," she murmured. "I keep telling myself that same thing." Sela awarded Leland a smile. "How are you doing?"

"I have good days and bad, but the good news is that I have days at all."

Pastor Grant had joined them at the hospital along with some of the other members of his church. Some of them Sela recognized, but a few of them she hadn't met until today.

"Let's gather together for prayer," Pastor Grant suggested.

In the waiting room, they gathered in a semicircle. A few people waiting for word on their own families joined them.

Hands held, heads bowed and eyes closed, they waited for Pastor Grant to begin interceding on their behalf.

"Most Blessed Father, on this day and all days, I ask that You guide the hands of the doctors, nurses and anyone who comes into contact with our brothers and sisters facing surgery this morning. Ease the pain and heartache of all the people here who are all having a hard time right now. I ask that You lay Your hands on Your child Rodney as he needs Your help now. Heal him in body, mind and spirit. Show him Your love—show him Your mercy, show him that You work miracles. This I ask through Christ Our Lord. Amen."

"Thank you, Pastor. I'm glad you're here today." Sela tried to keep her voice steady. "I feel a lot better having you here while Rodney's in surgery."

"I appreciate you calling me and keeping me informed."

"I can't believe this—we're going through all this again. One minute he was getting better, then all of a sudden, there's an infection and now Rodney has to go through a second transplant."

"It's a blessing that they were able to find another so quickly," Ethel stated. "I'm thankful for that. I hate that someone else had to lose their life… It's a precious gift."

Sela nodded in agreement.

Someone approached her from behind. "Mrs. Barnes, would you like something to eat or drink?"

She tossed a glance over her shoulder. "No, thank you. I'm not hungry."

Rita walked over and embraced her. "Try to drink a cup of water, hon."

"I don't think I can even hold that down."

"I just got off the phone with your mama. I'm supposed to call them back when Rodney comes out of surgery. They have their whole church praying for him."

Sela nodded.

Leah was getting cranky, so Junior stood up and took her by the hand. "I'm taking the girls down to get something to eat," he announced. "Marcus, you and Leon want to come?"

Roman decided to go with them.

Sela walked over to an empty seat and sat down. She was grateful that no one attempted to engage her in conversation—she didn't feel like talking.

Four hours drifted by.

"This is taking a long, long time," Lacey complained.

"Shh." Ayanna curled her finger, insisting that her sister come sit by her.

Lacey stomped over. "What?"

"I want you to do something for me, little miss. Could you help me with this puzzle? I know how much you like to do word searches and I just can't find all the words."

Grinning, Lacey dived in.

Her twin got up and crawled on Sela's lap.

Another two hours passed.

Sela's nerves began to get the best of her. She'd bitten her bottom lip, drawing blood.

Ethel pulled out a tissue and handed it to her. "That's an annoying habit. You should stop doing that to yourself."

Before Sela could utter a reply, Dr. Winston walked slowly towards them, a look of sadness on his face.

Sela shivered as a feeling of dread slithered down her spine and began pulling at her sleeves. Rita walked over, lending her strength as she embraced her.

Tears welled up in Sela's eyes and overflowed. Before Dr. Winston said the words, she knew. It was as if a part of her had vanished into thin air.

"Mrs. Barnes…too much rejection…problem appeared to be the antibodies…we did all we could…I'm sorry…died at four forty-five…"

Sela heard Ethel scream. Out of the corner of her eye, she caught sight of Roman holding her as she grieved.

She looked down at her own hands—her arms…arms that would never hold Rodney again.

Numb, she glanced around at the group of people standing around them.

Beside her, Rita was saying something to her, but Sela couldn't make out the words. Pastor Grant was talking to the doctor; her children were crying and Pastor Grant's wife was hugging Ayanna, while another member of the church held Leah and Lacey.

The room suddenly began to spin, everyone merging into a blur.

Darkness descended upon her with a vengeance.

Chapter Thirty-Two

❧

The children spent Sunday afternoon with their grandparents. Ayanna had dropped them off before she left for work and Sela would be picking them up.

She drove to Chapel Hill humming to the music playing on the radio. When Sela arrived at her in-laws' house, she found Leah nearly hysterical.

"Leah, honey, what's wrong?"

The little girl only cried harder.

Sela looked to Marcus and Leon for answers. "What happened?"

Lacey answered for her twin. "She's upset because Grandmother fussed at her for not eating all her food."

"What?"

"Leah kept saying Grandmother gave her too much food.

I told her to be quiet and just eat her food but she didn't listen to me. I ate my food, Mommy."

Shock yielded quickly to fury. "Where's your grandmother?"

"In the den, I think."

Pointing to the door, Sela instructed, "Y'all go on and get into the car. I need to have a talk with your grandmother."

She stormed through the house looking for Ethel. "Mrs. Barnes, I need to speak with you."

"I'm back here," Ethel responded.

She found her mother-in-law in the kitchen.

"What is it?"

"Mrs. Barnes, Rodney's been gone for two months, and Leah is still grieving for him. Don't force her to eat. If you can't be more understanding, I'll keep her home."

"I haven't done anything to harm Leah. I don't want her to get sick."

"And she won't. She's eating, but she just can't eat a large serving. She eats small portions. Right now I think that's about all her tummy can take. She does eat more frequently."

"You shouldn't let her have so much ice cream, Sela. I'm worried that the poor child is just going to waste away."

"I am limiting how much she eats, Mrs. Barnes. You don't need to fuss at her about this. She can't handle this right now."

"This is foolishness. If you let her, Leah will eat nothing but ice cream all day long. What are you going to say when the other children want to do the same thing, or decide they want nothing but a diet of candy? Huh?"

"I've already explained to the other children that Leah is grieving and this is her way of coping. Ice cream is comfort food for her. It used to be mine, so I understand. It's not like this is all she eats. She eats her food. Just not as much as before."

Ethel sucked her teeth. "It needs to stop."

"Just don't upset her, Mrs. Barnes. That's all I'm asking."

"Why must you always accuse me of doing horrible things to the children? Do you actually believe that I'd do something to harm my grandkids?"

"I don't want to fight with you, Mrs. Barnes. I'm just asking you to back off Leah. Please give her some time to adjust as best she can. I haven't accused you of anything."

"My poor Rodney is probably turning over in his grave over the way you've treated me."

"Oh, please," Sela shot back. "You're the one overreacting."

Ethel gestured towards the arched doorway. "I think it's best for you to leave. I won't have you disrespecting me in my own home."

"You need to remember that when you're in mine," Sela shot back. "Since we're on the subject, I'm tired of you and your husband just popping over uninvited. I would prefer that you call me first. If you want respect, then you need to respect me as well."

Ethel sent a glare her way.

"When it comes to my children—please let me make the decisions. No more haircuts, birthday parties or deciding what my children eat."

"Those children are my grandchildren, Sela. Whether you like it or not, I *do* have some say-so in their lives."

"Not really," she argued. "Mrs. Barnes, I know you love them. I do know that. I love my children, too, and I won't do anything to harm them. You have to learn to trust me—trust that I know how to handle Leah. How to handle all of them."

"I'm not trying to take your place, Sela. Why do you feel so threatened by me?"

She broke into laughter. "*You've got to be kidding me.* I can't believe you said that to me."

"You're saying this isn't true? Rodney seemed to think it was. He told me so."

Stiffening, Sela asked, "When did he tell you this?"

"Rodney always talked to me about you," Ethel gloated. "He said you were threatened by me."

She couldn't believe what she was hearing. "You're lying. Rodney wouldn't say something like this."

"Mom, when are we leaving," Leon yelled from the living room. "I want to go home."

"I'm coming," she yelled in response.

She and Ethel eyed one another warily.

"These are *my* children…remember that."

"I am not going to let you cut us out of their lives."

"If you keep disrespecting me, you won't have to worry about seeing them. I'll keep them away from you."

"Don't you dare threaten me."

"It's not a threat—it's a promise." Sela turned toward the door. "Now if you will excuse me, I need to get *my* children home."

She was shaking by the time she made it to the car. Sela was ready to give up—she'd done everything to get along with Ethel. Now they were back to square one.

* * *

Derek appeared on her doorstep fifteen minutes after they arrived home.

"What's wrong?" he asked her when she opened the door. "You look like you're upset over something."

"I'd like to hang Ethel Barnes out to dry. That woman gets on my last nerve. Every time I think we're getting somewhere…"

"What's going on now?"

Sela gave him a brief recap of her conversation with Ethel.

"They're still grieving," Derek offered up as explanation. "And they have a lot of anger over Rodney's death."

"So do I," Sela responded. "And frankly, I don't give a flip how they feel about anything."

Derek surprised her by bursting into laughter.

Her anger melted and Sela began laughing with him.

"Rodney would've had a fit if he'd heard me say something like that in reference to his parents."

Derek agreed.

"I feel so inadequate when it comes to dealing with my in-laws. I really want to keep my promise to Rodney, but it's hard."

"Promise?"

She nodded. "Rodney made me promise to be there for his parents—for some unknown reason, he believed that one day they would need me. I don't have a clue why—but it's what he believed."

"Give them a chance, Sela."

"I have," she argued. "Derek, they hate me. Roman and Ethel Barnes hated me from the moment they found out I was pregnant. Then to top it off—I'm black. Ethel almost had a stroke."

"I remember."

"That's right. You were there."

"Rodney didn't want to tell them alone."

"I thought once they saw how much Rodney and I loved each other, they would eventually accept me."

"You can't grow together unless both sides are willing to participate."

Sela didn't respond.

"Did you hear me?"

"Yeah. Derek, I've tried so many times to get along with them…I really did and I just don't have it in me anymore. I really want to keep that promise, but I don't think it's possible."

"Have you given your relationship over to God?"

"Not really," Sela admitted.

"That's what you're going to have to do—give them to God. You can't do any more, so let God handle them."

"I know nothing is too big for God, but…" Sela shook her head. "But sometimes I can't help but wonder if even God can change those folks."

Chapter Thirty-Three

"Hey, Mom," Ayanna greeted as she walked into the house. "Jay and I came by to see if you wanted to see a movie with us."

Placing her hands on her hips, Sela wore a big grin. "Yeah, right. Like you two really want me tagging along. I don't think so…."

"We're really serious. You've been wanting to see this movie."

"Mrs. Barnes, we want you to come with us," Jay insisted. "We'll have a good time."

"I think it's really sweet what you're trying to do, but I'm gonna say no. I've got some work to do for the business. Payroll is tomorrow."

Sela reached out to hug her daughter. "Thanks so much

for the invitation. I appreciate it." She hugged Jay next. "Next time, okay?"

"Mom…" Ayanna began.

Shaking her head, Sela blew her a kiss. "I'll go with you another time, honey. I promise."

"Okay." Ayanna and Jay headed to the front door. She tossed a glance over her shoulder, saying, "I'll give you a call tomorrow."

Waving, Sela nodded. "Have fun tonight."

When she was alone again, Sela glanced around the silent living room. Since Rodney's death, the house just didn't feel the same.

In the kitchen she made herself a salad. This weekend, her children were spending time with her in-laws. Sela prayed they would have a good weekend. "If Leah comes home crying—that's it," she muttered. "I've had it with that woman."

The next day Rita showed up and convinced Sela to have dinner with her.

"You really didn't have to take me to dinner, Rita," she stated after they were seated by the hostess at the Mayflower Restaurant. "I could've cooked something for us at the house."

"I wanted to get you out of the house. I figured this might be a hard day for you."

Sela waved her hand in dismissal. "You don't have to worry about me. I'm okay."

"Things any better with your in-laws?"

Sela shook her head. "I don't think it'll ever be."

"I wouldn't say never. Things could change. Something could happen to change your relationship forever."

She laughed at the mere thought of getting along with Ethel and Roman Barnes. The idea was simply too far-fetched.

Sela picked up her menu and scanned the contents. "I'm in the mood for some chicken, I think."

"I want fish," Rita announced.

"Hmmm, that sounds good, too."

"The stuffed flounder is wonderful here."

Laying her menu down, Sela decided, "Maybe I'll order that. I haven't had any fish in a while."

"Outside of in-law drama, how are you really doing?"

"Rita, you don't have to keep asking me that. Honey, I'm okay. I'm managing to move forward. The kids are back in school so I'm home alone during the day. I actually enjoy the time alone. I get a lot of work done. Barnes Trucking just picked up two new contracts."

"I'm proud of you, Sela."

"It's not easy because I miss Rodney so much. I'm scared, but I know I have to be strong for my children. They're watching me—I catch them all the time."

"I remember when Chuck Boyd died. That man was the love of my life—I just knew we would get married one day. The day I found out that he'd been killed…it was the worst day of my life."

"I remember how hysterical you became. They had to nearly carry you out of the church."

"I loved Chuck and I believe he loved me, too. People think when you're that young you don't know anything about love, but I did. I knew that I loved this guy—truly, deeply loved him. Chuck was the other part of me."

"You still miss him?"

Rita nodded. "I visit his grave almost every Saturday. I go right after my workout."

"You go out there to talk to him?"

She nodded a second time. "In a way I feel close to him."

"I went to see Rodney this morning. I put some fresh flowers on his grave and…and I just talked to him. I really needed to talk to him."

"I understand totally. I'll tell you what—next time you plan on going to the cemetery, let's ride out there together. I'll visit with Chuck while you spend some time with Rodney."

"I'd like that."

Junior was in the kitchen fixing a sandwich when Sela arrived home thirty minutes later.

"Have a good time?" he asked her.

"I did," Sela confirmed. "How are your studies coming along? You haven't said anything."

"Okay. I got Professor Singletary this time. I knew it was gonna happen."

"For your Biology class?"

Junior nodded. "I'd drop it if I didn't need it."

"Son, you're a smart young man," Sela stated with a smile. "You can do it—just study, take notes and keep the lines of communication open when it comes to your professor."

Sela made herself a cup of hot tea.

She and Junior sat down at the breakfast table talking while he ate his sandwich.

"Did you have a good time?"

"Yeah. I did." Sela broke into a short laugh. "Your Aunt Rita is crazy."

Junior grinned. "I could've told you that."

When they finished talking, Sela cleaned up the kitchen before heading off to bed. Her eyes landed on the photo that graced the bedside table.

Rodney had been gone for three months today.

Earlier she and the children had taken flowers to the cemetery.

Marcus was the only one who didn't seem to enjoy the monthly visits at his father's grave, choosing instead to sit on a stone bench a few yards away.

"I miss you so much," Sela uttered as she climbed in bed. "The children and I miss you terribly. Marcus…he's taking this so hard… He's still meeting with Pastor Grant. I don't know if it's helping though. Sometimes I get a glimpse of the little boy he used to be… We all have been affected by your passing. Leah…she never wanted ice cream until you left us. She wants ice cream morning, noon and night…"

Releasing a long sigh, she arranged and plumped up her pillows. "I'm glad you're not suffering anymore, but I just hate the fact that you had to leave us for your healing."

Reaching out, Sela picked up the photo and laid it on Rodney's side of the bed. "I'm not sure I can do this alone," she whispered.

She blinked back tears and sniffed. "I'm so scared."

Chapter Thirty-Four

❧

The next day, Junior and the boys cleaned out the garage while Sela and Ayanna moved more of Rodney's things in there.

They spent most of the day cleaning out the other closets and old moving boxes that hadn't been opened in months.

Sela was in a "throwing out" mood.

After dinner, she called Derek and invited him over.

He arrived half an hour later.

Sela held the door wide open for him. "Hey, Derek. Thanks for coming by so quickly. I have those boxes in the garage."

Sela guided him through the house to the den. "How are things going with Kim?"

"Good. She's a real nice lady."

"You two have been dating for what? About six months now?"

"Yes," Derek confirmed. He eyed her as she moved an open Bible out of the way for him to take a seat.

"What were you doing?"

"I just finished cleaning up the kitchen. I was about to try and study the Bible. I'm working on my relationship with God."

"Good for you," he exclaimed. "So what are you reading?"

"I was reading different selections from the book of Psalms. It's where I can usually find my peace whenever I'm troubled."

Derek nodded in understanding. "I go there myself."

"Do you have some time to talk?"

"Sure."

Sela pressed the Bible to her heart. "Derek, I'm trying so hard. I really am. Sometimes though, I just feel like I'm not getting anywhere with my in-laws. I had to fire one of the drivers—things are just crazy right now. It makes me wonder what I did to deserve all this."

"Paul gives us a clue in how to find benefits when we experience disagreeable experiences. He wrote, 'Let us exult and triumph in our troubles and rejoice in our sufferings, knowing that pressure and affliction and hardship produce patient and unswerving endurance and fortitude develops maturity of character.' I think Paul was showing us how to get blessed fruit off of the bitter trees of life. Remember this advice is coming from a man who said, 'As sorrowful yet always rejoicing, as poor yet making many rich, in good reports and bad reports, as having nothing, yet possessing all things.'"

"So what do you think God is trying to show me?"

"It could be that God may be asking you to change your attitude or realign your thinking more with His sovereign plans for your life. The Lord is far more interested in helping us become mature in Christ than giving us what we want. One of the things I had to learn is to trust the Lord despite all the adversity."

"It's easier said than done."

"Paul teaches us how to exult and triumph even in our troubles. Our heavenly Father knows what it best. He never allows anything to come into our life that we are unable to handle. The Bible tells us to count it all joy when you encounter various trials. You have to remember that God is working all things together for your good in ways you may not understand or appreciate at the time."

"Rodney used to say that all the time. But that's what I'm talking about. To me, there was no sense in Rodney's death. He fought so hard and we all prayed… God said no. I don't get it."

"Sela, allow Him to mold you and make you after His will while you are waiting, yielded and still. Let Him have his own way with you and your family."

Derek thumbed through the Bible as he continued talking. "Paul teaches us that adversity may come into our life to expose areas of weakness, deficiency or sins of faulty attitudes. Many times the Lord slams the door in our face because we may not be willing to deal with certain deficiencies in our attitude."

Sela nodded in agreement. "I can see that."

"Do you remember the story of Jonah?"

"Yeah. He was the one running away from what God wanted him to do."

"God said 'no' to Jonah because He wanted His word

preached to the people of Nineveh. God may have said 'no' to you because He has prepared you to do something you may have been refusing to do for a while. Or we have to consider that this was Rodney's healing. Maybe God didn't say no like you think. Rodney's in no pain any longer. And he's with Jesus. We can't be sad about that."

"You're right. I'm just being selfish."

"Nobody enjoys having their shortcomings pointed out, but God uses criticism to force us to focus on areas where we fall short of the glory of God."

"I know that I do need to change my attitude. I realize that."

"Make a choice to turn the controls of your thinking, attitudes, emotions and behavior over to God. Cast all your care upon Him, Sela, because He cares for you. The only other option to growing better through life's experiences is to become bitter and resentful."

"I just wanted God to make Rodney whole again."

"We all wanted that, Sela. But think about what Pastor Grant said—our bodies are temporary, but our spirits are whole. God doesn't spare us pain because suffering draws us apart from worldly cares and brings us closer to Him.

"Sela, have you truly ever given your life to Christ?"

She considered his question for a moment before shaking her head no.

"Would you like to do it right now?"

Tears in her eyes, Sela whispered, "Yes."

Derek took her by the hand. "Pray this prayer with me— Dear Lord, I acknowledge that I am a sinner."

Sela repeated his words.

"I believe Jesus died for my sins on the cross, and rose again the third day. I repent of my sins. By faith I receive the Lord Jesus as my Savior. You promised to save me, and I believe You, because You are God and cannot lie. I believe right now that the Lord Jesus is my personal Savior, and that all my sins are forgiven through His precious blood. I thank You, dear Lord, for saving me. In Jesus's name, Amen."

Sela opened her eyes and her heart.

Derek was smiling. "God heard you, Sela and He saved you. I personally want to welcome you to the family of God."

Chapter Thirty-Five

❦

Sela and Derek stayed up late sitting in the family room talking. When she glanced up at the clock, it read 2:30 a.m.

Running fingers through her hair, she exclaimed, "I can't believe it. We've been up all night."

"I get excited talking about God and what He's done in my life. I guess I get carried away."

Getting to his feet, Derek uttered, "I'm so sorry for keeping you up."

Sela stood up, too. "I want you to know that I really appreciate your support, Derek. You've been such a wonderful friend. I don't think I could've made it this far without you and Rita. For the first time since Rodney's death, I feel like I can make it."

She covered her mouth to stifle her yawn.

"You go on up to bed. I'll see myself out and I'll check on you later this week."

She yawned again. "Thanks again, Derek." Sela walked him to the front door, saying, "I really appreciated our conversation. I needed this."

When Derek drove away, Sela walked back into the family room and stretched out on the sofa. She was too tired to even make it up the stairs.

Four and a half hours later, she woke up the boys first, then she went into Leah and Lacey's room.

"Come on sleeping beauties…."

Lacey shot up in bed. "Morning…"

"Good morning, baby. Did you sleep well?"

"Uh-huh," she responded. "I got up and went in your room and you weren't there. Where were you?"

"I fell asleep on the couch downstairs. I was up late talking to your Uncle Derek."

Standing over Leah, Sela gently shook her, trying to wake her up. "It's time to get up for school."

Leah moaned, then covered her head with the comforter.

Sela laughed. "Leah, honey. It's time to get up."

"No-oo," she whined. "Don't want to."

"Well, I guess you're going to miss my famous chocolate chip pancakes, huh?"

Leah pulled the covers away from her face and opened her eyes. "You made some pancakes?"

"I sure did."

The children drifted down the stairs one by one where Sela had breakfast waiting for them. She sat on the sofa in the family room, barely awake.

Forty-five minutes later, the kids were ready to leave.

She was a zombie by the time the children left. Sela couldn't make it to her bed quick enough—she was so tired. She couldn't blame Derek for keeping her up so late, because she was the one firing question after question at him.

Sela stole a peek out the living room window when she heard a car pull into her driveway. She wanted to cry when Rita got out of her car.

"I'm so tired," Sela moaned. All she wanted to do at the moment was crawl into her bed and get some sleep. She couldn't even summon a smile for her friend when she opened the front door.

Rita didn't seem to notice Sela's dark mood.

"Hey. I thought we could have breakfast together."

Walking farther into the house, Sela nodded. "Derek and I stayed up very late talking."

"About what?" Rita questioned as they headed to the family room. "Don't tell me he's already trying to step in Rodney's shoes. I know better than that."

Sela tossed a glance over her shoulder. "He's not like that, Rita. Derek is a really nice guy."

Rita dropped down on the sofa beside Sela. "He's all right."

Sela yawned. "I'm so s-sorry."

Rita stood up. "You're tired, so go on to bed. I'll stop by here on my way home this evening."

"Okay." She yawned a second time. "I want you to go shopping with me sometime this week."

"What are you buying?"

"I want to redecorate my bedroom."

Rita sat back down. "Sela, are you sure you're ready to do this?"

"It's something I think I need to do for me. I'm not trying to erase Rodney's memory…I just need to begin a new phase of my life. Rita, every time I walk into my bedroom, I expect to see Rodney lying in there—it's like my brain hasn't fully realized that he's no longer here."

"Honey, it takes time…."

"I know. But each time it happens, my heart breaks all over again."

Rita nodded in understanding. "I'm so sorry, Sela. I hurt for you and the children. Rodney was a very good man." She broke into a wide smile. "He sure loved you. From the moment that man laid eyes on you—he was in love."

"I was so scared of dating him. I didn't know what my parents were going to say or do—I just knew my father was gonna kill him."

"Girl, you used to have me lying for you, so you could sneak around with Rodney. My grandmother wanted to kill me when she found out."

"My parents knew I had a boyfriend, but they just didn't know it was Roman Barnes's son. My mama thought that Mrs. Barnes was gonna pull all our furniture out of the house when they found out I was pregnant. She stopped shopping at Barnes Furniture Store right then and there."

Rita burst into laughter.

"Rodney was so brave, Rita. The way he stood up to both my parents and his—I was so proud of him. He's never left my side until now…."

"I wish things had turned out differently."

Sela gave her a sad smile. "So do I."

Rita checked her watch. "I need to get going. I'll come by later on and we'll make definite plans for shopping." She rose to her feet.

Sela stood up and walked Rita to the door. "I'm going straight to bed," she stated with quiet emphasis. "I don't think I'll even answer the phone for a couple of hours."

"Why don't you just turn off your phone?"

Sela shook her head. "It might be the school."

"They'll call me if you don't answer. I'll come by here if there's an emergency. Turn off your phone and get some real sleep, Sela."

She embraced Rita. "Maybe I will…. Thanks."

Ten minutes later, Sela was in bed fast asleep.

Ethel and Roman had the children for the weekend. They were going to Virginia. Initially, Sela didn't want them to go, but Lacey and Leon had practically begged to go with their grandparents.

Roman had gone behind her back and told the children of his plans to take them to the Kings Dominion Amusement Park near Richmond, Virginia. Sela was furious at first, but when she saw just how badly her children wanted to go— she relented. But not without telling Roman what she thought of his tactics.

He'd then turned the tables on her by saying Rodney had made him and Ethel promise to take the children to the amusement park. Something he and Sela had done for the past ten years.

So she was alone.

Ayanna had gone to Atlanta with Jay to meet his family. Junior was hanging out with some friends around town, but had already called to check on her twice.

She decided to spend her time reading Rodney's journal and reflecting back to much happier times. Sela loved day-dreaming because it allowed her to spend time with her husband.

Curled up in Rodney's favorite oversized leather chair, Sela ran her fingers lovingly over the black leather journal. She opened it and began to read his final entries.

July 13

"I wake up at 6 in the morning and just stare out my window sometimes. When I'm looking out there, I'm not just looking at the blue sky or the clouds, which I've seen more than my share of lately. What I see is just that: I'm able to wake up and look out my window.

There are those days that I am filled with a lot of pain, but then there are those days when I'm simply grateful to feel anything at all.

When it's all said and done, I am a lucky man to have married a beautiful and loving wife. To have 6 beautiful children. To have two of the most devoted parents in the world. To be a child of God. Yes, I am a lucky man."

"I'm the lucky one," Sela whispered. "There will never be another man like you." Her eyes watered.

She wiped at them and turned to the next page.

July 16

"Today is not a good day. It's raining outside and matches my mood. I just had to pretend to enjoy fake, saltless eggs practically covered under a layer of pepper and watery grits that tasted horribly.

My head hurts, my teeth hurt and my sinuses are driving me up the wall; I hurt so much that the nurse gave me Tylenol #3. Here comes Dr. Cookson. I hope he has good news for me."

Down at the bottom of the page Rodney had written:

"No good news. Just more tests. Leland just came by to tell me to keep a stiff upper lip. Sometimes I wish I were more like him. Despite his bad days, Leland always has a positive attitude.

Everything itches like crazy! The tapes they use to dress cuts and wounds also make me itch so I have been demoted to the use of paper tape."

Sela turned the page to read Rodney's last entry.

"Today is my son's birthday. I am so blessed to have been able to share this day with my family. This day is almost like my birthday, too. We just found out that I'm getting a new heart. I'm scared and excited. I pray that God will send his angels to guide the hands of the medical team that will perform the transplantation.

There are no words to express the emotions my family and I are experiencing. The children are at the windows in my room hoping to get a peek at the helicopter bringing my new heart. A gift from heaven. I am saddened that this gift is mine at the expense of another life, but I am so grateful to this unnamed person's family.

I'd never been a real fan of organ donation, but after being on this side of things, I know that if I had the chance to do it all over again, I would be a donor.

Before I go, I want to add this one thing. Sela, if you are reading this, then I must be gone—I didn't survive the transplantation. Please know that I love you always. My life was never wasted, nor filled with regret. I have been blessed to have all I could ever want in life. Do not mourn me, Sela, as I am now with my Heavenly Father.

Rejoice in the knowledge that in being saved by the blood of Jesus—I shall now have eternal life.

Raise our children as you have done throughout our marriage. Be happy and live. Live out the rest of your life without bitterness. Seek the Lord in all things. I love you and I know that I can go peacefully because I leave you in good hands—Jesus's. I entrust my family to Him."

At the bottom of the page, he wrote, "*Well, I got the call. It's time.*"

Sela wiped her eyes and closed the journal. "I don't know that I could have been as brave as you, Rodney."

Another tear fell.

"I want that kind of faith in You, Lord," she whispered. "I want to believe without a doubt that I can find my peace in You for all things. My beloved Rodney had it and I want it, too."

"We're home, Mommy," Lacey screamed as soon as she entered the house on Sunday night.

Sela had been working upstairs in her office. She rushed down the stairs to greet her children when she heard their voices.

Leah rushed to her, arms opened wide. The impact of their connecting caused Sela to sway. Hugging her tightly, she uttered, "I missed y'all."

"We missed you, too," Leah gushed. "I wanted to come home last night, but Grandmother said we should just stay with her."

Sela held her temper in check. "I guess she wanted to spend more time with y'all." Over Leah's head, she eyed Ethel.

Marcus and Leon gathered their luggage and took it upstairs.

"I want some water," Lacey decided.

"Grab a bottle out of the fridge," Sela stated. "Leah, hon. Go with your sister."

"It's not my business, but I really don't think it's wise to have men staying over at the house," Ethel stated as soon as the children were out of earshot. "I didn't think you were ready to start dating again. Rodney's barely been gone a good four months yet."

Sela gave her a confused look. "Mrs. Barnes, what in the world are you talking about?"

"I know Derek spent the night here."

"He did no such thing," Sela snapped in anger. "Anyway, what were you doing?" She folded her arms across her chest. "Spying on me?"

Ethel pushed away an errant curl with the palm of her hand. "I have better things to do with my time than to keep an eye on you, Sela. The girls told us."

Sela made a mental note to speak to Leah and Lacey about volunteering information when Ethel left.

"I'm sure you didn't count on my finding out."

"I wasn't trying to hide anything, Mrs. Barnes. Derek and I are friends—he was Rodney's best friend. Not that it's any of your business, but we stayed up late talking. Derek didn't spend the night."

"Humph."

"It's the truth," Sela insisted.

"Humph. Whatever's happening under this roof is between you and God." Ethel licked her lips nervously. "Eh…Roman and I had a discussion recently. We think it's better if the children came to live with us." She added quickly, "At least for a little while. It would give you time—"

Sela interrupted her. "*No.* No way. I am not going to give you my children."

Ethel retreated back a step. "There's no need to be so rude about it, Sela."

"I am more than capable of raising my own children. Despite what you may think, I've done a pretty good job."

"Humph…" Ethel muttered in response.

"It's best that you leave my house now before I do something I regret," Sela warned.

"Those children are my flesh and blood. I'm not going to just let you wipe me and Roman out of their lives. I know that's what you're trying to do. Rodney never had a problem with my getting on them if they needed it." Ethel gestured toward her. "But you—you challenge me on every turn."

Sela's voice rose an octave. "This is crazy. You are the one running your mouth and accusing me of inappropriate behavior. With Derek no less. Derek and Rodney were best friends. He is my friend. *Nothing more.*"

"I only know what your children saw," Ethel countered.

Pointing to the door, Sela screamed, "Get out of my house! Now!"

Lacey and Leah ran into the room with Marcus on their heels.

"Mom?"

Her eyes traveled to Marcus. "Take your sisters to the family room, hon."

"You okay?"

"I'll be fine," Sela uttered, her eyes never leaving Ethel's face.

"Are you and Grandmother mad with each other?" Lacey asked.

Ethel pasted on a smile. "Your mommy and I are just having a discussion, dear." She made a move toward the front door. "I'm on my way out anyway."

Marcus and Lacey embraced her before leaving the room.

Leah moved until she was standing with Sela.

"You're not going to give me a hug?" Ethel inquired.

Leah didn't respond.

"She's tired," Sela offered.

"We'll finish our discussion later."

Sela shook her head. "We're done, Mrs. Barnes. I've said all I have to say on the subject."

When Marcus called out for Leah, the little girl looked up at her mother. Sela gave her a reassuring smile and said, "Go on, honey. There's nothing to worry about."

Leah observed them for a moment before leaving.

Ethel glared at Sela when they were alone again. "If you try to keep us from seeing the children—we will sue you for custody." She threatened in a low voice.

"Keep your nose out of my business and we won't have a problem, Mrs. Barnes. I mean it. You have no say-so over how I raise my children or what I do. Understand?"

Sela opened the door and held it open. "Goodbye."

As soon as Ethel left, Sela called Ayanna to see if she could drop the children off for a few hours. She needed to see Rita.

Chapter Thirty-Six

❧

"I'm so glad you're home," Sela uttered when Rita opened her door. "I really need to talk to you."

She walked into the living room and sat down.

"What's wrong?"

"You're not gonna believe this—Ethel and Roman Barnes just threatened to sue me for custody of my children." Sela muttered a string of curses under her breath.

"Honey, calm down. Let me make you some tea."

Rita strode in the kitchen with Sela following her.

"You do know they're just saying that to get under your skin. They can't be stupid enough to believe that they can take your children."

Turning her mouth downward, Sela muttered, "I don't know what to believe. Rodney's gone and now they want to take the children. They believe I took their son from them so now they are planning to get revenge."

"I think you're overreacting, Sela." Rita poured hot water into a cup and pushed it toward her. She handed her a tea bag.

"You don't know them like I do. Rita, they want my children." She chewed on her bottom lip. "I should've seen this coming on."

"Well, they are not gonna get them. Honey, you have absolutely nothing to worry about."

Sela took a sip of her tea. "I don't trust them."

"They were just trying to upset you, Sela." Rita leaned forward against the kitchen counter. "It's an empty threat."

"You really think so?"

Rita nodded.

Sela inhaled and exhaled slowly. "I hope you're right. I've already lost Rodney—I can't bear losing my children, too." She pulled on her sleeves.

Rita stilled her hand. "You don't have to worry about it. There is no way in the world a court of law would agree to a custody change. Okay?"

She nodded.

"I mean it, Sela. Your in-laws don't have a leg to stand on. They are just running off at the mouth."

Some of the tension began to slip away as Sela sipped her chamomile tea. After a moment, she said, "You're probably right. I don't know why I was so worried. I'm a good mother to my children."

"I want to play outside," Lacey complained.

"I said no," Sela stated. "You need to finish cleaning your room and then you need to do some reading."

Lacey folded her arms across her chest and pouted. "You're mean. Just like Grandmother says."

Sela whipped around. "What did you just say?"

"N-nothing."

"Don't lie to me, Lacey Denise Barnes. Now repeat what you just said."

Averting her eyes, the little girl whispered, "I said that you're mean just like Grandmother says."

"When did she say this?"

"She always says it."

Sela sat down on the chair in her bedroom. "What else does your grandmother say about me?"

"Mommy…"

"Tell me, Lacey."

"She says that you don't want us to spend time with them now that Daddy's gone to heaven. She says that you don't think about how we feel."

Sudden anger lit Sela's eyes. She got up and walked over to one of the windows. Staring out, she said, "Lacey, I don't want you listening to things like this. Your grandparents…" She walked over to where her daughter stood. "Let's have a seat in the family room. I think we should talk."

"I don't wanna make Grandmother in trouble, Mommy."

She's done that herself, Sela decided. "Honey, you're not getting anybody in trouble." She sat down and gestured for Lacey to sit on her lap. "There's something you should know."

"What is it?"

"Your grandparents and I have…we have some problems and we are trying to find a way to work them out." Sela searched for the best way to explain her relationship with Ethel and Roman Barnes.

"I don't think they like you, Mommy."

She played with her daughter's ponytail. "It doesn't matter whether they like me or not. You—your brothers and sisters—are their flesh and blood. Your grandparents love you very very much."

"I want them to love you, too."

"Honey, I don't want you worrying about this. I will work this out with your grandparents. We all want what's best for you and I need you to understand this. Okay?"

"Mommy, are you happy?"

"I guess. Why?"

"I would feel bad if someone didn't love me. I would be sad."

"I have all the love I need from you and your brothers and sisters. You don't have to worry about your grandparents and me, precious. We're going to work this thing out."

Sela kissed the top of her daughter's head. "I love you so much."

"I love you, too, Mommy. That's why I feel so sad. I'm gonna tell Grandmother that she has to love you, too."

Sela broke into a short laugh. "Ooh, sweetie…you don't have to tell her that."

"I am gonna tell her, Mommy. I don't want us to be mad with each other. Daddy wouldn't want it, either."

She knew Lacey spoke the truth. Guilt seeped from her pores. "I'll make a promise to you, little miss. I'll do the very best I can to make sure I don't fight with your grandparents any more. I promise."

Lacey beamed. "That would make me so-oo happy, Mommy."

"Okay then."

"I'd be happier if I could go outside."

"Not until you clean your room and do some reading," Sela shot back with a laugh.

Her turbulent relationship with Roman and Ethel was getting out of control. Sela replayed Lacey's words over and over in her mind. It was Rodney's most fervent desire to have his parents and Sela get along.

Hadn't she tried? What else could she do?

Sela didn't want to share in any blame for the rift with her in-laws. She preferred to believe that it was Ethel and Roman who kept widening the gap between them.

Despite who was at fault, she couldn't allow this feud to continue. Sela had made a promise to Rodney and to her children.

It was up to her to keep her vow.

Ethel called Sela later that day to say, "Roman and I want the children to spend next weekend with us. We're flying down to Florida and bought tickets for them, too. We plan to take them to Disney World."

Sela didn't bother to hide the anger from her tone. "I certainly hope those tickets are refundable."

"Excuse me?"

"I'm sorry, but they won't be able to go. I thought I'd made myself clear. You should have consulted me before you went off buying plane tickets."

"Why can't they go with us? Do you have plans for them?"

Sela tapped her fingers on the granite countertop while she talked. "Mrs. Barnes, I don't intend to let you or your husband near my children if you can't respect me. I don't go around badmouthing the two of you to the kids. I don't appreciate you talking about me in front of them. It makes them very uncomfortable."

She heard Ethel's deep sigh on the other end.

"What was it that I supposedly said?"

"I'm not gonna go into all that," Sela uttered. "I'm sure you know exactly what you said. I know we have issues with one another, but I don't broadcast it to the kids."

"I don't appreciate your tone, Sela."

"I'm afraid this is the best I can do. Mrs. Barnes, I mean it—you can't see my children until you can find a way to treat me better. I'm not taking any more disrespect from you or your husband."

"Why do you always have to make this about you?"

"I'm not gonna argue with you," Sela sniped. "I've said what I have to say. Until things change, you are not to see or talk to my children. *Understand?*"

"I—"

Sela didn't let her finish. "I've got to be somewhere in an hour. Goodbye, Mrs. Barnes."

She hung up without waiting for a response.

An hour later she met Rita for lunch.

"Maybe I was too harsh," Sela wondered aloud after giving Rita a brief summary of what happened between her and Ethel.

"I don't think so. You told her exactly how you felt." Rita picked up a menu and began to scan it.

Sela did the same. "I didn't know what to say when Lacey told me that her grandmother didn't like me. She said it made her very sad."

"Ethel should never put those children in the middle like that. How could she?"

The waiter arrived to take their orders.

When he left, Sela responded, "She's such a witch."

"She really needs to get over herself, if you ask me. How long does Ethel expect to carry on this feud? This is getting ridiculous."

Sela agreed. "Now with Rodney gone, I kind of thought they'd go back to ignoring me, but it's not like that. They are now trying to turn my children against me."

She reached for her water glass and took a sip. "I'm not gonna let that happen. I'll fight them tooth and nail."

"I got your back, girlfriend."

Sela burst into laughter. "I may have to take you up on it, Rita. I don't trust Ethel or Roman Barnes. They may actually try to fight me for custody."

Their food arrived.

While they ate, their conversation turned to a more pleasant topic.

Chapter Thirty-Seven

❦

Sela stared down at the legal documents in her hand.

Muttering a string of curses, she rushed over to the telephone and dialed her in-laws' number.

"You have lost your mind," she shouted when Roman answered the phone. Sela wasn't able to control her temper. "You are not getting my children."

"We have nothing to say to you," he uttered nastily. "Talk to our attorney."

"I don't—"

Roman hung up without preamble.

Stunned, Sela stared at the phone.

"Mom?"

Startled, she turned around to face Ayanna. "Hey…"

"You okay?"

Sela nodded. She was filled with so much rage, she

couldn't speak. She stood there clenching and unclenching her fists.

Ayanna surveyed her mother's face. "You don't look okay. What happened?"

Without saying a word, Sela handed the documents to her daughter.

"I can't believe this," Ayanna uttered. "Why are they doing this?"

Shrugging, Sela admitted, "I don't really know. Maybe this was their plan all along."

Fury flashed across Ayanna's face. "I'm gonna call them. I'm not gonna let them break up our family."

Sela placed a gentle hand on her daughter's arm. "Don't. I can handle your grandmother. I don't want you children getting caught up in the middle."

Ayanna's eyes glittered with unshed tears. "This is wrong, Mom. It's so wrong."

"Honey, I'll take care of your grandparents. I'm gonna go see Derek. Do you mind watching the kids for me?"

"I don't mind. Go ahead."

"Now promise me you'll let me take care of this situation. I don't want you saying anything to your grandparents."

"I promise."

Sela kissed her on the cheek. "I'll be back shortly."

Twenty minutes later, she walked into Derek's office.

"You bring the papers with you?" he asked her.

She nodded and held them out to him. "Here they are."

Her eyes bounced around the office, taking in the floor-to-ceiling windows and cherry-stained bookshelves. There were law books stacked on the couch and on the coffee table. Derek worked out of a home office that had been converted from the two-car garage.

Sela took a seat while Derek read the legal document.

"I never thought they would do something like this," he uttered as he pushed his glasses up his nose. "What prompted them to do this?"

"I guess I did," Sela responded, then explained, "Derek, a couple of weeks ago, Mrs. Barnes and I got into it over some things she's been saying to the children about me. After that I wouldn't let the kids go over to their house."

"Sela…"

She held up her hand. "Derek, hear me out. It makes my children uncomfortable to hear me trashed by them. They shouldn't have to go through this."

"You're right," he agreed.

"Can they do this, Derek?"

"Unfortunately, yes." He added after a brief pause, "It doesn't mean they have a leg to stand on."

Sela leaned forward in her chair. "Tell me what I need to do."

"Hey, you," Sela muttered as she sat down in front of Rodney's grave. "I need to talk to you."

She rearranged the dying flowers. "I'll bring you some fresh flowers on Saturday, babe. The reason I came out here is because I want you to know what your parents are doing. First, let me say that I've tried, Rodney. I really have."

She sat there staring at his name engraved in the marble. "Okay, so I haven't tried all that hard. But you know it's because your high-and-mighty mama gets on my nerves."

Sela rubbed her arms, trying to ward off the November chill. "Your parents are suing me for custody of the children. Derek says they don't have a leg to stand on, but I hate being put in this position in the first place. Your parents have a lot of money, Rodney. I don't know what they'll do."

After she vented, Sela felt a little better. She still worried that Ethel and Roman could actually end up with the children.

"I can't let that happen. I'm going to see them."

In the car, Sela called Ayanna. "Honey, I'm going to try and talk to your grandparents one more time. I'll be home right after that."

"Take your time, Mom."

"Say a prayer for me."

"I will."

Half an hour later, Sela pulled up in her in-laws' driveway.

"I told you to contact our attorney," Roman blurted out.

"I know what you said. I came to talk to you and Mrs. Barnes. I can't believe you really want to put my children through this."

"We're looking out for our grandchildren."

Roman was about to close the door, but Sela planted her foot in the way.

"How can you do this and say you love them?" she questioned. "Tell me that."

He didn't respond.

"You know what? I don't think you love them at all. You're just trying to take my children because I took Rodney from you," Sela accused. "Rodney married me because he loved me—you and your wife need to get over it."

"You and Rodney should have never gotten married in the first place," Roman sneered. "You never took anything from us—he was still our son."

"Your son chose me as his wife," Sela shot back. "You and *your* wife, on the other hand, are nothing but a couple of racists."

Roman turned beet-red. "I…I'm…" he sputtered. "We are not racists. The Bible clearly states that you and Rodney shouldn't have gotten together."

"Oh, yeah? Where in the Bible did it say that?"

"Second Corinthians 6:14 says, 'Be ye not unequally yoked together with unbelievers…for what fellowship hath right-eousness with unrighteousness.' Interracial relationships are wrong, Sela. They go against the will of God." Roman paused a moment before continuing, "I have nothing against blacks personally. I just believe that everyone should marry within their own race."

"I may not have been in the Word very long," Sela countered, "but I do know that this particular scripture you quoted merely discourages the union of believers with non-believers—not one race with another."

"What is *she* doing here?"

Sela looked past Roman, her gaze meeting the hostile glare of Ethel.

"I was just discussing the Bible with your husband," she stated.

"Oh, really?" Ethel countered. "What would you know about it?"

"I know enough to tell you this. If you oppose interra-cial relationships, then do it because it's your personal preference. But don't go around trying to insert God and His word between the lines to justify your reasons." Sela sighed in resignation. "All Rodney ever really wanted was for us to get along. He wanted us to be a family." She broke into a bitter laugh. "Before he died, Rodney actually made me promise to try and heal the rift between us. Well, I've tried— this is it."

She held up her hand to silence the objection she knew would be coming. "You've already made it clear that I'm not a member of this family. That's fine because I wouldn't want to be associated with a couple of bigots." Sela paused.

Shaking her head in sadness, Sela stated, "My children love you and you both say you love them. Well if you do, please start acting like it. If you continue with this foolishness, they are the ones who will be hurt. All I ask is that you think about what I've said."

With those parting words, she turned and left.

Chapter Thirty-Eight

❧

Sela eased into a seat near the back of the church. She'd made an impromptu decision to attend Bible study.

"Tonight we're going to start our family relationship series," Pastor Grant announced. "The topic is 'dealing kindly with an erring one.' Our scripture comes from the twenty-third chapter of Luke, the twenty-seventh to the thirty-eighth verses."

I really need to hear this, Sela decided. She hoped the pastor's words would help her in dealing with Ethel and Roman.

"Do you have a forgiving spirit?" Pastor Grant asked the audience. "One becomes a Christian only by experiencing the forgiveness of God through what Jesus Christ did on the cross in atonement and perfected in His resurrection from the grave…."

Sela followed along in her Bible as Pastor Grant talked. When the study ended, Sela made her way to the front of the church. She waited on the sidelines for the minister to finish up his conversation with another member.

"This was so timely," she told Pastor Grant when her turn came to speak with him. "I really needed to hear this today. It was really relevant to what I'm going through right now."

"Has something happened?"

"Just that my in-laws hate me," Sela murmured. "Pastor, Rodney's parents are trying to take my children from me."

They sat in the back of the church talking.

"You have to forgive your in-laws by releasing them from any obligation to make things right."

"But Pastor—" Sela began.

"You have to forgive as Christ forgave, Sister Barnes."

After a moment, Sela nodded. "I know you're right, Pastor. I'm just so angry with them for the way they've treated me over the years."

They talked for another ten minutes.

Sela stood up. "Thanks so much for taking time out to speak to me, Pastor."

"It's always a pleasure, Sister."

Pastor Grant escorted Sela out to her car.

"Thanks again. I'll see you Sunday."

That evening, Sela fell to her knees to pray. "Heavenly Father, I come before You to say thank You for all the blessings You've bestowed upon me. I thank You for helping me push ahead after losing Rodney. We are still struggling to come to grips with his death but…Lord, we're trying. Lord, I ask that You come into my heart and help me forgive the wrongs against me by the hands and mouths of Roman and Ethel

Barnes. Pastor Grant spoke earlier about forgiving as Christ
did. I want to forgive them the same way Christ forgave. But
I'm gonna need your help, dear Lord. I can't do it without
You. In Jesus's name. Amen."

A whisper of peace settled in her heart as Sela rose to her
feet. She knew that God would work everything out.

Sela was stunned to see Ethel and Roman standing on her
porch two days later.

Keeping her voice down, she said, "I don't want to make
a scene in front of the children, so I'm asking you to leave
quietly please."

"Mom, I asked them to come over," Junior announced
from behind her. "I think it's time we all sat down and had
a little talk."

Ayanna suddenly appeared beside her brother. "I agree totally. This has gotten completely out of hand."

Sela moved out of the way to let Ethel and Roman into
the house.

She led the way to the family room.

The girls were upstairs in their room playing with dolls
while Leon was watching cartoons in the basement. Marcus
had been in his room playing with a new PlayStation game.
"We should be able to talk in here without interruption."

She waited until her in-laws were seated before dropping
down onto the oversized stuffed chair. Sela eyed her oldest
son, wondering why he would invite his hateful grandparents into their home after all they'd done to her. In a sense
she felt betrayed.

"Dad would be so upset with all of you," Junior began.

"My grandparents suing my mother for custody. How could you do this to his memory?"

Ayanna chimed in. *"How could you do this to us?* Grandmother, we all know how you feel about Mom. You and Grandfather have never hidden your hatred from us. To be honest, it upsets me—*always has.* To a child, if you speak badly about either of his or her parents, you are speaking badly about him or her. That's how we all feel. This is our mother and we love her." Ayanna paused a heartbeat before continuing. "Y'all are always talking about how smart I am or how good I'm doing in school. Y'all say that about all of us."

Junior nodded in agreement.

"Well, where do you think it came from?" she asked. "Dad was a good father to us, but he was gone a lot. We know he had to make a living and build up his trucking business, so we didn't mind, but it was Mom who was here at home with us. She helped us with our homework. It was Mom who really disciplined us."

"If you think we're so wonderful, then it's because of not only Dad—Mom, too," Junior contributed. "Pastor Grant once talked about the responsibility of grandparents. He said one thing grandparents shouldn't do is dishonor the parents of their grandkids. A house divided can't stand. This is not the legacy my dad wanted for us."

The words of her children brought a tiny smile to Sela's face. *Yeah,* she cheered them on in silence. *Tell 'em.*

"Mom," Ayanna began. "You have to take responsibility for some of this tension, too."

Her smile disappeared. "Excuse me?"

"You were always trying to make Dad choose between you and his own mother. Just like y'all are trying to do with us."

"Yanna's right," Junior agreed. "You and Grandmother know how to press each other's buttons and you do it well. But it's time to grow up. We lost our father. We need all of you to help us get through this." He shook his head sadly. "Dad's not even been gone that long."

"Grandmother," Ayanna murmured. "And you, too, Grandfather. Please do not discuss my mother in a negative way around me or my brothers and sisters. We deserve so much better than that. You both want us to respect you—well we are asking the same of you. Please respect the fact that this is our mother for better or worse. She was your son's wife for better or worse. No matter how y'all feel about her—we love her. *Dad loved her.* Nothing will ever change that."

"And this lawsuit… That needs to end, Grandfather. Yanna and I will not let you split our family up. My mom is not a bad mother and she hasn't done anything wrong. All she wants is respect. Don't criticize her or try to belittle how she raises my brothers and sisters. She didn't do so bad with me and Yanna, did she?"

Ethel spoke up. "We were only looking out for you children…."

"What it looks like to us is that you're trying to punish my mom for marrying your son," Ayanna countered. "Grandmother, I don't mean to be disrespectful, but you really need to get over it. They were married for twenty years, and if Daddy were still alive—they would still be married. Suing Mom for custody is wrong and y'all know it."

A tear ran down Ethel's face as she nodded. "I'm so sorry."

"We didn't think about how this might have affected all of you…" Roman gave a heavy sigh. "We were so angry when your mother said we couldn't see you. I guess we wanted to fight back in some way."

Junior turned his gaze to Sela. "Mom, we don't want you badmouthing our grandparents, either. Like calling them racist. Leah asked me a while back what the word meant."

Heat crept up to her cheeks as a wave of shame flowed through her body.

"If they really were racists, do you think they would have anything to do with us?" Junior inquired. "Why don't y'all talk about what's really going on?"

"The only thing that Junior and I really want to say is that we love y'all. And we want to be a family. A *real* family. We don't want to have to go to court or put our siblings though that drama."

Junior spoke up. "Pastor Grant once said that the greatest thing we have to give is our lives. We need to be people who are safe to come home to—no matter what our children or grandchildren have done. Each of us will leave a legacy and the life we choose to live will have an impact on those who come behind us that is far greater than what we can imagine."

"We need to show the future generations how to live and lead a Godly life, show them how to love and show them how to forgive," Ayanna stated.

"We'll drop the custody suit," Roman announced.

Ayanna and Junior glanced over at Sela, who nodded.

"We know y'all may never be friends, but I hope and pray that we can at least put forth more effort to get along. This is something Daddy wanted really bad. This was his biggest wish. He told me this before he had surgery—when he was waiting for his new heart."

"He said the same thing to me," Sela confessed. "He made me promise to try."

"We made the same promise," Ethel announced. "You're right, children. Rodney would be so ashamed of us."

Sela put her hands to her face, wiping at her eyes. "Mr. and Mrs. Barnes, I owe you an apology. I'm sorry for my actions and very ashamed for my part in all this. I've had so much anger and resentment towards y'all…"

"Why?"

She couldn't believe Ethel had the nerve to ask that question. "Think about the way you and Mr. Barnes have treated me. All these years, you've hardly ever acknowledged me. You come to my house unannounced. You decided when my children need haircuts or you give them parties without asking or inviting me."

"Sela, we never meant any harm," Roman stated. "We were just trying to help you. We love these children just as much as you do and we treat them as our own. I'm sorry we stepped on your toes. It was never our intention."

"I hear what you're saying, but I have to admit that I'm not convinced of your sincerity."

Red-faced, Roman sat up in his seat. "I beg your pardon.…"

Sela held up her hand. "Let me finish, please. I say that because of the dismissive attitude you and your wife have where I'm concerned. Practically every time you say something about me it's negative. *Am I wrong?*"

"I believe we can say the same about you, Sela," Roman shot back.

She thought about it for a moment. "You're right, Mr. Barnes."

Junior cut in. "So what are y'all gonna do about it? Things have to change."

"Sela, I won't come over unannounced anymore. We'll call first."

"I'd appreciate that." The first step was taken.

Sela and her in-laws spent the rest of the evening discussing ground rules and working toward having a better relationship—a real relationship.

Chapter Thirty-Nine

❧

"Honey, you would've been so proud of your children. Ayanna really got your parents to listen to reason. She and Junior stuck to their guns. I'm just so glad that they've dropped their suit for custody."

Sela pulled at the weeds around his grave. "I wish you were still here with us. I miss you so much, Rodney." She paused a moment before saying, "There are days when I'm so mad at you for leaving. I know you didn't have much choice in the matter, but I hate it. I hate that death has to be so much a part of our lives. It's selfish, I know, but I want you back. I want you home with us."

She heard footsteps behind her and turned around. "Mrs. Barnes…"

"I…I didn't know you were here."

"I wanted to bring some fresh flowers and clean around

the grave." Sela eyed the flowers Ethel carried. "The flowers are beautiful."

"I thought Rodney might like them."

"I'm sure he will." Sela gathered her belongings together. "I know you must want some time alone with Rodney, so I'm gonna leave. We've had some time to talk."

Ethel nodded and murmured, "Thank you."

"You're welcome." Sela turned to leave, but Ethel's voice stopped her.

Gesturing around with her hand, she said, "You know this is just for us—the living. Rodney left this place on July twentieth. Funerals are for the ones left behind. This is for the ones left, too. We come out here for ourselves."

Sela faced her mother-in-law. "I know. It gives us a chance to find some closure, I guess."

"Does it help you?"

"Some," Sela admitted. "But not much. How about you?" She walked back over to the grave and sat down. Her eyes traveled to a headstone not far from Rodney's. "I've never noticed that before."

She pointed. "Have you seen this before?"

Ethel followed her gaze.

In the shade of a live oak tree, a tombstone of a woman bore her name, the years of her life and only one word.

"Waiting…" Sela read aloud. "What do you think she's waiting on?"

"Sunday," Ethel answered. "For the day when God will raise the dead."

"Oh."

Her mother-in-law changed the subject by saying, "I can

still remember giving birth to Rodney. I didn't know if I'd ever be able to have a child. I had three miscarriages."

"I never knew that. I'm sorry."

"I envied that about you, Sela. I wanted a house full of kids. I wanted Rodney to have a little sister and a little brother."

"He wanted siblings."

Ethel gave a wry smile. "Rodney would get so angry when his friends had baby brothers and sisters. There was this time when he tried to buy his friend Ricky's little sister for two dollars."

Sela threw back her head and laughed. She'd never heard this story before.

Ethel burst into laughter, too.

They sat there talking and laughing as they arranged the flowers around Rodney's grave.

When they finished, Sela and Ethel walked back to their cars.

"You…you do a good job keeping the grave clean and neat. Thank you."

"You're welcome," Sela murmured.

Humming, she climbed into her car and drove away.

Today, she and her mother-in-law had reached a milestone.

Three days later, they reached another milestone.

The kids invited Roman and Ethel Barnes for dinner. Sela wasn't sure they were going to accept, but they did. She and Ethel had had a pleasant afternoon by Rodney's grave, but that didn't mean her mother-in-law was ready to accept her with open arms.

"Wow, the food smells delicious," Sela complimented when she came downstairs. "And the table looks beautiful."

"I helped do the table," Lacey announced. "Leah folded the napkins. I didn't do that because they kinda got on my nerves."

Grinning, Sela murmured, "Really? They got on your nerves."

"Yeah."

Ayanna burst into a short laugh.

Sela glanced around the kitchen. "What do you want me to do?"

"You don't have to do anything, Mom," she responded. "Just relax. Everything is gonna go okay. You'll see."

Sela played with the sleeves of her shirt. Her eyes strayed to the clock. Roman and Ethel would be arriving any minute.

Leah walked over and climbed in her lap. "I'm glad we like Grandmother and Grandfather again. I really missed them."

Sela planted a kiss on her daughter's chubby cheek. "They missed you, too."

"Let's not be mean anymore. Okay?"

A wave of shame crept up her back. "Okay, sweetie. We're all gonna do our best to get along."

"You promise?"

"I promise," Sela replied.

The doorbell rang.

Leah clapped her hands in glee. "They're here….

"We're gonna have a good time tonight, Mommy."

Sela summoned up a smile. "Lord, please don't let this night be ruined. They've worked so hard on this dinner…."

Fortunately, it was a success.

* * *

"I think last night went well," Sela stated as she and Rita strolled through the Triangle Town Center Mall. "Roman and Ethel Barnes were very cordial. We weren't surrounded by a lot of tension like before."

"That's wonderful."

Sela shrugged in nonchalance. "They even played a round of bingo with the twins."

Rita gasped in surprise. "You're kidding."

"I'm serious. They looked like they were having a good time, too."

Shaking her head in disbelief, Rita stated, "Wow. I can't believe it. Your in-laws are always so stiff. Especially that Roman Barnes."

"We're all trying to make this work. It's not about us—it's the children." Sela stopped at a sale rack in Dillards department store. "Ooh, I love this dress."

Rita fingered the silk wrap dress. "It's nice. You should buy it."

"I don't know…." Sela pulled the garment off the rack and held it against her body. "You really think it'll look good on me?"

Nodding, Rita responded, "That's the dress for you. Red looks great on you, Sela."

Grinning, Sela walked over to a nearby full-length mirror. "I'm gonna get it. I'll wear it for Thanksgiving."

"Are your parents still coming up?"

Sela shook her head. "We're actually gonna spend the holidays with my sister. Shelly invited all of us to her house."

"That's nice," Rita said. "You'll have a great time."

Rita selected an emerald-green sweater and handed it to Sela. "Hold this for me, please."

They made a few more selections before making their way up to the cash register.

On the way out, Sela passed a man who reminded her of Rodney. She stopped in her tracks.

"What's wrong?"

"Nothing," she murmured. "That man over there reminded me of Rodney. That's all."

Rita followed her gaze. "He does look a lot like him."

"The holidays are the hardest for me," Sela confessed. "I do okay for the most part until then."

"That's why I think it's a good idea that you're going out of town. You and the kids shouldn't be alone for Thanksgiving."

Sela couldn't agree more. With Thanksgiving and Christmas coming, she was worried about her children. Those holidays were special days for them. *I miss you, Rodney.*

Chapter Forty

❧

Sela woke up early Thanksgiving morning. She showered and dressed quickly before joining her mother downstairs in the kitchen.

"Morning, Mama," she greeted.

"I thought you'd sleep in. Y'all didn't get in until late last night."

"We'd planned to leave earlier, but Ayanna had to work later than she first thought." Sela poured herself a cup of coffee. "I'm glad we came."

"Me, too. I couldn't stand the thought of you and the children being alone for the first Thanksgiving since Rodney passed." Althea glanced over at her daughter. "How you doing, baby?"

"Usually on Thanksgiving, Rodney would have each of us say what we're thankful for—this year…" Sela paused for a moment before adding, "I'm not sure what I'm thankful for or even if I'm thankful at all."

Sela took a long sip of coffee. "There are days when I feel like I understand all this—you know, life in general. I know that death is a phase we all must go through… I miss Rodney so much, Mama. Some days I'm real angry about it all. Other days, I know that he is with the Lord and while that makes me feel good—I can't truthfully say that I'm happy about it. I'm not happy that Rodney is dead and I don't think I'll ever be okay with it."

"I know what you mean, baby."

"I'm being selfish, I know. But Mama, it's not just for me. I look at my children…my babies…it nearly breaks my heart to see the pain they're going through. We all miss Rodney so much. Leah is just really getting her appetite back. You know she wouldn't eat anything but ice cream for the longest time."

"How is Leon doing? Is he still getting in trouble at school?"

"No, not really. He's doing so much better. Junior spends a lot of time with him and Marcus. So does Derek. He's so quiet—he internalizes so much."

"Your brother's been thinking about taking them camping next summer. He's gonna talk to you about it."

Nodding, Sela took another sip of her coffee.

"Why don't you eat something?"

"I'm not hungry."

"Sela, when was the last time you ate a good breakfast?"

She searched her memory. "I can't remember. I eat breakfast with the kids every now and then."

"When Rodney was alive, you used to eat breakfast every day."

"It was *our* time. I don't have that anymore."

Her mother embraced her. "I wish I could take this pain away from you and the children. I'm so sorry you're hurting, baby."

"When I dreamed of my future with Rodney, I never saw a time when I would be alone without him. I never dreamed that he would die. Now I think of death all the time. I'm terrified of losing my children, Mama. I'm so scared."

"Honey, listen to Mama. Death is not meant to frighten us. For the Christian, death is simply an interlude until we have eternal life with our Heavenly Father. We have no control of how and when it comes, but we have to put our faith and trust in God for salvation."

"Death has a great way of making us reevaluate life— that's one thing for sure. It's definitely taught me what is really important in life. I just can't get past the grieving though and I feel guilty about it, Mama."

"You don't have to feel guilty. This may seem hard to believe, but remember that the Lord knows grief, too. His son was put to death upon Calvary. God is a good God, baby. He understands your feelings and He loves you so much, Sela. He just wants you to put your trust in Him. Give the children back to the Lord. Ask Him to send His guardian angels to keep watch over their lives. Trust in Him to keep them safe."

"I know what you're saying, Mama. I'm trying to do all that. I really am."

"Happy Thanksgiving," Shelly greeted as she joined Sela and their mother in the kitchen.

"Morning," Sela muttered.

Shelly embraced her. "Hey, girl. How did you sleep?"

"Okay." Sela changed the subject. "Where's Rusty? Is he still sleeping?"

"No, he's taking a shower. He'll be down in a few minutes." Shelly reached for a loaf of wheat bread. Opening it, she took out two slices and stuck them in the toaster. "I'm starving." She glanced over at Sela and asked, "Have you eaten breakfast already?"

"I'm not hungry."

Sela didn't miss the look her sister gave their mother. "Shelly, I'm gonna eat something later. You don't have to worry about me. I'll be fine."

"May I have some more turkey, please?" Lacey asked.

"I just gave you two slices," Ayanna complained. "What are you doing? Sucking it down?"

"I like turkey."

"Can I have some more chicken, please?" Leah held out her plate towards Sela. "And some mashed 'tatoes and gravy."

Sela blinked back her tears. Her baby was eating more and more. "Yes, sweetie. You sure can."

Leah gave her a big beautiful smile. "I love mashed 'tatoes."

"I know," Sela responded.

"Your Mama loves them, too," Althea interjected. "When she was a little girl, that's all she wanted. That and French fries. Then when she got older—it was baked potatoes."

Leon and Marcus snickered over their plates.

"You need to eat the food that's on your plate," Lacey stated. "Before you get more bread. Marcus, you know if you eat all that bread—you gonna get full."

Junior pointed his fork toward Lacey's plate. "Little miss, you need to worry about the food that's on your plate."

"She need to mind her own business," Marcus muttered. "And stay out of mine."

Althea broke into a short laugh. "Son, you ain't old enough to have some business."

Laughing, Marcus reached for his water glass.

Amused, Sela played with the food on her plate. Her heart heavy, she tried not to show any signs of sadness. Thanksgiving was a holiday both she and Rodney looked forward to celebrating. It was a special time for her family and just didn't feel the same without him.

"Mommy," Leah prompted. "You didn't eat your 'tatoes. They're real good. Taste them."

Sela stuck a forkful into her mouth.

"Good, huh?"

Smiling at Leah, she nodded. Sela sliced off a piece of turkey and put it in her mouth.

She was keenly aware of her family watching her. "Okay," she muttered. "None of you have to worry about me. I'm fine." Sela wiped her mouth on her napkin. "Really, I am."

"I miss Daddy," Lacey blurted out. "This Thanksgiving would be really special if he were here with us."

"I agree. But even though Dad's not here physically, I know he's here in spirit." Junior reached for a roll and placed it on his plate. "He's in our hearts."

"I'm just glad that Daddy's not in any pain any longer," Ayanna contributed. "I didn't want him to die, but I hated seeing him suffer. He always tried to hide it, but I knew."

Sela's eyes grew wet as she listened to her children talk about Rodney.

Marcus shocked them by sharing his feelings, "I was real mad at Dad for dying. It…it just hurts real bad…on the inside. Sometimes, I don't want to talk because I…it just hurts too much."

"Sugar, you know your Daddy wouldn't have left this earth if he had any say in the matter, don't you?"

"I know, Grandma."

"Rodney loved y'all and your mother more than his own life. That man woulda died for y'all. I know it's hard not to be sad, but try to remember all the good times. Cherish those memories 'cause nobody can take them from you."

Sela gave her mother a grateful smile.

Chapter Forty-One

❧

"I've included your Christmas bonuses with your paychecks. I thought I'd give them to you early. Consider it an early Christmas present."

Sela's employees gave her a round of applause.

Smiling, she held up her right hand to quiet them. "We'll meet again right after the first of the year," Sela announced.

She and the children had made it through the Thanksgiving holidays and in two and a half weeks Christmas would come.

Sela adjourned the meeting.

Junior came from around the table to stand beside her. "You did a great job as always."

"Thanks, son. I feel very blessed to have the employees we have. They are dedicated and hardworking. That's why I gave them their bonuses early. They deserve them."

"Well if you don't need me any longer, I'm going to get on outta here, Mom. I want to do some Christmas shopping before I have to go to work."

Sela embraced him. "Thanks so much, sweetie. I love you."

"I love you, too."

"I need to do some shopping of my own. I haven't been in the mood. I just want the holiday season over."

Junior nodded in agreement.

After seeing her son out, Sela went upstairs to her bedroom.

She strolled to the back of her closet and pulled out a huge shopping bag of presents.

Looking toward the ceiling, Sela said, "I guess you knew that you wouldn't be here. That's why you were so insistent that I go out and get these presents."

Sela didn't think she would ever get used to the silence that hung in the air of her bedroom since Rodney's death. It wasn't a peaceful quiet—instead it was unsettling. Like being part of a bad dream.

Life continued to move forward beyond Rodney's time on this earth. Christmas was looming before her and while it was once her favorite holiday—this time she dreaded it.

I'll get through it, she vowed silently. *I'll do it for the children.* No doubt Rodney would be on their minds as well, but Sela would do her best to make this Christmas as memorable and special as all the ones in the past.

She knew Christmas wasn't just about celebrating with gifts. It was the celebration of Jesus's birth. Rodney always insisted on them attending the Christmas Eve church service and Sela would keep up that tradition. She'd learned the importance of worshipping as a family.

The children were thrilled when she made the decision to give her life to the Lord. They loved church and were happy to have her attending every Sunday with them.

The best gift she could give them was her salvation. Sela's only regret was that all this had come about after Rodney's passing. He would be so proud of her.

Ethel was fighting depression, so Sela invited them to have Christmas dinner with her and the children. She and Roman hoped that spending time with her grandchildren would help her mother-in-law get through the day.

All of them had managed to make it through Thanksgiving, but Christmas was a very special holiday for their family.

Rita, Derek and his girlfriend would be coming by as well. Sela was grateful for all of the support, but she determined to be strong. She had to be.

For her children.

For Rodney.

"Y'all were wonderful tonight," she complimented when they arrived home from church. Stroking Leah's cheek, she said, "You were a good little shepherd."

"I wanted to be Mary, but there were too many lines to remember. I thought I might forget 'em."

Junior chuckled. He was carrying Lacey, who'd fallen asleep during the drive home. "I'm gonna take her upstairs to bed."

"I'll be up there shortly."

"Mom, can we open one of our presents tonight?" Leon asked. "Pleeze?"

She awarded him a smile. "Honey, it's late. If you go on up and get into bed, Christmas morning will be here before you know it."

"I wish Daddy could have seen me in my play tonight at church," Leah stated softly. "I wish he could be here with us for Christmas, too."

The room grew quiet.

Junior bounded back down the stairs. His eyes searched the faces of his siblings and his mother. "What's wrong?"

"We were just thinking about Daddy," Ayanna answered.

He scratched his head. "Me, too."

Sela's eyes traveled over to the six-foot tree standing in her living room near the marble fireplace. Presents were beneath the decorated Christmas tree and spilling out towards the sofa. There was only one thing missing—Rodney.

Sela was in bed by eleven o'clock.

When the clock struck half past, all of her children had found their way into her room and were scattered all over her floor with pillows and blankets.

She lay in bed reading a book Rita purchased for her until she became sleepy.

When the clock struck one-thirty, Sela put the book away. Pulling the covers up to her chin, she snuggled close to Leah and Lacey, who were in bed with her.

Junior sprung up suddenly. He glanced around the room.

Their eyes met.

"Merry Christmas, Mom."

Smiling, Sela responded, "Merry Christmas to you, Junior. Now get some rest while you can," she uttered in a loud whisper. "The twins are gonna be up at the crack of dawn."

* * *

Ayanna picked up a box and read the label. "Mom…this says that—"

"It's from your father," Sela finished for her. "He had me do his Christmas shopping early. Just in case he wasn't going to be here to do it himself."

The room grew silent.

Lacey broke the silence. "You coulda just said that Santa brought them here for Daddy."

"Would you have believed me?" Sela questioned.

"I'on know. I might have."

Leon handed Marcus a present. "This is for you."

"That's from me," Lacey announced. "I bought it for you."

Marcus reached over and hugged her. "Thanks, little miss. I got you one, too."

"Here, Mom, this is for you." Ayanna passed Sela a present.

"Thanks, sweetie, but I told you not to worry about me."

"It's not from me."

Sela read the label. "This is from your father." Surprised, she glanced over at Ayanna. "Where did this come from?"

"Dad had me pick it up," Junior answered. "He wanted to surprise you."

"He certainly did accomplish that." Sela tore open the small present. Inside was a black velvet box. She opened it and gasped. "Oh, it's stunning," she murmured.

Ayanna got up and came over to view her mother's gift. "Wow. It's beautiful, Mom."

Sela's eyes watered. "It's what I always wanted." The sapphire and diamond tennis bracelet matched the wedding set Rodney presented to her on their wedding anniversary.

She reached up to wipe the tears rolling down her cheeks. Rodney had taken care of everything—even down to his last days.

All of the children were pleased with their presents, but it was the gifts from Rodney that they seemed to cherish the most.

The smaller children spent most of the morning playing with their toys while Ayanna and Junior helped Sela in the kitchen.

Around noon, Rita showed up bearing gifts for everyone. Derek and Kim arrived fifteen minutes later.

"Merry Christmas," Sela greeted.

Derek hugged her. "Merry Christmas to you, too. What you cooking? It smells good in here."

"I have a chicken in the oven along with some stuffing and macaroni and cheese." She gestured toward the dining room. "You're more than welcome to stay and eat with us."

"Thanks for offering, but Derek and I promised to have dinner with my parents," Kim responded. "They want to get to know him better."

Rita walked out of the kitchen. "That chicken is really smelling good."

Sela glanced over her shoulder. "Did you check on the macaroni?"

"I took it and the stuffing out of the oven. Ayanna went upstairs to shower and get dressed. Jay's on his way over."

Sela smiled at the mention of Jay's name. He was really a nice young man and seemed to truly care about her daughter. Ayanna looked happy.

Even Rodney would approve.

"What are you smiling about?" Rita inquired.

"I was thinking about Rodney. He didn't really get to know Jay, but I know he would like him. He'd want him to get a haircut…but I know he would approve of Jay's relationship with Ayanna."

Rita agreed. "He's got it together from the way he talks. He comes from a good home."

Ethel and Roman arrived.

Sela had never seen her mother-in-law look so sad. Greeting her with, "Merry Christmas" just didn't feel right. She walked over, stopping a few inches away from Ethel.

Taking her hand, Sela barely noticed the contrast in their skin color. Pain crossed all racial lines.

"We will get through this day as a family. We don't have to pretend that we're not hurting. We will remember the holidays before—laugh, cry—whatever you feel like. And we will never forget how much Rodney loved us."

Ethel embraced Sela, then burst into tears. "I miss my b-baby soo m-much. I miss h-him."

Rubbing her back, Sela murmured, "I know you do. I miss him, too."

It took a moment for Ethel to compose herself. Sela sent her upstairs to one of the guestrooms to freshen up while she checked on the food.

The children rallied around their grandmother, giving her hugs, kisses and presents, trying to cheer her up. Ethel seemed to brighten up until Sela handed her the gift from Rodney.

She was a little emotional, but gathered herself as she read the card from her son. Ethel held the handmade quilt close to her heart.

Rodney had commissioned a local woman to design the quilt and add photos of Rodney from birth to adulthood. Sela had suggested he include pictures of him with Ethel, knowing her mother-in-law cherished those moments with her son.

"This is exquisite," she murmured, fingering the antique lace trim. "I love it."

Rodney had put just as much thought into his father's gift as well. Roman collected toy soldiers, so Rodney purchased the new series from World War II as soon as they became available.

Thirty minutes later, everyone sat down to eat dinner.

Roman prayed over their meal and took his son's place in slicing the turkey.

As Sela glanced around her dining room table, she sent up a silent prayer of thanksgiving. She couldn't have asked for a better Christmas.

Chapter Forty-Two

&

Sela wanted to sleep through Valentine's Day.

Instead, she decided to make a trip to the cemetery after dropping the children off at school.

The air still held a chill in the air, but Sela didn't care.

She sat a bouquet of red roses on top of Rodney's headstone. "Hey, babe…happy Valentine's Day.

"I wasn't sure how I'd feel today…I wasn't sure I could handle it. I thought it would depress me, but actually…" Sela paused for a moment. "Actually, it's not a bad day."

She pulled a handful of weeds while she talked. "The children are progressing well. Rodney, they're doing so good in school. They still miss you of course. They're never gonna forget you."

Sela sat there for a while, eyeing other people gathered at a nearby grave.

Turning back to face the headstone, Sela traced Rodney's name with her fingers. "I miss you, too."

When she returned home, Sela found Junior's car parked in the driveway.

She called out his name when she entered the house.

Junior walked from the kitchen into the foyer. "I was hungry so I made myself a sandwich. I did the invoicing already and I'ma take the deposit to the bank before I go to class."

"Thanks, sweetie." Sela embraced her son. "I really appreciate your helping me. I've made a decision. I think you should be paid for all you're doing to help me with the company. I'm putting you on payroll."

"Thanks, Mom. I can sure use the extra money. My books are getting more expensive by the day."

"Your father and I told you that we'd take care of your books."

"I know, but I figured if I could handle paying for them—no need to bother you unless I have to."

They talked for a few minutes more before Junior left.

Sela made her way upstairs to her bedroom. She smiled when she spotted the present and envelope on her pillow.

Humming, Sela walked over and picked up the card. Her breath caught in her throat.

"Rodney…"

The writing on the card was in her husband's handwriting.

"Sela,
I didn't know if God would allow me to be here with you another Valentine's Day, and if not—I can only

imagine how hard this day must be for you. Honey, if I could, I would never leave you and my beautiful children. I love you. I hope you are enjoying the bracelet you received for Christmas. I know how much you love sapphires and diamonds, so with that in mind— enjoy your Valentine's present.

Your loving husband,

Rodney

Sela ripped through the layer of wrapping paper. This time the gift box held a sapphire and diamond necklace with matching earrings.

Holding them close to her heart, Sela released tears of happiness.

In March, her wedding anniversary rolled in, bringing Sela to tears. She sat in her family room with photos from the year before when she and Rodney renewed their marriage vows.

After the surprises from Rodney during Christmas and Valentine's Day—Sela couldn't help but be disappointed when nothing materialized.

Shortly after six o'clock that evening, the doorbell rang.

"Leon, can you get the door, sweetie?"

"Yes, ma'am."

She didn't hide her surprise when Roman and Ethel strode into the room. "What are y'all doing here?" Sela inquired. She dabbed at her eyes with a tissue.

"We knew today would be an emotional one for you," Roman began. "So we came over to take the family out to a big fancy dinner. It's what Rodney would want. We're going to honor him by celebrating your marriage."

More tears followed, only this time they were tears of happiness. Sela rose to her feet and embraced Roman. "Thank you so much...."

She hugged Ethel next. "I'm so touched by your thoughtfulness."

"Go on upstairs and put on something beautiful. Today is still your day—yours and Rodney's."

Chapter Forty-Three

By April, Sela felt like she had everything under control. She was comfortable running Barnes Trucking and had even picked up two new accounts. The ache in her heart was still there, and she suspected it would always be. Rodney had been the love of her life.

Sela sat on the window seat in her office staring out at the blooming flowers in her backyard. Spring was here and with it came the bright explosion of colors in flower beds all over Raleigh.

The telephone rang.

Sela walked over to her desk. Recognizing the number on the caller ID, Sela answered, "Hey, Mama."

"Happy birthday to you…" Althea sang.

Sela busted up with laughter. "Thank you, Mama."

"So what are you doing to celebrate?"

She sat down behind her desk. "Ayanna and Junior are taking me and the kids out to dinner."

"That's so sweet and thoughtful."

"I think so. They're wonderful kids."

Althea's tone grew serious. "Sugar, you know you can't just wrap yourself up in your kids. Rodney wouldn't even want you to do that."

Playing with the pen on her desk, Sela questioned, "What are you trying to tell me, Mama?"

"I think it's time for you to move on. Get out there and start meeting people. Now I'm not saying you have to get married or nothing. I'm just saying that you need to find something to do outside of being a mother."

"I don't have time for stuff like that, Mama. Leon and Marcus keep me running with their after school activities. Besides, I am not one of those women who feel they just have to have a man. I was so blessed to have Rodney in my life. I just can't see getting a better man than that. I think I should quit while I'm ahead."

"I hear what you're saying, Sela. Believe me I do."

"Mama, I'm way too busy to even think about dating. Maybe a few months down the line, but for now…I'm just getting my life back on track. I'm fine."

Sela heard a click on the phone line. "Mama, I've got another call coming in. I'll call you back later. Okay?"

"Talk to you then. 'Bye, sugar."

Sela answered the incoming call. "Hello…"

"Mom, Grandfather is in the hospital," Ayanna announced. "I went to pick up the stuff Grandmother bought for me and she was on her way to Duke. Grandfather wasn't at home when he got sick—he was out on the golf course."

"What happened?"

"I don't know. I'm gonna see if I can get someone to switch with me at work tonight and then I'm going to the hospital."

"I'll call Rita to watch the kids and I'll meet you there."

"Thanks, Mom. After Daddy…"

"I hope your grandfather will be okay."

"I do, too. Mom, you should have seen Grandmother. I thought she was gonna faint or something. She's real scared."

"I know exactly how she feels." They talked for a few more minutes before hanging up.

Sela arranged for Rita to come watch the children. While she waited for her friend to arrive, she went to her room and prayed for Roman's life.

Rita arrived a short time later. Sela rushed out of the house and into her car.

Her mind became clouded with memories from Rodney's stay at Duke University Hospital as she drove along the highway.

She found Ethel standing near the nurses' station. Sela couldn't remember ever seeing the woman look so pale. "Mrs. Barnes, how is he?"

"They're running tests…I don't know anything."

"How are you holding up?"

"They think it may be his heart. A heart attack." Ethel's eyes grew wet. "He wouldn't get tested. He was afraid to find out."

Sela took her mother-in-law by the arm and led her over to a nearby chair. "Would you like something to drink?"

She shook her head. "No, thank you."

Sela pulled a tissue out of her purse and handed it to Ethel, who gave her a grateful smile.

Wiping her eyes, Ethel stated, "I kept telling him to get that test done. We needed to know…he wouldn't hear of it."

A doctor came out thirty minutes later.

"Mrs. Barnes?"

Ethel rose to her feet. She glanced over at Sela and whispered, "Don't leave me, please."

"I won't," she promised.

Sela escorted Ethel over to where the doctor was standing.

When he mentioned heart failure, Ethel swayed and had to be seated.

Sela wrapped an arm around her and tried to offer comfort. "It's gonna be all right, Mrs. Barnes. Dr. Shriner says that it can be treated. It's not like Rodney where it was too late."

Ethel wiped her eyes. "I can't go through this again," she whispered.

"We are going to put Roman on ACE inhibitors to reduce the work of the heart and slow down any losses in the heart's pumping ability…."

Sela handed a tissue to Ethel. "This time is different," she reassured her. "I can feel it."

"I should've insisted that Roman be tested. His father…Rodney…" Ethel clenched her fist against her lap. "He's never liked going to the doctor, you know. And Roman hates hospitals."

"I'm not crazy about them myself," Sela confessed.

A few minutes later, they were allowed to see Roman.

The hospital room brought a host of painful memories to the forefront. Here Sela was again with monitors beeping and displaying graphs and numbers. Attached to Roman's chest and arm were various lines and IVs. He looked as pale and as frightened as Rodney was the first time he was brought in after the stroke.

Roman gestured toward his wife, summoning her closer to the bed. Sela stayed near the door in case he wanted her to leave. The last thing she wanted to do was upset him.

When Ethel glanced over at her, she said, "I think I should wait outside."

"No," she responded. "Don't leave."

Sela's eyes strayed to Roman. "I don't want to upset him."

"Stay…" he grunted. "I-It's okay."

Sela remained near the door and pretended not to hear any of the conversation between Ethel and Roman. While standing there, she searched her memory. After all the research she'd done when Rodney was first diagnosed—surely she could come up with something….

"Talk to your doctor about a ventricular assist device, Mr. Barnes," Sela blurted without preamble.

"What's that?" he asked.

"It's a type of mechanical heart that is surgically implanted in the patient's chest during an open-heart surgery. A left ventricular assist device helps the heart pump what they call, oxygen-rich blood to the rest of the body, while a right ventricular assist device helps the heart pump oxygen-poor blood to the lungs for more oxygen. I read some cases where people need both. It's been an option for people who are waiting on a heart transplant to survive."

"But Roman's condition isn't that serious," Ethel interjected.

"I know. I read that in some cases, LVADs have been given to people who have disease-weakened hearts in order to give it a chance to recover."

"How do you know so much about this?"

"Because I was hoping Rodney could've gotten one, but he couldn't. His heart had sustained too much damage. I've done a lot of research on treatment options for cardiomyopathy. I wanted to know everything about the disease and what was available to treat the condition."

Dr. Shriner strolled into the room.

"Doctor, my...my daughter-in-law was just telling us about a device. A left..." Roman looked past the doctor to where Sela was standing.

"Left ventricular assist device," she finished for him.

Dr. Shriner nodded. "It's used as a treatment of congestive heart failure when heart transplant is not possible, and when the heart needs a rest to heal itself. The use of a left ventricular assist device is certainly an option for you, Roman. In patients with advanced heart failure such as yourself, the device has resulted in an improved quality of life. Time and the device could give your heart a chance to heal."

"This requires major surgery though."

Sela could see the fear in Roman's face. He was deathly afraid of surgery.

Dr. Shriner nodded. "Part of the device is implanted in your heart and abdomen, and part remains outside your body."

"How would this device work?" Ethel inquired. "I've never heard of it."

"The left ventricular assist device is an electromechanically driven pump, about the size of a human heart," Dr. Shriner explained. "Which is implanted within the abdominal wall. It provides circulatory support by taking over most of the workload of the left ventricle, the heart's main pumping chamber."

Sela pulled a pad out of her purse and made notes as she listened to the doctor.

"Blood enters the pump though an inflow conduit connected to the left ventricle and is ejected through an outflow conduit into the body's arterial system. The system is monitored by an electronic controller and powered by primary and reserve battery packs, worn on a belt around the waist or carried in a shoulder bag, or by a small bedside monitor. The controller will be connected to the implanted pump by a small tube containing control and power wires through the skin."

"I read somewhere that the recipients must take blood thinners to reduce the risk of stroke. Is this correct?" Sela asked.

"Yes. That's absolutely correct," Dr. Shriner confirmed.

"Are there any restrictions?" Roman wanted to know.

"The rechargeable batteries must be changed three or four times a day, and the bandages around the cable to the battery must be changed daily and kept dry. Showering is allowed, but swimming is not."

Dr. Shriner patiently answered all of their concerns before leaving.

Sela knew Roman and Ethel had a lot to discuss so she readied to leave. "I'm gonna go. I'll call and check on you later, Mr. Barnes."

He nodded. "I'm glad you were here," he mumbled.

She awarded him a smile. "Ayanna and Junior plan on stopping by this evening."

"I'll be here."

"Bye, Mrs. Barnes." Sela headed to the door. She stopped in her tracks when she heard her name called. Sela turned around.

"I think it's time you stop being so formal with us. Just call me Ethel."

"Okay. I can do that."

Smiling, Sela left the hospital room. "Thank You, Heavenly Father...."

Chapter Forty-Four

❧

Sela walked fast, her heart racing and her breathing labored, as she breezed through the long sterile corridor of Duke University Hospital in Durham, North Carolina.

She spotted her mother-in-law standing near the surgery unit reception area and increased her speed. As she neared, Sela glimpsed Ethel's pale, tear-streaked face and noted the way her hands trembled when she swiped at her eyes.

"Ethel, I'm so sorry I'm late," she stated in a rush. "I ran into some traffic on the way here from Raleigh."

"They took Roman to surgery just a few minutes ago." Ethel pulled at the folds of her salmon colored cardigan, her eyes constantly darting to the clock on the wall behind the reception desk.

"He's gonna be fine." Sela took Ethel gently by the arm and led her over to the small waiting area. "Why don't you sit down?" she suggested. "And I'll get you some coffee."

Ethel's voice was barely above a whisper when she spoke. "Don't leave me, Sela. Just stay here with me, please."

"I won't go anywhere." Sela sat down beside Ethel. "I'll be right here."

Ethel seemed to relax a little. She'd never seen her mother-in-law look so scared. Deep down, Sela wasn't as confident as she tried to appear. She was afraid for her father-in-law as well. Cardiomyopathy had already struck the Barnes family twice and the results were tragic.

Shuddering at the thought, Sela placed a hand to her nose to ward off the sterile, antiseptic smell of the hospital that caused her stomach to twist with nausea and threatened to make her gag. Over the last year, she'd spent way too much time here. As much as Sela tried to think otherwise, Duke Hospital was a painful reminder that death stood lurking around every corner.

"How are the children?" Ethel asked suddenly. "I meant to call them back last night, but Roman and I spent most of the evening talking about our life together. It was midnight before we knew it."

"I understand," Sela murmured. "They're fine. Leah was just calling to tell you that she's doing better with her reading. Marcus and Leon just wanted to let Mr. Barnes know that they were praying for him."

"They are wonderful children. You've done a great job with them, Sela. I'll have to make sure I call Leah and tell her how proud I am of her."

Swelling with pride, Sela responded, "She's doing so well. Leah wants to read chapter books now, while Lacey is still struggling some with the early reader books. I still have to force her to read at least twenty minutes every day. But Leah—she has a real love for reading like Rodney and me."

Ethel smiled. "Lacey's more like Marcus when it comes to reading, I guess."

Sela agreed. "That boy can't stand reading. I've tried everything, including comic books, but nothing seems to interest Marcus. When they get out of school on the thirtieth of this month, I'm gonna make sure they all spend this summer doing some reading every day."

"You know, Rodney was like that when he was a young boy. Then when he turned thirteen—that all changed. He read everything he could get his hands on. Maybe Marcus and Lacey will change as they get older."

"I certainly hope so." Sela glanced up at the clock hanging on the wall. It felt like they had been sitting there for hours, but in reality, it had only been forty minutes.

She stole a peek out of a nearby window. It was a beautiful spring morning in May. The sun was already out and shining bright. She longed to be outside basking in the sunlight—anywhere but here in this hospital, surrounded by death and sickness.

Shoulders drooping, Sela slumped against the chair as her eyes darted upwards to the clock hanging on the wall opposite her. "I keep thinking that this place is becoming all too familiar."

Ethel nodded in agreement. "Roman was so terrified. He's

never liked doctors or hospitals. Too many of his friends have died while undergoing surgery."

"I never pictured Mr. Barnes…eh, I'm sorry…Roman afraid of anything."

"He's always been my protector," Ethel murmured with a smile. "The day I met him, he swept me off my feet." She shifted in her seat. "That was a long time ago."

"I can see how much you love him."

Ethel turned to Sela then. "I could always see how much you loved my Rodney. That's the one thing I never doubted about you. I knew you loved him."

"He told me once that his dream was to experience the type of love you and Roman share. I don't think I really appreciated that until now."

Sela's eyes strayed to the clock.

Ethel followed her gaze. "Sitting here and waiting like this drives me crazy." She hid her trembling fingers in the folds of her sweater. "I can't stand all this waiting."

Sela wrapped an arm around her mother-in-law. "Roman is in God's hands. We just have to believe that he's gonna be fine."

Reaching over, Ethel held Sela's hand in a viselike grip. "I can't lose him. Roman is my life."

Nodding in understanding, Sela responded, "I know how you feel. Rodney was my life, too. But you don't have to worry about this because Roman is not going anywhere." A smile tugged at her lips. "Besides, he's way too stubborn."

Ethel wiped at her eyes and smiled. "You're right about that. Roman is indeed a stubborn man."

When a young woman carrying a clipboard strode over

to the waiting room, the soft chattering around them came to an abrupt halt.

"I need to speak with the family of Edgar Richards?"

A petite woman stood up. "He's my husband."

Sela overheard the woman being told, "Mrs. Richards, your husband came through surgery fine. He's…"

She stole a peek at Ethel. "You okay?" Sela asked. Ethel looked as though she was about to fall apart at any given moment.

Her mother-in-law nodded in response. "I'll just be glad when this is all over and Roman's back home with me where he belongs. I keep thinking about the last time we were here. *With Rodney*. I can't bear that kind of loss again."

Sela's heart twisted with grief whenever she thought of her husband. "That's not gonna happen, Ethel. Rodney was very sick long before we knew what was going on. This time is different."

As she and Ethel sat waiting for some word on Roman, Sela prayed that her father-in-law's life would be spared. Their family had been through too much already.

While they waited, Sela's stomach churned and her mind drifted back to the past. It wasn't all that long ago that she and her in-laws were barely civil to one another. Now here she was—sitting with Ethel, waiting to see if her father-in-law would survive the condition that had taken her beloved Rodney ten months ago.

When Sela felt she couldn't bear another moment in the hospital, she heard her father-in-law's name called.

"They're done," Ethel muttered. She stood up quickly.

Sela rose to her feet and followed her mother-in-law. Walking across the room, she prayed that the news would be good.

She listened quietly as the hospital representative explained what would happen next.

"Once you're in the back, one of the nurses will take you to see your husband. He's still under the anesthesia but should be waking up shortly...."

Sela inhaled deeply before plunging forward through the heavy, double doors leading to the surgical ward. She still felt queasy and placed a hand to her stomach.

They neared the room where Roman lay and Sela's footsteps slowed.

Ethel paused and turned. "Are you okay?"

Sela leaned against the wall and shook her head. "I think I need to stay out here. You go on in."

"Sela..."

"I'll be fine," she assured her mother-in-law. "I think I just need to get some air."

Ethel reached out and took Sela by the hand, giving it a gentle squeeze. "I won't be long. I just want to know that Roman's okay."

Sela pasted on a smile. "Go ahead. I'll be fine."

"You're not leaving, are you?"

"No. Just need to get some air. Hospitals make me nauseous at times."

"Since Rodney's death?"

Sela nodded. "I'll be right back."

She turned around and walked towards the nearest exit, her hand still pressed to her stomach, willing it to settle down.

Outside, Sela felt somewhat better. After a moment, she strolled back into the hospital where she navigated to the first bathroom she saw.

Sela wet a paper towel and bathed her face. The bathroom mirror suggested she looked like she'd had little sleep and didn't feel well.

She wasn't certain how she scraped up the bravado to open the door and walk down to the room where her father-in-law lay after his surgery, but she soon found herself standing beside Ethel.

"Is he still sleeping?" Sela inquired in a low whisper.

"He woke up briefly," Ethel answered. "But couldn't keep his eyes open. The doctor said everything went well."

"Junior's coming by after his class this morning," Sela said to distract her.

"That boy is destined to be a doctor. He came by the house last night to make sure we understood what was going to happen. Junior's not even in medical school yet, but he's already reading all these medical journals and articles."

"He wants to be a cardiologist," Sela announced.

"He told us. I'm so proud of him."

"I am, too."

Sela changed the subject abruptly. "Ethel, I want to ask you something. It's something I've wanted to ask for a long—"

"It's not that I didn't like you, Sela," Ethel interjected. "It most certainly had nothing to do with your being black. I had dreams for Rodney. I wanted him…I wanted him to be more than a truck driver."

"I wanted Rodney to go back to college but he didn't want to, Ethel. He chose to be a truck driver. He loved his job."

"I know," Ethel acknowledged. "But it didn't stop me from wanting more for him."

"I still believe that my skin color bothered you. I know it bothered Roman. He said as much."

"Sela, we were worried how children born to interracial parents would be raised. We worried over how they would be treated by society. We've heard the stories—we lived through the civil rights period. I didn't want Rodney or any of his children to go through something like that."

She studied Ethel, trying to measure her sincerity.

"We tried to reach out to you several times, but you had this wall up. Roman called it a chip on your shoulder. After a while…we just stopped trying."

"You never made me feel like I was a part of your family."

"You're right, Sela. We didn't. For that, I'm truly sorry. It wasn't until Junior and Ayanna sat us all down to talk—I realized then, we were all acting very foolish. My only regret is that we weren't able to do this while Rodney was still alive."

Sela agreed. "This was his deepest wish."

Ethel reached over and took Sela by the hand. "Please forgive us for the pain we caused you."

Sela placed her other hand over Ethel's. "I forgave you a long time ago. And I want to ask the same of you."

"I know Dad's probably shouting all over heaven," Junior stated as he joined them. He took a seat on the other side of Ethel. "Praise God for all He has done."

Sela glanced over at her son. "Junior?"

"Mom, losing Dad…changed me. I've been talking with Derek and I've given my life to Jesus."

Ethel's eyes filled with tears.

Sela embraced her.

On the other side, Junior hugged her as well.

They sat like that until a nurse came out to speak with them.

"Mr. Barnes is awake now and he's asking for you."

Sela closed her eyes and said a silent prayer of thanks. When she opened them again, she found Junior watching her.

She reached over and hugged him. "Your grandfather's gonna be fine. I just know it."

Epilogue

Three months later

Marcus met Sela at the front door. "Is Grandfather really okay? He's been going to the doctor a lot."

Stepping around him, she ran her fingers through his short curls while giving him a reassuring smile. "He's doing wonderful."

Giving her a look filled with suspicion, he questioned, "You sure?"

Sela met his gaze and confirmed, *"I am."*

She took Marcus by the hand and led him over to a nearby chair. She sat down and patted the empty space beside her. "Honey, it's not like it was with Daddy. Your grandfather is doing really good."

"Then why did you have to go to the doctor with him and Grandmother?"

She surveyed his face. "Because they asked me to, Marcus. Why all the questions?"

"I just want to know if his heart is as sick as Daddy's was. Is he gonna need a new heart, too?"

"Nope." Sela broke into a smile. "All the tests that the doctors ran after they removed the device Grandfather had to wear show that his heart has fully recovered from the illness."

She fought back tears when she heard his audible sigh of relief. Marcus hugged her.

"Honey, it's okay," Sela murmured when she felt her shirt getting wet from her son's tears.

"I just don't want to lose Grandfather, too."

She sat there holding him until Marcus pulled away.

"So, where's everybody?"

"Yanna's helping Leon with his homework. I don't know what Leah is doing—she was in her room drawing. Lacey is in my room playing with my trucks."

"Your trucks?"

"Yes, ma'am." Marcus's face twisted into a frown. "Mom, you need to buy Lacey her own trucks. She's always bothering mine and they're not for babies. I don't even play with them. *I collect them.*"

"I'll talk to her. Okay?"

He nodded.

Later that evening, Sela walked into Leah's room. "What are you working on?"

"It's a picture of something I dreamed last night."

"Can I see it?"

Leah handed it to Sela.

"It's a picture of our family. That's Grandfather and Grand-mother over there. See, Grandfather has a new heart…that's why it's bright red—because it's new."

"Is this me over here?" Sela asked. "It looks like we're on a bridge. You and your brothers and sisters are standing in the middle. Your grandparents are over here and I'm on the other side."

"It's what I saw in my dream. See y'all are walking to the middle—where we're standing. We're coming together."

Leah's words had a chilling effect on Sela. "We're…you saw us coming together?"

The little girl nodded.

"What's this up here?" Sela gave it a closer look. "Is this an angel?"

"It's supposed to be Daddy," Leah explained. "I didn't draw him very well." Pointing, she asked, "But can you see his smile? He has a real big one—that's why his face looks kind of funny. He's very happy."

Sela's eyes grew wet with unshed tears. "Why is he so happy?"

"Because this is his dream—he wanted us to be a family. Daddy died so that we could come together."

Sela's mouth dropped open in her surprise. "Leah, honey…where are you getting this? Who have you been talking to?"

"Just Daddy," she responded. "He visits me in my dreams, Mommy."

Sela stared down at the drawing again to hide the tears in

her eyes. "I see another person." She pointed to the picture. "Right here in this corner."

"That's the Lord. He's watching us and everything we do. He keeps us safe."

"You are such a smart little girl. You don't realize it, but you've taught me so much with your drawing."

"I have?"

Sela nodded. "I think you're right. Your father's dying has brought this family together. I've realized something else. Life itself is enough reason to praise God."

"Amen," Leah responded.

Laughing, Sela asked, "Do you have any clue as to what I'm talking about."

"Not a clue, Mommy. I'm glad I made you smile though." Pointing to the picture, Leah asked, "Where are you going to hang my picture?"

"I know just the place—where your grandfather can see it every day. In his office. What do you think of that?"

"It'll make his heart feel so much better."

Hugging Leah to her, Sela couldn't agree more.

Once, twice, ten times a bridesmaid!

Made of Honor

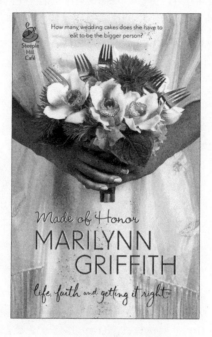

On sale January 2006

Dana Rose has a closetful of unflattering bridesmaid's dresses and a whole lot of stress! Between an ex who married someone else and opened a shop right across from her, and an unwelcome visit from her siblings, Dana has had it up to here. At least she's got the Sassy Sistahood to help her along.

Steeple Hill®

Visit your local bookseller.

JACQUELIN THOMAS
FRANCIS RAY
FELICIA MASON

HOW
SWEET
THE
SOUND

HOW SWEET THE SOUND features three beautiful and inspiring love stories born out of musical collaborations. Discover how love blooms in the most unlikely of situations.

Visit your local bookseller.

Steeple Hill®